MEAN AND SHELLFISH

Tamar Myers

**SEVERN
HOUSE**

First world edition published in Great Britain and the USA in 2021
by Severn House, an imprint of Canongate Books Ltd,
14 High Street, Edinburgh EH1 1TE.

Trade paperback edition first published in Great Britain and the USA in 2022
by Severn House, an imprint of Canongate Books Ltd.

severnhouse.com

British Library Cataloguing-in-Publication Data
A CIP catalogue record for this title is available from the British Library.

ISBN-13: 978-0-7278-8929-4 (cased)
ISBN-13: 978-1-78029-772-9 (trade paper)
ISBN-13: 978-1-4483-0510-0 (e-book)

All Severn House titles are printed on acid-free paper.

Typeset by Palimpsest Book Production Ltd.,
Falkirk, Stirlingshire, Scotland.
Printed and bound in Great Britain by
TJ Books Limited, Padstow, Cornwall.

This book is dedicated to Rich and Terri Keffert

ACKNOWLEDGEMENTS

I would like to thank my publisher, Kate Lyall Grant, at Severn House for the opportunity to write this book. I would also like to thank my editor Sara Porter for her wisdom and skilful guidance.

In addition, I am very grateful to my literary agent of twenty-eight years, Nancy Yost, of Nancy Yost Literary Agency. I want to give a shout-out to the entire team there, most especially Sarah, Natanya and Cheryl.

Last, but not least, I would like to thank Barbara Savage for her recipe. I met Barbara in Thailand twenty-five years ago, when our families booked the same package tour of the River Kwai and environs. Part of the tour included an elephant-back ride through the jungle. Because only three passengers were permitted to ride in each howdah, and Barbara had two children, my husband and I agreed to let her young son Daniel ride with us. We have been friends ever since. As I see it, allowing a stranger to ride along in one's howdah can be the foundation of a lasting friendship.

ONE

A woman's hunch is worth two facts from a man. That's just a fact, and it's something that I know from ten years of experience helping local law enforcement solve murder cases in and around our bucolic village of Hernia, Pennsylvania. Unfortunately, the majority of these untimely demises have occurred at my bed and breakfast, The PennDutch Inn. One local wag went so far as to suggest that I rename my otherwise charming establishment Cabot's Cove, a reference that went totally over my extraordinarily large, horsey head.

Please bear with me while I introduce myself more fully. My name is Magdalena Portulacca Yoder. I am currently happily married to Dr Gabriel Rosen, a retired cardiac surgeon from New York City (that has not always been the case – the happy part, that is). The reason that I have not adopted my husband's surname is that I made the mistake of doing that when I was married the first time. To a bigamist. That is when I became Hernia's first official inadvertent adulteress. That is to say, I had absolutely no idea that Aaron Miller was married when I promised to be his wedded wife to death do us part. The trauma of our wedding night, and the subsequent nightmares in which I was assaulted by a turkey neck, were all in vain. Well, I guess if I am being completely honest, they did prepare me for wedding night number two.

At any rate, I am a Conservative Mennonite woman. Both sets of my grandparents were Amish, and I am related by blood to approximately eighty percent of them. My dear husband, on the other hand, is Jewish. We are, as the Bible states, 'unevenly yoked'. Given that the original prohibition was against pairing an ox with a donkey, and my husband is quite a bit larger than I am, that leaves me playing the part of the ass.

We have two wonderful but very disobedient children. Gabe claims that their contrariness is due in part to that fact that they are very clever and are being raised to be independent thinkers.

Our adopted daughter Alison is nineteen, a pre-med student at the University of Pittsburgh, and her brother Little Jacob, age five, is being home-schooled by his father. It was either that, or let him start high school, as he had already mastered all the other requisite work in-between.

Just so you know, I take absolutely *no* credit for Little Jacob's inordinate amount of brains. Gabe shouldn't take credit for them either. Little Jacob's smarts are a God-given gift. If either of us starts taking credit for what is good in our children's lives, then we will have to take credit for the bad as well. That's a conclusion I came to when my younger sister Susannah fell in love with a truly wicked man by the name of Melvin Stoltzfus, and then finally ended up serving time in the state penitentiary for aiding and abetting an accused murderer.

I won't bore you with the long history of the PennDutch Inn. Just believe me when I say that folks with enormous amounts of money like to get a little abuse when they dish out their dole. I'm not referring to physical or verbal abuse – or, heaven forfend, sexual abuse. What I mean is that every now and then, the uber-wealthy enjoy 'roughing' it a bit. This enables them to once again appreciate the luxuries to which they'd become inured. This is especially true when their abuse of choice contains an element of education, something about which they can elaborate upon ad nausea at their next dinner table.

At the PennDutch Inn one gets the privilege of toting in one's own valises and then lugging them up my impossibly steep stairs. (By the way, whinging is penalized by a penalty of fifty dollars per complaint.) For a mere one hundred bucks more than the standard room rate, one may opt for the thrill of cleaning one's own en-suite room. For a fee of just fifty dollars more than that, a guest may select a room that doesn't have its own bath, and clean it, as well as the public bath. There are additional fees for privileges of mucking out the barn, cleaning the chicken coop, plucking butchered chickens, and ironing bedsheets with flat irons heated on a wood-burning stove.

The point of all this is to give our guests a genuine Amish experience in this corner of Pennsylvania Dutch Country. The fact that we aren't Amish doesn't matter; my grandparents were Amish, and I am quite capable of replicating their lifestyle here at the PennDutch Inn. Of course, in this spirit, all cell phones will have been confiscated at my front door. Not that they would have been much good to their owners for long, as there are no electric outlets in the guest rooms for recharging the dang things. Neither are there any electric lights. Guests are given oil lamps when they retire at night. Also, I've seen to it that the upstairs radiators don't work – Amish rely on heat from wood-burning stoves downstairs to rise up through the floor and supply sufficient heat to keep their large families from freezing. Gabe believes that this is the reason the Amish are really into making quilts.

Any rational person might conclude that my business model was insane. Who would squander their precious leisure time to work their manicured fingers to the bone, while staying at an establishment where so many guests have been stabbed, poisoned, or merely shot? Surely even the report of just one such incident would be one too many, never mind a baker's dozen. But *au contraire*. Like moths to the flame, folks vie for reservations, usually requesting to stay in specific rooms from their understanding of the crimes having occurred therein. Often guests arrive clutching yellowed newspaper clippings of their favourite atrocities, or stories printed from the internet.

So my business has thrived, and I have become a prosperous woman. Scripture instructs us to give freely to those who are not as well off. Actually, it goes a mite further than that. In the Gospel of Luke, Jesus tells the rich man that in order to get into Heaven he needs to sell everything that he has and give the money away to the poor. The rich man walked away from the deal.

Now *that* is a hard teaching which only a small minority of Christians follow. I certainly don't, because scripture also states that the key ingredient to one's salvation is faith, not poverty. Not that my finances are anyone's business except for the government's, but I donate a great deal of money to charities scattered throughout the county, the country, and even abroad. I also single-handedly support the Hernia Police Department, the Hernia Lending Library, and our small but fascinating Museum of Local History and Peculiarities.

I wasn't bragging, mind you – merely stating the obvious:

I can afford to retire whenever I choose. In fact, I was mere weeks from doing just that when the Babester begged me to put off the day when we'd have the inn and children all to ourselves again. 'Babester' is what I sometimes call my handsome hunk of a husband. Those occasions are more frequent now that I've at last managed to snip the apron strings of steel that wired him to his mama. And to think that all it finally took was bringing his older sister to town and suggesting to his mother that she might prefer to live with her daughter rather than with me.

Anyway, we had just started getting dressed one morning – the Babester in blue jeans and a denim shirt, and me in a fake Amish outfit to go with my fake Amish accent, suitable for greeting new guests – when he casually brought up the issue. At first, his request went flying over my head, despite me being five feet, ten inches tall.

'Hon,' he said, 'if you don't mind working just an extra week or two, my cousin Miriam Blumfield texted and said that she wants to stay with us until the Billy Goat Gruff Festival.'

'*What?* She's coming all the way from Australia for some silly parade?'

'Sweetheart,' Gabe said, an edge creeping into his voice with every word, 'you're the one who thought up this silly parade. Ma can't help it that she was elected Citizen of the Year and gets to be pulled across the bridge in the goat cart.'

'When does your cousin plan to arrive?'

'Um – well, today.'

'*What?*'

'Calm down, Mags. You'll hardly know she's here. She'll be so busy hanging out with Ma and me, you'll barely get a chance to greet her.'

'I can't believe this! You having the chutzpah to foist your cousin on me at the last minute, and after what your mother did to ruin our town's annual fiesta.'

'What did Ma do?'

'Your mother stole that election,' I said, 'and you know that. Everyone in the village of Hernia knows that.'

I didn't need to look at my husband to know that he was glaring at me. When Gabe glares, his dark brown eyes function like a heat lamp.

'You just don't like my mother,' he said. 'You've always hated her, and without cause. What you refuse to see is that she is a warm and caring woman, who has made countless friends since moving here.'

Ida Rosen *warm* and *caring*? That was akin to describing a boa constrictor as a creature fond of giving hugs. Gabe was wrong, I didn't dislike his mother; I hated her. Yes, I know, as a Christian, I am supposed to love her, and believe me, I have tried. And tried. But that woman is *impossible* to love. I do know that is what the Good Lord expects me to do, but please bear in mind that neither Jesus nor the Apostle Paul had mothers-in-law. I'm just saying.

I struggled to say something that was at least not terribly offensive. 'But why does your cousin have to stay with us? Your sister's house has plenty of room, and that's where your mother *lives*, for crying out loud.'

'Mags, it only makes sense that she should stay here. We own an inn, for *crying out loud*.'

Nobody likes to be mocked, least of all me. But I was proud of Gabe for keeping business and family concerns separated. Not too long ago, he never would have even considered steering a cousin to my inn.

'How much of a family discount should we offer her?' I asked agreeably.

'*What?* You can't be serious, Mags! Miriam's my cousin. We grew up together. We're not going to charge her a single penny.'

I swallowed hard, for I was already beginning to drown in regret for yet unspoken words. 'Um . . . OK. But the Billy Goat Gruff Festival and the parade are a full week away. Why does she have to stay here the entire time? You have heard that saying about company and fish both beginning to smell after three days, haven't you?'

Gabe shot me his wounded, little boy look. Despite the fact that my husband is in his early fifties, his dark, soulful eyes, rimmed by long black lashes, are easily turned into powerful, guilt-inducing weapons.

'Mags, try to keep in mind that the ways of the world are a little more complex than they are here in bucolic Hernia, Pennsylvania. Miriam said that in order to get the best ticket price, she had to book it as part of a tour.' He chuckled. 'She'll be ditching the tour group as soon as she lands stateside, of course.'

'Of course,' I said. Who was I to judge this unscrupulous cousin of my husband?

'Besides, this will give Miriam and me a chance to get reacquainted. As adults. We used to fight all the time when we were kids.'

'That's nice, dear,' I said as I pulled heavy cotton tights up and over the bottom half of my sturdy Christian underwear.

'I'm sure I've mentioned that she's my only living relative on Ma's side of the family, but that the two of them haven't spoken for thirty-five years, when she was only twenty-one. That's when I last saw her.'

'Yes, dear,' I said, as I struggled into the top half of my sturdy Christian underwear. The Babester refers to this piece as my 'over-the-shoulder-boulder-holder'. Trust me, that's wishful thinking on his part. Either that, or my dear husband has periodic flashbacks to a past life wherein he lived as an ordinary citizen of Lilliput.

'Of course, you remember why Cousin Miriam and Ma parted ways, don't you?'

'Unh-huh, but why don't you refresh my memory, dear.' My atrophying brain didn't actually need any refreshing. His beloved 'Ma' was the reason.

Miriam and her parents had decided to take one last family trip over the Christmas break of Miriam's senior year of college. They chose scuba diving on Australia's Great Barrier Reef. Tragically, on the last day of their vacation, Miriam's parents never resurfaced, and their bodies were never recovered.

Miriam refused to give up on searching for her lost parents and is said to have spent an enormous portion of her inheritance chasing down every rumour of people, alive or dead, who were said to have shown up on remote strands of coral, or islets that were hitherto uninhabited by humans. Meanwhile, Ida Rosen, her deceased mother's sister, pleaded with the young woman to return to America to finish the school year and graduate with her class. Miriam was due to enter Harvard Medical School in the fall along with her cousin Gabriel Rosen (even then known as the Babester).

But Miriam would not listen to her aunt. In fact, she eventually grew so annoyed with Ida's incessant nagging, that she gave her aunt a sexual directive that was anatomically impossible. Ida never contacted her again.

While Gabe had been 'refreshing' me on his version of why poor Miriam had turned on her only remaining maternal relative, I had quietly continued to dress. Now, looking in my mirror (a luxury that true Amish don't have) I saw a reasonable facsimile of one of our local Amish women. Any minute the doorbell would ring, and our first guest would arrive, and their experience would start off in high gear.

I smoothed my crisp white apron over my black dress. 'So, dear,' I said, as I sinfully admired my reflection, 'when is your cousin arriving?'

'Any minute now.'

I froze. '*Excuse* me?'

'I'm sure I told you that as well, hon. She's supposed to get here early, before the other guests, so that we can get her comfortably settled in down here before all the hubbub begins.'

'What do you mean by *down here?*' I said.

'In our room, of course. Didn't I tell you that one, or both – I can't remember which – of her legs was bitten off by a saltwater crocodile, and that she's been confined to a wheelchair? We can't possibly expect her to drag herself up your impossibly steep stairs using just her arms.'

'Coconut crumpets!' I cursed. 'No, you didn't tell me. I suppose then that *we're* supposed to sleep in one of my guest rooms?'

Gabe winked. 'Those guest rooms are cozy, right? And we can bunk Little Jacob over at his gam-gam's house. You know how she adores him.'

The doorbell rang.

'Hold that thought, mister,' I said.

TWO

Unless Gabe's cousin Miriam was a six-foot, five-inch-tall Texan who wore cowboy boots and a ten-gallon hat, she was not our first caller that morning. Standing beside the man, maybe just half a step back, was a woman wearing cowgirl boots and a one-gallon hat. It's possible the hat that the old gal was wearing didn't even hold more than two pints, given that she barely exceeded five feet in height.

'Morn'n, ma'am,' he drawled. 'Mah name is Tiny Hancock, and this heah filly is my purty bride of forty-seven yeahs, Delphia, and we look forward to parking our saddlebags here for the next three days and eatin' vittles' with y'all, around y'all's communal campfire, so to speak.'

I've had a passel of Texans as my guests over the years, but none that ever sounded like Tiny Hancock. Well, two could play that game.

'*Velcomen to zee PennDutch Inn,*' I said in my best fake Pennsylvania Dutch accent. *Mi namen ist Magdalena Yoder und zee eez—*'

'Stop it right now, you two,' barked Delphia Hancock in a voice barely a smidge above a baritone. 'Neither of you is any good at accents. Now get in on inside; there are flies out here.'

'Yes, Mother,' Tiny said, and practically pushed me back into the inn. If he had actually pushed me, I'd have screamed bloody murder, in hopes that My Beloved would have heard me and rushed to my defence.

'Oh dear,' I said, once I'd gathered my wits, 'I thought that you two were a married couple, so I assigned you to the same room. I didn't realize that you were mother and son. But I must say, Mrs Hancock, you do look young enough to be Mr Hancock's wife . . . er, younger sister, you know.'

If I'd heard Delphia Hancock laugh in a crowd of strangers, and my back was turned, I'd have been quite certain that she was a man. Her husband's laugh was a full octave higher than hers.

'Just so you know,' I said, 'I discriminate against no one, and you're not the first transgender woman to stay here. I'll admit that at first I didn't believe there was such a thing as transgendered persons, because they aren't mentioned in the Bible. Then my husband, who is a physician, pointed out that there are scads of medical conditions that aren't mentioned in the Bible. I mean, do you recall reading any biblical passages about conjoined twins?'

Instead of being comforted by my words, which were meant to show inclusion, the Hancocks laughed even louder. That both mystified and irritated me, but at least it brought my husband ambling out of our bedroom and through the dining room. I was relieved to see that he was still dressed in the Amish costume that I'd made him wear, including the fake beard, cheesy though it was.

'What's going on?' he said, ignoring his lines. 'What am I missing?'

'Your charming fake Amish wife thinks that I'm transgender because I have a low voice,' Delphia boomed.

'I didn't say that there's anything wrong with it,' I hastened to say. 'The Good Lord made us who we are and loves us all equally!'

'Hon, what have I said happens when one assumes?' Gabe said self-righteously, as he ripped off the beard.

'One makes an *ass* out of *u* and *me*,' I said. 'Pardon my French, folks.' But everyone ignored me.

'How did you know the Amish bit was an act?' Gabe said.

'Perhaps it's because my wife, Dr Delphia Hancock, is a distinguished linguist and could tell immediately that your wife was faking it with her Amish dialect.'

'Not everyone is as astute as you, Dr Hancock,' my devastatingly handsome husband said with his trademark smile.

I groaned inwardly. Gabe is a medical doctor, a cardiac surgeon, who has performed heart transplants. I knew that he didn't like the fact that in America, a person with a Doctor of Philosophy degree and a person with a Doctor of Medicine degree both had the word 'doctor' in their professional titles. In his mind, that was like comparing a strawberry to a fruit salad. To his credit, he is a somewhat modest man, who only expresses that feeling to his mother – or so I've been told. By his mother.

'And the man who just complimented you,' I said to Delphia, 'is the famous, Harvard-educated, heart-transplant surgeon, Dr Gabriel Rosen. He completed four years of college, four years of medical school, five years of general surgical residency, and a three-year cardiothoracic fellowship.'

'Mags,' Gabe said, his tone chiding, 'that was completely out of line.'

'Was it?' I said. 'Since when is sticking up for your spouse a crime?'

'Now kids, play nice,' Tiny said, 'or Father's going to have to spank you and put you to bed without any supper.'

I can tell you that Gabe and I were both dumbfounded by Tiny's outrageously inappropriate comment. Our unspoken emotions must have registered on our faces because Delphia put her hands on her hips and, like a mouse that could roar, hollered up at her husband in a voice lower than his.

'You apologize to these nice people, Father,' she said. For the record, I wouldn't even consider calling my husband 'Father'. First of all, the Babester is . . . well, enough said on that subject. And secondly, the Bible tells us to call no man 'Father' but God.

'Aw, shucks, Delphia, I was only joking around. They know that.'

'Apologize now,' Delphia barked, 'or you're the one who will be going to bed with a good hard spanking and without any supper.'

Tiny hung his huge head, which, for the record, is even larger than mine. 'Yes, Mother,' he said to his wife in a tiny voice. 'Dr Rosen and Mrs Rosen, I apologize for the spanking comment.'

'And the comment about withholding supper,' Delphia growled.

'Yeah, that comment as well,' Tiny said.

'Apologies accepted,' Gabe said.

'So we're good then, right?' Delphia demanded.

'Well, I'm quite sure that Dr and Mrs Rosen are,' I said sweetly, 'but what about Miss Yoder?'

Tiny, who by now was fully inside my lobby, had yet to remove his hat. Unless he was an Orthodox Jew, I was going to fine him five dollars for being ill-mannered.

'Who is Miss Yoder?' Tiny said.

'*Moi*, dear,' I said. I could feel my sweetness dissolving like artificial sweetener when it meets hot coffee.

'Her name was all over the brochure that I gave you when I booked this place, Father,' Delphia said.

'Are you sure that we're talking about the same brochure, Mother? I couldn't get past the photo of the woman on the back cover. She looked like a real battleaxe.'

'You'll have to forgive my husband,' Delphia said. 'He suffers from foot and mouth disease.'

'This disease is usually seen in young children,' Gabe said.

'What Delphia means,' I said, 'is that her husband tends to stick his foot *in* his mouth.'

'Oh,' Gabe said, and to his credit, he blushed. Although I have lived a sheltered life, growing up a Conservative Mennonite, of Swiss Amish ancestry, I seem to have picked up more idiomatic expressions than my husband. I believe the reason for this is because I have operated a full-board inn for two decades. My clientele, although most of whom have been very wealthy, have come from all over the country, bringing with them their colourful expressions.

At any rate, before the aforementioned 'battleaxe' had a chance to formulate her own response, a van barrelled up the driveway in a spray of gravel. The second the driver slammed on the car's brakes, he, or she, leaned on the horn for an interminable length of time. I realize that I have been known to embellish my stories on rare occasions, but this time I'm almost positive that I heard Elmer Gantry's mules bray two farms over, and then Silas Marner's pack of coon hounds pick up their refrain. Then again, perhaps the infernal noise had driven me temporarily around the bend.

'Great gobs of clotted cream,' I swore angrily, 'I have half a mind to pelt you with scones.' Thank heavens the honking was so loud that the Hancocks didn't appear to have heard me swear and deliver my most un-Mennonite threat of violence.

The four of us rushed out, our hands over our ears. When the driver of the van, a woman, saw us, she took her hand off the horn and smiled broadly.

'G'day, mates. Which one of you handsome blokes is me

cousin, Gabe?' Miriam had the deeper, raspy voice of a smoker. Believe me, if she lit up, she was going to have to light out.

'That would be me,' I said, still rather annoyed. I meant it as a joke, of course.

'Crikey, mate,' the new arrival said, 'you haven't changed a bit since college. Same soft girlish skin. I see you've kept all of your hair too, so you're doing better than me, mate. There were two crocs that attacked me that day and nearly did me in. One got me leg' – she gestured at the robe that covered her lap and the pedals on the floor – 'and the other croc nearly bit me skull in half and took all of me scalp, as well as one eye.' She gestured at a hideous black wig that looked as if it might have once been part of an inexpensive Halloween costume.

Big Tiny gasped in horror, which was an appropriate response in my book. But diminutive Delphia's reaction was to snort softly and roll her eyes. Never had I witnessed a disabled person be treated with so much disrespect.

Poor Miriam was doomed to spend the rest of her life wearing wigs or head wraps in order to cover up what must be serious scars. The coarse synthetic wig hair was long, styled with a part in the middle, and she wore it with the left side brushed forward so that it mostly obscured half of her face.

However, despite the heavy layer of foundation that Miriam had trowelled all over her face, I could still catch the outline of a grotesque scar that ran from the outside of her jawbone up to her eye socket, which was covered by an eye patch. This was not your run-of-the-mill black patch either; this patch bore the image of a heavily veined eyeball sporting a neon blue iris. Clearly this poor woman needed my pity, not my anger, nor even my scorn. It was time to step up to the plate and shower her with the love and compassion that my faith required of me, even if I had to grit my teeth the entire time.

'Welcome, dear. Any cousin of Gabe is a cousin of mine. Although, I dare say, if you wish to return the compliment, you would do well to first give it a lot of thought. Until my grandparents' generation, all of my ancestors were Swiss Amish and married exclusively among themselves for four hundred years. My grandparents were fifth cousins, five different ways. They were even double second cousins. This means that I am my own first cousin. Give me a sandwich and there you have it – voila, I am a family picnic.'

'My, you are garrulous,' Miriam said in her charming Australian accent. 'You remind me of the budgerigars of my adopted homeland.'

The Hancocks laughed, which I thought rather rude of them.

'You mean digeridoos,' I said, 'don't you? That's the name of the instrument that you're thinking of.'

Gabe took my elbow gently. 'Budgerigars are parakeets,' he whispered in my ear. 'I don't think that she meant it as a compliment. Miriam, how about you open the back and I'll get your wheelchair, so that we can get you into the house?'

'I thought you'd never ask, cousin,' she said.

Gabe hadn't even blinked when he'd seen how much his beautiful cousin had changed. Ever the kind and chivalrous man – at least to other women – he hurried to meet her needs.

Miriam waited until Gabe was fully occupied retrieving her chair, and the Hancocks were on their way back inside before she addressed me again.

'Cousin Magdalena,' she said, 'please be a doll and come around to the other side of the car and get Fi-Fi for me. My precious baby hasn't had a potty break since I left Pittsburgh International Airport.'

'Excuse me?'

'My dingo.'

'OK,' I said, 'you've had your fun, but the joke is over. It's been a long day, and it's only just begun.'

'Hmm,' Miriam said. 'Should I tell Cousin Gabe that you simply refuse to help me?'

'Help you with what?' said Gabe, who'd returned *riding* in Miriam's wheelchair. Not only was the conveyance motorized, but it had so many switches and gadgets, one would think that with the addition of a small propeller, and a pair of ironing boards to serve as wings, one could get the chair airborne.

'I won't help her get her *dingo* out of her ding dang car,' I said with a sardonic laugh. 'Imagine that.'

'Yes, the dingo,' Gabe said. 'Uh, Mags, I should have warned you about that. I'm afraid it's a real, wild Australian dog.'

THREE

Boy, did I see red! Incidentally, if the average person sees red, metaphorically speaking, when they are angry, what colour does a totally colour-blind person see when they feel that emotion? Perhaps darker shades of grey?

'Actually, she's only half dingo,' Miriam said. 'Otherwise, customs wouldn't have allowed her into the country. And she's ever so tame; I hand-reared her. You know, bottle-fed her as a pup after her dog mum abandoned her immediately after giving birth to the litter.'

I'm rarely given to tantrums, but this time I stamped one of my boat-sized feet. 'This is impossible! I can't believe it, if it's true. I have a firm "no-pets" rule on my establishment, and my husband knows this.'

Gabe shrugged, before winking at Miriam. 'Magdalena, please keep in mind that this is a special occasion. Miriam flew all the way from Australia to see Ma be honoured as Hernia's Citizen of the Year, in hopes that it will mend the rift in our family. Fi-Fi suffers from *canine separation disorder* and cannot be boarded, so what was Miriam to do? Surely we can make *one* exception, can't we? For dear old Ma? For me?'

Frankly, Gabe's mother is about as dear to me as a case of poison ivy, or that bit of parsley stem that gets stuck between one's back teeth at a church supper, and is driving one crazy, but there's not a toothpick to be found for twenty miles around. Her son is a different story. He is the father of my children, and the man who shares my bed. It is no secret hereabouts that I'm married to a mama's boy, and ours has been a rocky marriage. But I'd made a solemn vow to cleave to my husband until 'death do us part' and unless Cousin Miriam was the Grim Reaper – and I wouldn't have discounted that – we were both still quite alive and kicking.

'Anything you say, dear,' I said.

'Congratulations, Cousin Gabe,' Miriam said gaily, 'you finally found that subservient woman that you went on and on about when we were in college. Is that why you finally married a Christian? Because her scriptures state that a wife should obey her husband?'

Gabe was about to lift Miriam out of the van, but he straightened and looked at me. 'Hon, I don't remember any such conversations. Besides, you know Ma, she never would have approved of a mixed marriage back then.'

'She still doesn't,' I said.

'That's right!' Gabe said, sounding greatly relieved, as if I'd exonerated him of Miriam's implication that I was a meek pushover. As a matter of fact, I struggle with the very scripture to which she'd just alluded.

I was sorely tempted to treat Miriam to a sample of my personality that was distinctly not subservient, but my conscience intervened. Had not the poor woman suffered enough already, what with being maimed and disfigured by the jaws of two of the world's most fearsome predators? Now only in her early fifties, quite possibly she still had two or three decades ahead of her to live in a wheelchair, half-blinded, and without a scalp.

'I'll go get Fi-Fi,' I said. I didn't say it meekly, but humbly, as a good Mennonite woman ought to. We are, after all, experts on humility, and justifiably proud of it.

'Good girl,' Miriam called out, as I started around the car. 'Oh, and there's an old shower curtain in the back of the van that you can lay on top of the mattress, on her side of my bed. Fi-Fi is *mostly* housebroken, but she *is* half dingo, so I can't guarantee anything. Not even that your sheep will be safe!'

I pivoted on the sole of my left brogan with half the grace of a drunken ballerina. But having never seen a sober ballerina, that's just a guess, mind you. In a flash I was back at my starting point.

'Oh, no. Oh, no. We're putting you in *our* room, and you're getting *our* bed. If you think that ding dang dong dingo of yours is going to make doo-doo in our bed, then you're a ding-a-ling!'

'She meant pee-pee,' my clueless husband said, 'not doo-doo.'

'Then the three of you can share a room,' I said, 'in another establishment.'

Miriam had a deep, throaty laugh. I could have imagined it coming from Delphia's throat.

'Well,' she said, 'your not-so-little woman is not as subservient as I imagined. She's got a spark in her after all. If I didn't have a Sheila of me own back in Cairns, I could fancy this one.'

Let it be known that my Achilles heel is susceptibility to flattery. And like just about everyone whom I've ever met, I have a need to be liked – at least by someone. However, my desire for others' approval has never even caused me to fantasize about doing the mattress mambo with another person of the same gender.

'You're not my type, dear,' I said. 'I'm afraid that I've recently become virulently anti-Antipodean.'

Miriam stared at me, obviously without a shred of comprehension. At last she turned to her dear Cousin Gabe for a translation.

'It means that she hates Aussies,' he said. 'But she was only joking; two of our best friends are from Melbourne.'

At that Miriam cackled so hard that poor Fi-Fi, who still hadn't been walked, howled pitifully. Woe was me, because my pebble-sized heart was beginning to soften.

'You are quite a character,' she said when she could control herself. 'I rather think I like you. Yes, I'm sure of it. You and I are going to get along famously.'

'Don't count your chickens before they hatch, dear,' I said. 'You may stay here on two conditions: the first is that you pay a one-time, non-refundable fee of five hundred dollars for your pet to stay with you in your room. This fee does not include any charges for whatever damages your dog might cause. The second condition is that you understand and sign a waiver that states that although you may sleep in my bed, that mutt of yours will not. I'll be moving our son's old crib into the room and placing it next to your side of the bed. It has a pee-pee proof mattress on it, and since we won't be having any more children, that demi-dingo of yours can chew on its wooden slats all it wants.'

Miriam clapped her hands happily. 'You're a fair dinkum mate.'

'Back at you, toots,' I said. Of course I didn't have a clue to what she'd just said.

'She said that you're a true friend,' Gabe said, who can read my mind – just not when I need him to.

Hypocrite that I am, I flashed Miriam a wan smile. 'Wonderful,' I said. 'Now I think I'll make like a bee and buzz off. It's time to wake my little one and feed him breakfast.'

'But you have to walk her dog,' Gabe said.

'No, you do,' I said.

'*What?*'

'You heard me, dear.'

Gabe grabbed my hand and pulled me aside. 'Mags,' he hissed, 'have you no mercy? Don't you see that she needs help getting into her wheelchair?' Incidentally, one can only hiss when saying a word that includes the letter 'S'.

'No, darling, she doesn't need help. Miriam isn't handicapped – she is very handicapable. She has one very good leg, one prosthetic leg, and two very strong arms.'

'How do you know?' he demanded.

'Because she has to have functioning legs under her lap robe in order to drive, and she *drove* all the way here from Pittsburgh International Airport. This van isn't equipped with handicap controls. Anyway, you can bet that Miriam has strong arms, and a good grip as well, because she would have needed them to steer around all the potholes and deer carcasses on the turnpike.'

'Good point,' Gabe conceded. 'Now what?'

'Leave that to me,' I whispered.

'Are you two lovebirds done plotting my demise?' Miriam called in a voice that managed to be both plaintive and playful at the same time.

'Ages ago,' I said brightly as we returned to where she sat, still inside the car. 'We settled that before you came. We're going to bore you to death, and then dip you in milk chocolate, roll you in chopped peanuts, and sell you at our Billy Goat Gruff Festival this weekend.'

'Excellent! What a way to go – except for the actual demise part.'

'Miriam,' I said, 'do you need some assistance getting into your chair? I'd be happy to put you in it.'

'*You*, Magdalena?'

'Of course me, dear. I am, after all, a farm girl, born and bred. I've been slinging bales of hay up into the loft since I was knee high to a grasshopper.'

'Crikey! If you aren't just about the most amazing woman I've met in a long time. Bright, beautiful, and as strong as a wallaby on steroids. You're everything a girl could want.'

'Feeling wanted can be a powerful aphrodisiac,' I said, 'but you can stop flirting with me, Cousin Miriam. There isn't a snowball's chance in the Devil's abode that you could lead me to commit adultery with you.'

'Mags,' Gabe said sternly, 'how could you even think such a thing?'

Miriam had the audacity to pull a hurt face. 'Am I that hideous? Is it my eye patch?'

I shook my head. 'No, your eye patch is quite clever. You're just too short for my taste.'

'Mags!' Gabe chided, 'That's beneath you.'

'Do you mean because I'm in a wheelchair?' Miriam said.

'No,' I said. 'I'm just not attracted to someone who is under five feet eight. That's my bottom line. Six feet would be better.'

'But I'm five eight!' Miriam cried. 'At least I was – before that old salty got me leg.'

'Maybe,' I said.

'Mags!' Gabe said.

'I *am* five feet, nine inches tall,' Miriam said. As she spoke, she managed to slip out from beneath the steering wheel and was presumably standing, and straight as a soldier at attention. However, since she had also managed to extract the lap robe with her and wrap it securely around her waist in the twinkly of an eye, it was impossible to discern which leg was flesh and bone, and which was prosthetic. Or for that matter, how long her legs were. As far as I could tell, Miriam might only have been five feet tall and wearing ten-inch platform shoes.

'You *see*,' Gabe said triumphantly.

I'm quite sure that a clever retort was about to issue forth from my thin, withered lips, when the shortest male to ever have stolen my heart ran up from behind and threw his arms around my waist.

FOUR

'Mommy, Mommy,' my five-year-old cried. 'Auntie Freni said to tell you that she is beside huhself and that Mona is cwhying.'

For the record, my son, like many American children his age, still cannot pronounce his 'R's, and unlike my husband, I refuse to insist that he does. After all, even most Brits can't pronounce their 'R's when they appear at the end of a word.

'Well, looks like I'm being summoned,' I said.

'Wait,' Gabe ordered. 'You can't leave; you still haven't walked Cousin Miriam's dog.'

My dear, sweet son, fruit of my once barren womb, released my thickening waist. 'This lady has a doggie? Where?'

'Come on, Little Jacob,' I said. 'Off we go. Back into the house, dear.'

'Oh, what a handsome little devil you are,' cooed Miriam. 'The spitting image of your daddy when he was your age, you are. I bet you've got the sheilas chasing you even now.'

Little Jacob stood rooted to the spot. 'I don't got no cheetahs chasing me,' he said hotly, ''cause they would have catched me alweddy. They'ah the fastest animals on the eawth. Don't ya know anything, lady?' (Note to my gentle weaduhs. Since it is too hahd to twanslitewate the speech of vewy young Amehwicans, I shall cease forthwith.)

'That's my boy,' Gabe said proudly. 'He's a verifiable genius. Still too young to start first grade in public school, but he's already reading at tenth-grade level.'

'Good on ya, mate,' Miriam said, and held out her arms. 'Come give your Cousin Miriam a welcome kiss.'

My son shook his head vigorously. 'No. You're a strange lady and I don't like you.'

'Little Jacob!' Gabe said. 'Come here and apologize now.'

'No.' Little Jacob crossed his arms defiantly.

Gabe glared at *me*, not at our son. 'I said, "Come here".'

My son adores his father. Likewise, Gabe adores and dotes on his son. That's all well and good. Unfortunately Little Jacob is keenly aware that the one who wears the pants in our family has never actually slipped into a pair of trousers. When the roles of 'good cop, bad cop' are required, it is Yours Truly who is stuck with being the 'bad cop'. Always. That is to say, it is invariably left up to me to discipline our son. Gabe's admonishments mean almost nothing to Little Jacob.

'Magdalena,' Gabe said, his face turning red, 'make your son obey.'

'Go back in the house at once, Little Jacob, and tell Aunt Freni that I'm coming,' I said, and off he ran.

'There,' I said, 'are you satisfied?'

'That's not what I meant,' my dear husband growled, 'and you know it!'

'It's not? Oh, crikey, you know how rattled I can get when surprises are sprung on me. Speaking of which, poor Freni will be bouncing off the walls by now, having heard that she has to cook for your Aunt Miriam as well.'

'I'm not his *aunt*,' Miriam snapped. 'I'm his first cousin. His mother is my aunt.'

'Oh,' I said coyly. 'I'm sure that was already established, but I forgot and was judging by your appearance and, as I'm sure that you must be aware, having lived such a long life, appearances can be deceiving. It's just that you and his mother could be twins.'

Know when to walk away, and know when to run, *n'est-ce pas*? Actually, I tried to stride away nonchalantly, like I imagined a self-satisfied Parisian might do if she'd just delivered a so-called 'zinger', but given my gangly physique, it was more of a pitiful lope. As scripture points out, our sins will always catch up with us.

Freni, who has been the primary cook here at The PennDutch Inn since its inception twenty-five years ago, is a genuine Amish woman. In addition to being my late mother's best friend, she was closely related to both of my adoptive parents, as well as my birth parents. That's because both sets of parents were Mennonites of Swiss Amish ancestry, a group that had inbred for centuries. Is it any wonder that I lope when I mean to stride?

At any rate, my dear octogenarian cook and cousin is stout, lacks all semblance of a neck, and wears spectacles so thick that one could start a roaring fire with them given some kindling and a few seconds of sunshine. Although she won't admit it, Freni has reached the point where she can't always do everything by herself, so now we have Becca as well.

Thirty-one-year-old Becca's full name is Rebecca, but Little Jacob, who as I said has trouble with his R's, has always called her Becca. Rebecca, whose parents are both Mennonites, is also related to me. Her father is a Professor of English Literature at Penn State, and her mother is a homemaker. I have reviewed Rebecca's genealogical chart, and if I wasn't college educated myself, I could be tempted to conclude that the young woman is the daughter that I had 'unawares'.

Granted, we don't look exactly alike, but not every woman resembles her mother. To put it kindly, Rebecca resembles a brown-eyed mule wearing a straw hat, minus the hat. In addition, she is knock-kneed, and walks with a most unusual gait. There, I won't say another negative thing about the way she looks, except that she has exceptionally large teeth. Perhaps I shouldn't have said that much, because who am I to talk?

Where we differ the most is in our personalities. Rebecca is as sweet as maple syrup, but as slow as molasses outdoors on a January day. And I don't mean mentally slow, either. Rebecca makes a tortoise seem like an Olympic sprinter. In the spirit of Christian charity, I shan't dig much further into her myriad personality faults other than to say that as a waitress, she is utterly incompetent. But again, she is as sweet as maple syrup.

One might reasonably ask why it is that I should employ Rebecca. The answer is simple: I have to put my money where my big mouth is. You see, my people are pacifists. We do not believe in taking human lives. We refuse to go to war, we are against the death penalty, and yes, we believe that abortion is taking a human life, so we are against that too. (Gabe, by the way, is pro-choice, but he is still against the death penalty.)

At any rate, since I believe that the mother should keep the baby until it is born (although I do hold out for exceptions), I believe that it is my responsibility to see that the child is provided for afterwards. Rebecca was single, working at a minimum pay job, and sharing an apartment with three other women when she became pregnant. At that point she'd been estranged from her parents for a dozen years over something which I will not share, simply because I am not one to gossip. Quite possibly it might have involved a few drugs, petty theft, and more than a wee bit of sex, but again, my lips are sealed. Now, where was I going with this?

Oh yes, one Sunday morning the wretched woman, heartbroken and feeling hopeless, sat next to me in church. It was the first time that Rebecca had been in the Lord's house since heading off to college at the age of eighteen. Even if she hadn't been nine months pregnant, I wouldn't have recognized her. Long story short, I invited the weeping woman back to eat Sunday dinner with us. I gave her a roof until the baby was born, found her a roof afterwards, and then employed her at a decent salary. After all that Rebecca decided to give her baby up for adoption.

One need not worry that I am a saint; I have more detractors than there are ears of corn in a dairyman's silo. The important thing is that my family loves me, and that my young son adores Rebecca. The fact that both my elderly kinswoman/cook and my hunk of a husband find the young woman in question more irritating than a pebble in one's shoe – well, I keep praying that the Good Lord will change their hearts.

When I returned to the lobby of the inn I found Delphia Hancock fit to be tied. She was swivelling and spinning so aggressively in the office chair behind the check-in counter that the swirling black cloud above her head had a difficult time keeping up. Her husband Tiny, however, was sitting calmly on the counter with one boot and sock on the floor. It took me a minute to wrap my mind around the fact that he was cleaning his toenails with one of my paper clips.

'Howdy again, ma'am,' he drawled.

'Don't you be all sweet to her,' snapped Delphia, swivelling to a stop so fast that the storm cloud above her head collapsed in on itself and disappeared. The little woman hopped off my chair and advanced on me like a bantam rooster would on another cock encroaching on his harem. Instead of pecking me with a beak, she repeatedly jabbed the air with a miniature finger. The claw-like nails on said digit came so close to my dress that at one point a talon caught a small snag on my bodice and created a noticeably larger one.

'The service here is deplorable,' she raged. 'What did you expect us to do while you held that gabfest out there with that creature?'

I was not amused. 'First of all, you will not speak disrespectfully about a person who is disabled. And secondly, you will pay for this,' I said while trying to smooth out the snag.

'So now you're threatening me?' Delphia snarled. 'You lay a hand on me and I'll have you arrested for assault.'

'Down girl,' Tiny said. 'I think Miss Yoder was referring to her dress.'

'What dress?' Delphia said. 'That's a cheap, knock-off costume. I've seen better ones at party supply stores.'

'My land o'Goshen,' I said. 'This is the genuine article. I bought it from my Aunt Irma Rhody's estate, and she was a pious Amish woman, who was wearing this very same dress the day that she died. It was a very clean death, mind you; Irma drowned in the mill pond standing on her head.'

'She's pulling your leg,' Tiny said with a deep-throated chuckle.

'It isn't funny,' Delphia said to her husband. She turned abruptly to me. 'For your information, Miss Yoder, it wasn't Aunt Rhody who drowned in the song, it was the old grey goose. I suggest that in future, if you plan to mock your guests, at least go to the trouble of getting the lyrics right.'

'Mock, smock,' I said, quite justifiably annoyed. 'I was merely trying to inject a little levity into what was rapidly becoming a somewhat heated discourse.'

'That was your doing,' she said. 'Now, what I want to know is where's your bellhop? Because if you think we're going to carry our own luggage around this dump, you've got another think coming.'

'Me thinks not, dear,' I said. 'I do know that you read your contract thoroughly because you initialled and signed all the right places. At any rate, part of the charm of this establishment is that you get to pay through the nose for the privilege of schlepping your own bags up my impossibly steep stairs, while viewing it as a cultural experience. For an extra one hundred dollars a day you also get the additional privilege of cleaning your own room. Mr and Mrs Morris, who have yet to arrive, have already claimed the honour of mucking out the barn, for a mere two hundred dollars a day. However, my cook and her husband, who are a genuine Amish couple, have graciously offered to allow my guests to muck out their outhouse for the paltry sum of five hundred dollars.'

'Yippee,' said Tiny, 'now this is what I call a yee-haw vacation. Sign us up for mucking out the poop shed. Say, what kind of cattle ya got?'

'I have two Jersey cows. The most beautiful girls you've ever seen – except for my daughter, of course.'

Tiny laughed. 'Pardon me, ma'am, but them is sissy cows.'

'They most certainly are not!' Then the Devil got into me and urged me to be snarky. 'I suppose that you ride bareback on a wild mustang whilst rounding up your long-horn steers?'

Delphia snorted and stomped a foot the size of an ear of 'baby' corn. 'Will you two bovine-brained blowhards just shut up already, so that a gal can hear herself think?'

'Excuse me,' said a new voice. It belonged to Rebecca. Who knew how long she'd been standing in the doorway to the dining room and eavesdropping? The woman certainly had a talent for it.

'Rebecca, dear,' I said patiently, 'not now. Can't you see that I'm busy?'

'But ma'am, that man is here.'

'What man?'

'You know, *that* man.'

'I have no idea to whom it is that you refer. Has Little Jacob got his breakfast?'

'Yes, ma'am.'

'That's all then.'

'No, it isn't,' she said placidly.

I frowned disapprovingly, hoping that this alone would send her scurrying back to the kitchen. Ha! Silly me. One of the gal's less endearing characteristics is that she is more stubborn than a team of mules. She didn't move a muscle; except for her vaguely human features, she might have been a mule carved out of stone.

'Then please explain, dear,' I said, praying for Christian charity.

After all, how would it look if I upbraided my staff in front of paying guests who might yet be heathens, or Presbyterians? Or worse yet, Anglicans? What sort of example would I be showing them? Why, they might think that I was a full-time, intentional hypocrite, like some televangelists are, instead of the accidental, part-time hypocrite that I become when I am stressed out.

'The man who always wants to speak to you alone,' Rebecca said. The resentment in her voice was almost palpable to me. Rebecca had a wide mouth to accommodate her exceptionally large teeth, and she had a bizarre way of pulling back her lips after slowly enunciating each word. Her ears were unnaturally long and narrow – I am sure that the Good Lord had His reasons – but they added to her mulish appearance.

'Tell him I'll be right there,' I said.

'You're not going anywhere,' Delphia said. 'Not until we get a few things settled here first. For instance, we're still waiting on a bellhop. I simply *refuse* to do without.'

Rebecca smiled at Delphia. 'When that man comes to see Miss Yoder this early in the morning, it can only mean one thing.'

'Yee-haw!' Tiny said, as he tossed an imagery lasso in my direction.

'Rein it in, cowboy,' I said. 'That mysterious man is our Chief of Police, and as Mayor of the Village of Hernia, *I* am his boss. A visit from Chief Toy Graham this early in the morning means that someone has been—'

'Murdered,' said Rebecca. Only after having stolen my thunder did she see fit to bolt from the room.

FIVE

Toy and I retreated to the privacy of his cruiser with our steaming mugs of coffee and a dinner plate stacked high with Freni's freshly baked cinnamon buns. I planned to enjoy two of them, and I knew that Toy would polish off the rest.

I waited until Toy had devoured a bun and slurped his way

through part of his coffee before speaking. Don't get me wrong, Police Chief Toy, who hails originally from Charlotte, North Carolina, has impeccable manners, but he is a bachelor and needs fuel to run the gears inside his handsome head. I mean, one wouldn't think of flipping on a light switch during a power outage, would one?

'Lay it on me,' I said. 'Who, what, when, where, and why. All the details that should be included in a properly written piece of journalistic reporting, but seldom are anymore.'

The dear boy – he is after all, only in his early thirties – smiled. 'The world would be a better place if you were its mother, Magdalena.'

I sighed. 'I suppose you meant that as a compliment.'

'What else could it be?'

'Hmm,' I said. Why were some men so clueless? So what if I was mostly happily married, twenty years older than him, and yes, a mother? That still didn't mean that I wanted *him* to fit me into the 'mother' slot.

'Moving right along,' he said, 'the murder victims were a married couple: Gerald and Tanya Morris.'

I gasped, spilling what was left of my coffee all over my fake Amish dress. The plastic-like fabric doesn't breathe and is practically waterproof, so that it really didn't matter. Nonetheless, it irritated me and drove me to swearing.

'Bite-size custard tarts,' I said.

'Why, hush your dirty mouth,' Toy said in his genuine Carolina accent. 'Magdalena, by your reaction, I take it that you know this couple.'

'I know *of* them. They were scheduled guests for this week, due to arrive at any moment. Surely you've heard of them as well. They're the renowned sociologists who wrote that best-selling book, *Brits with Buggies*. You know, about the ten suburban London couples, all of them wealthy, upper class folks, who decided to leave the twenty-first century behind and join the Amish community.'

'Yeah, I read that book. Those rich Londoners didn't fare very well traveling back in time, did they?'

'Sadly, no. One reason is because they didn't approach it from a spiritual angle. They weren't divorcing modernity because of its sinful influence; they were doing it for health and ecological reasons.'

'Right,' Toy said. 'The authors called them "New Age hippies".'

'Then of course,' I said, 'as you now know from living up here in the village of Hernia for the last seven years, although the Amish are not a closed group, for all intents and purposes they may as well be. Everyone is related to everyone else, they speak their own dialect, and they shun baptized church members who disobey the *Ordnung* – the community rules as laid down by the elders.'

Toy reached for another cinnamon bun. 'I could never be Amish. I could never give up my eighty-four-inch flatscreen, 4HD TV.'

'Good point, but put that bun down, dear, and tell me where Gerald and Tanya Morris met their Maker, and how?'

Toy coloured and immediately threw the bun back on the plate, so impeccable are his manners. 'Well, hold on for a bumpy ride, Magdalena, because the details are pretty gruesome.'

'More gruesome than finding a pickled body in a sauerkraut barrel?' I asked. 'Or discovering a corpse that has been flattened by a steam roller? Because these eyes have seen just about everything.'

The police chief shook his handsome head. 'Ma'am, I keep forgetting about what an awesome life you must have lived.'

'*Lived?* It's not over yet!'

'T-that's not what I meant, Magdalena. I was merely trying to compliment you.'

I graced him with an ambiguous sigh. 'Facts, dear. *Where*, and *how*. For now. Then together we'll try to figure out the motive.'

'In your cousin Sam's dumpster. The one behind his store. They were both shot with a small firearm and then she, having apparently survived that, was stabbed. But that's for the coroner to determine.'

'Hot water crust!' I said. Gabe had recently coaxed me into watching *The Great British Bake Off* and for some inexplicable reason, terms that I heard on that show found their way to my lips when I was stressed. Gone were the days when my worst swear words were 'ding, dang, and dong'.

Toy smiled. 'If you weren't my boss, Magdalena, I'd chide

you for being such a potty mouth. By the way, I love that show too.'

I cringed. My reputation as a Conservative Mennonite woman was going to suffer if word got around that I watched television other than religious programming. Leave it to some envious and somewhat imaginative harpy to say that I lollygagged all day on a cushy divan whilst devouring chocolate bonbons.

'More details, Toy!' I said, hoping to distract the young police chief. 'What time were the bodies discovered? And by whom?'

Toy lunged for the cinnamon bun and took a bite before answering. 'That's more bad news: they were discovered by Monotone Mona when she was dumpster-diving early this morning. She says she waited awhile before she called me because of the shock.'

'*Excuse* me?'

'Uh – which part?'

'The dumpster – whatever.'

'Dumpster-diving. Monotone Mona climbs into dumpsters outside of grocery stores on a regular basis to rescue foodstuffs that she believes to be still edible. Of course, we have only the one – Yoder's Corner Market – but she also goes into Bedford and Somerset on a regular basis.'

I was gobsmacked, rendered uncharacteristically speechless while Toy finished his bun.

'That's bizarre,' I finally said. 'That's got to be one for the record books.'

Toy wiped the back of his hand across his mouth. 'Actually, no. People have been doing it for years. Some do it because they can't afford to buy groceries, and others do it because they hate the idea of anything going to waste.'

'Well, I guess I learn something new every day. Why do you think that Monotone Mona does it? I've never been inside her house, but she keeps it up – at least on the outside – and she's never fallen behind on her village assessments as far as I can remember.'

Toy started to reach for the last cinnamon bun, but after glancing down at his still flat stomach, shrugged and gave me his full attention. 'Her house is well-maintained inside as well, Magdalena. It's actually furnished very nicely. I'm not an expert on antiques, but my mother knows a lot, and used to take me to shops, and auctions, all around Charlotte. In my opinion, Monotone Mona has some very nice pieces. She certainly has a lot of silver, and her electronics are all high-end.'

'In other words,' I ventured, 'the fact that she is literally eating garbage might be a choice on her part?'

'Possibly.'

'On a scale from one to ten, how upset did she seem to be when she made the call? And then later when you interviewed her?'

'Well, that's the thing, isn't it?' Toy said. 'With Monotone Mona everything she says comes out as the same flat droning note. She can put you to sleep just by saying hello. Magdalena, I've lived here in Hernia for eight years, not seven, and I still don't know her name. Everyone just refers to her as Monotone Mona.'

'Her name is Mona Boyer,' I said. 'You know, I should be ashamed of myself for having used that pejorative adjective earlier, no matter how apt. Mona's life story informs her current behaviour, just like everyone else's does, except that undoubtedly hers is more dramatic. You see, when she was about nine, her family was returning from a trip to visit family up near Erie and their station wagon slid off a country road during a blizzard. It ploughed over an embankment, into a deep snow drift, where it subsequently got buried under more snow. That was during one of our coldest winters on record. At any rate, it took six weeks for anyone to discover the wreck and by that time Mona's parents, three sisters, and two brothers were long dead.

'One of the back windows was open a crack, so authorities surmised that Mona ate snow to survive. No one had the heart to ask her what, if anything, she ate – although it was pretty obvious. Anyway, she didn't speak at all for almost a year. She was placed with her aunt and uncle here in Hernia, who lived in the same house that Mona lives in now. They were childless, and her aunt home-schooled her.'

'Holy guacamole!' Toy said. 'I wish I'd known all that before I interviewed her. It just goes to show you that you never know what's under the hood of another human being.'

'Yes,' I agreed, 'but would you have tried a different approach? Knowing what you know now? I can't imagine you being any kinder.'

'One can always be kinder,' Toy said. 'Hey, Magdalena, I've gotta get back to the crime scene, which is still active. I just wanted to fill you in personally. And you may wish to follow me back into town. Your cousin, Sam, is practically having a meltdown.'

SIX

Sam Yoder is more than just a cousin. He is a first cousin, a double second cousin – who knows what else? Given the intersecting bloodlines of the Amish and Mennonites of Amish descent, I wouldn't be totally shocked if Sam turned out to be my father, brother, and an uncle, all at the same time. (Only one of those would be mildly surprisingly, given that Sam and I are roughly the same age.)

The disconcerting thing is that Samuel Nivens Yoder has always harboured the hots for me. Through thick and thin (I've always been thin, whereas his wife Dorothy weighs well over four hundred pounds), Samuel has striven mightily to breech my sturdy Christian underwear. I refuse to yield an inch. So relentless are his attempts to know me in the biblical sense, that I am convinced that the only time that Sam will cease in his efforts are when he is dead, or else during the Rapture, when he is too preoccupied ascending into Heaven to think adulterous thoughts.

Imagine my state of mind when I discovered Sam sitting in a puddle of tears on his storeroom floor behind the grocery. When he looked up and saw me, he began to audibly sob. At that point I felt as awkward as a Brit in a lift with a chatty stranger. To hug, or not to hug, that was the question. Given Sam's lifelong obsession with me, and what lies beyond my sturdy Christian underwear, a mere act of compassion could easily be misconstrued. On the other hand, I was blood kin, as well as a neighbour, and supposedly a good Christian. Surely I might be able to get away with a couple of swift pats on the back.

I leaned over the stricken man. 'There, there,' I said, patting briskly as if I was burping a baby. A very *hot* baby.

'Where, where?' Sam responded.

'*What?*' I said. 'How can you joke at a time like this? You're in the middle of bawling your eyes out.'

'Quite true,' Sam said as he rubbed his eyes. 'But that's the same response that you always give when someone drags out that meaningless platitude "there, there". Isn't it? I figured what's good for the goose is good for the gander.'

'*Or* if we were Brits,' I said, 'the word would be "sauce".'

'Magdalena, you are a saucy, sassy woman, and a good friend. Thank you for trying to take my mind off things, even for a second.'

'Did it work? At least a trifle?'

'Do you mean just a small amount? Or are you speaking British again, and referencing a dessert? I can certainly go for the latter. It has booze in it, you know. Sherry, usually.'

'No, I didn't know that,' I said, 'and you better not know about the booze from personal experience.'

That made Sam smile. 'My favourite teetotaller of a cousin. I'll never convince you that Jesus drank wine.'

The truth is that my Jewish husband had already convinced me of that fact. As for what Sam puts in his mouth – well, that's none of my business, is it? Because as Gabe told me once, in Sam's store as a matter of fact: 'It's not your zoo, and they're not your monkeys.' Gabe was referring to some scantily clad tourists whom I wanted to lecture, but hey, my need to control the behaviour of others is something that even I cannot deny with a straight face.

'Jesus also drank water,' I reminded Sam. 'It says so in John, chapter four, verse nine.' Sam had begun life as a good Mennonite and then defected when he married that wild Methodist gal, Dorothy. What harm was there in drilling a biblical reference into his head now and then, before he forgot his upbringing altogether?

'You're feeding a monkey,' Sam said.

'*What?*' I said.

'I overheard what Gabe told you that day; I know what that expression means. I'm not your child.'

'Uh, you're absolutely right,' I said. 'May I sit down?'

He gestured to the floor in front of him. 'Sure.'

'On a chair, dear.'

Sam groaned as he stood, and then led me into his cramped office. Along the walls, stacked floor to ceiling, were boxes of candy and cookies. Sam's desk had been pulled into the middle of the claustrophobic room, and we sat on either side of it on metal folding chairs. Sam has been proud of his ability to keep overhead costs to a minimum.

With his head down, and his thumb pushing hard against the bridge of his nose, he began to speak in a low voice. 'I should have listened to Toy and not looked in the dumpster bin. What I saw will haunt me for the rest of my life. I'll never be unable to stop seeing those two bodies. Especially that horribly mutilated woman. I don't know how you do it, Magdalena.'

'I don't mutilate women, Sam.'

He glanced up. 'No more jokes, OK? When word of this gets out –which it will – it could mean the end of my business.'

'You're talking crazy,' I said. 'Why on earth would that happen?'

'I'll tell you why,' Sam said, close to tears again, 'because who in their right mind is going to want to shop at Yoder's Corner Market, knowing full well that two people were murdered out in back? Heck, it may as well have been me who really killed them.'

'Now you *are* talking crazy. You started working here for the previous owner when you were a teenager. Some of these people have been your customers for over thirty years. Others have known you their entire lives. No one is going to think that you murdered those two folks in the dumpster bin.

'Besides, take it from me, Queen Ghoul of the PennDutch, when the folks over in Bedford hear about this tragedy – which they will, in time for the evening paper – they will flock to this store like pigeons to a bag of spilled popcorn.'

Sam sniffed and straightened. 'Do you really think so?'

'I guarantee it,' I said.

'But what about Billy Goat Gruff Festival and the parade?' he said.

'What about it?'

Sam waved his freckled arms in all directions. 'Just look at all of this mountain of candy and cookies: they're special orders from the village parents to toss at the children in the parade when they "baa" like goats. What parent is going to trust picking up a candy order from a maniac who allegedly committed a double homicide? I mean, is there even going to *be* a parade now?'

'Don't be daft, dear,' I said. 'No one wants to disappoint the children. And you forget, we don't have an age limit on who gets to be a goat for a day. Last year we had some pretty old goats. Weren't there at least fifty folks from Deer Tick Assisted Living Facility all the way over in Monroeville?'

Sam smiled. 'You're right. That's why I advised some folks to add soft candy to their orders. Anyone who totters breathlessly along behind their walker, while trying to bleat like a billy goat, should not worry about getting his, or her dentures broken—'

The door to Sam's office was pushed open by the first eighteen inches of Sheriff Stodgewiggle's beer belly. Quite a bit more of his midriff followed, as well as jowls that resembled a large, jellied ham. Above the latter rode three quivering chins. Toy entered the room as soon as he could squeeze past this imposing edifice.

'I'm sorry, Sam,' Chief Toy said. 'It wasn't me who called the sheriff.'

Sam looked at me inquiringly.

'Nor was it me,' I said. 'You know how I feel about this man. After the way he treated me the last time someone died at my inn, I'd sooner have a root canal without novocaine than be in the same room with him.'

'Oh, quit your whining,' said the grossly overweight lawman. 'This is my county, and I can do what I want.'

Toy, bless his relatively bean-sized heart, puffed out his chest. 'Sheriff, you are infringing on my jurisdiction here. Hernia is my town. I am more than competent to investigate this crime scene. I strongly suggest that you return to Bedford or attend to more pressing matters elsewhere in the county.'

To watch someone the size of Sheriff Stodgewiggle belly laugh can be downright unnerving, so I didn't dare look any lower than his chins. To be fair, the sound of me laughing causes jackasses, of the four-legged variety, to leap their paddock fences and seek me out for a romantic rendezvous.

'Ho-ho-ho,' the sheriff boomed, 'you're quite an amusing little man. *More than competent.* It's no wonder you people lost the Civil War.'

Toy rested his balled fists on his slim hips. 'If my itty-bitty granny was in this room, she'd have jumped up and boxed both of your corpulent ears – one at a time. Her granddaddy fought in that war which, by the way, she called the War of Northern Aggression. In school I was taught to call it the War Between the States, because there was nothing civil about it.'

'Oh yeah? Your defensiveness leads me to believe that the three of you are trying to cover up for something.'

That did it! That hiked my hackles practically up to my armpits.

'Get out of my town, you bullying interloper,' I hollered. 'Go pick on a crowd your own size – like at a football game!'

'Are you fat-shaming me, Magdalena Yoder?'

'Indeed I am not,' I said. 'You did it to yourself with the sin of gluttony. Four burritos, extra cheese, two large orders of fries, and a supersize soda for breakfast. Then a dozen glazed doughnuts for your mid-morning coffee break—'

'Are you spying on me?' Sheriff Stodgewiggle hissed.

'I heard that's what you ate the morning I was waiting for my arraignment, when you had me arrested for a murder that I didn't commit. Some of the good folks who worked at the county jail that day said that you were ill, but instead you were feeding your bottomless belly. And they said it was an unusually light order for you.'

'Get out of my way, you idiot,' the sheriff roared, and barrelled out of Sam's office.

Toy waited a couple of minutes and then took me out back to the dumpster bin. By mutual agreement Sam remained inside. Even if he weren't going to take another peak at the pair of putrefying corpses, his absence was a good thing. I say that because it seemed like half of Hernia was already there, jostling to get as close as possible to the site where our village's umpteenth murder victims had been unceremoniously deposited. It was all our other police officer, Lucinda Cakewalker, could do to keep them from breaking through the yellow crime scene tape. In a village where seemingly nothing ever happens, we take our pleasures where, and when, we find them.

SEVEN

For pleasure these days I read the sort of books that fall into the genre of 'cozy mysteries'. No cozy mystery author worth her salt would even allude to such a gruesome scene as this. However, should one of those authors foolishly ignore this convention, she should at least have the courtesy to announce her attentions beforehand. If I was a writer of cozy mysteries I would state it thusly: 'Gentle readers, those with delicate constitutions are advised to skip over the following eight or ten paragraphs, as they may be a wee bit too intense for your well-bred sensibilities.' Then again, not being a novelist, what do I know?

Because the day promised to be a real scorcher, and the garbage bin was in full sun, Toy had wisely ordered that the lid remain open. The trapezoid shape of the bin, with the opening facing the store, prevented the public from seeing its contents, but it welcomed every fly in Hernia to come in to dine on the refuse of the past several days, plus the two new entrees. After staring at the corpses for several minutes, I'd seen all that I'd needed to know about what had happened to my prospective guests.

Once my head was out of the bin, I gulped for fresh air, and in the process I swallowed a fly. The rest of the horde I swatted away from the corners of my mouth, which I then wiped on my modest, elbow-length sleeve. Then I tugged on Toy's arm.

'Let's go back inside, dear. Sam's going to have to donate some mouthwash to the cause.'

Then once Toy and I were fully restored and refreshed, and Sam had been gently shooed from his own office, Toy got down to business.

'Now don't wimp out on me, Magdalena,' he said. 'You know that's why I dragged you down here. Besides the fact that this couple were your intended guests, you almost always see something that I've somehow missed. I swear, Magdalena, you should have become a professional detective, and not an innkeeper.'

'Ha,' I said. 'That's what Gabe says, except that he means it sarcastically. He also says that if I wasn't an innkeeper, the total number of murders in Hernia over the last twenty years would be a fraction of what it is today.'

Toy grinned. 'He's right. But enough about that. Let's get started: what did you learn?'

'The most obvious thing about this case,' I said, 'is that the killer has done this before.' As I spoke I scrutinized Toy's face to see if he agreed. All I could tell was that he didn't strongly disagree.

'Please explain,' he said.

'Well, for one thing, there isn't a blood trail across the parking lot leading to the bin. The asphalt is crazed with a jillion tiny cracks. It would have been impossible to clean up.'

'Not so,' Toy said. 'Pour hydrogen peroxide directly onto blood, and it eats it right up. That stuff is available in any pharmacy in the first aid section.'

'That may be so,' I said. 'But you'd need gallons of it to be able to clean the parking lot, the way this woman bled. He stabbed her in the aorta. My guess is that the killer brought a plastic sheet with him, rolled her body up in it, and then dragged her from the car to the bin.'

Toy shook his handsome head slowly. 'Then where's the sheet?'

I nodded my horsey head vigorously. 'That's it! I know it is.'

'What is? No wait! Answer my question: where's the darn plastic sheet? If he'd unwrapped her in the bin, and then pulled the sheet out, there *would* be one heck of a bloody mess to clean up.'

'Watch *your* swearing, dear,' I said sweetly. Episcopalians like Toy (America's version of Anglicans) sometimes use salty language.

'Explain that *darn* plastic sheet *now*,' Toy growled, 'or you'll have one *heck* of an irritated police chief on your hands.'

'Aye, aye, sir,' I said with a stiff salute, and in the process jabbed my thumb into the bridge of my prominent Yoder proboscis. 'You know that I am not a betting woman, but if I was, I would wager that you have not moved the bodies.' I paused long enough for another wrinkle to form on my fifty-some face, and when no confirmation seemed forthcoming, I plunged on. 'Anyway, dear,' I said, 'these bodies weren't just thrown into the dumpster bin – they were *placed* in it. The scene was staged. I think that when you move the woman's body, you will probably find the plastic sheet folded up beneath her.'

Toy was staring at me wide-eyed. But whether it was because he thought I was on to something, or was just plain nuts, he wasn't ready to say.

'I'm not going to take another look,' I said, 'but if you do, you'll see that the garbage is mounded up around her, as if to hide something. That will be the plastic sheet.'

He rubbed his lean, but strong, jaw. 'You're describing a psychopath. You know that?'

'Aren't most people who commit double homicides psychopaths?'

'Well, people do commit crimes of passion.'

'So you're saying those folks merely suffer from momentary lapses of good judgment?'

'Come on, Magdalena, now you're just being silly.'

I stood. 'That's me, all right: I'm just a silly old woman. A silly, billy, willy-nilly who doesn't care for frilly, but I'll leave you with the following bit of advice. Take a closer look at the front of the bin, on the side where the man is. The metal along the top front edge is fairly sharp, and not entirely smooth anymore. In a small stress fracture along the crease you will find a bright fuchsia thread. See if forensics in Bedford can match it to a snag in the gentleman's Hawaiian shirt.'

Toy shook his head. 'Magdalena, you're—'

'Silly.'

'I was going to say incredible, darn it!'

An uninformed onlooker, upon observing me peer into the dumpster, might have concluded that I was in shock, or incapable of experiencing a normal range of human emotion. Neither of those assumptions would have been correct. Alas, these peepers have beheld sights far grizzlier than that of the two bodies in the dumpster.

At any rate, instead of driving straight back to The PennDutch Inn, as I should have done, I left my son and guests in the quasi-capable hands of my nonetheless hunky husband and stopped by to see my best friend, Agnes. She and I grew up together, having even shared bathwater together when we were babies, so that gives us a special bond, if you ask me.

Agnes used to be a country gal but has lived in the heart of the village for the past four years. She shares her snug Cape Cod cottage with her two elderly uncles who are both committed nudists, and who both should be committed. The trouble is that Agnes won't stand for it, but then neither is she able to control their behaviour. Unfortunately, the sight of these two naked octogenarians striding briskly down the Primrose Lane, vigorously pumping their arms in unison, their still quite considerable body parts wagging in the self-generated breeze – well, this has become quite a draw with tourists, particularly amongst women of a 'certain age'.

However, Hernia does have a couple of attractions that are more family friendly. For instance, we have what bills itself as the World's Smallest Museum of Amish History and Memorabilia. We have a working blacksmith shop, where one can sit and watch real, working horses being shod while their Amish owners wait (next door is a car repair shop). One of our biggest attractions is our collection of Victorian-era homes with intricate scrolled woodwork along their wraparound porches. Guided tours are available every day at ten, two and four o'clock, except for Sunday during the summer months. Tickets for the tours cost twenty dollars for adults, and ten dollars for children. All the proceeds go into our local schools.

I knew that Agnes would be home from work, where she manages the upscale, eclectic restaurant, Asian Sinsations. Once upon a time, this was The Sausage Barn and was owned by Wanda Hemphopple, my second worst enemy. Back then the menu featured the three Amish food groups: fat, sugar, and starch. But Wanda made the mistake of trying to kill me and she ended up in the slammer. Her college-age daughter was given the restaurant but would have gone into bankruptcy had she not sought my help in running the place. I reinvented this greasy spoon with an imaginative menu and a new name for the joint, but enough tooting my own horn. The truth is, I couldn't have done anything for the place had it not been for dear Agnes.

Now where was I? Oh yes! Because Agnes has to get someone

to sit with her uncles while she's away from the house, the poor woman never goes anywhere on her days off. When I rang her bell, I expected to see Agnes. Therefore, I was thrown off guard when I beheld Uncle Fred in all his natural glory.

'Hel-*loo*, Magdalena.'

'Cover your shame, Fred. Or need I remind you what happened to Noah's son, Ham? Only this time the curse might be in reverse, given that I am a God-fearing woman and you are a heathen who has subjected me, unwillingly, to the sight of your abomination.'

Fred scowled and pursed his withered lips. 'You religious types are such prudes,' he said, before sauntering away. 'Ned,' he called over his shoulder in a loud voice, 'the doorbell was for you.'

I heard a toilet flush somewhere. 'Be right there,' Ned, the other brother, shouted.

'No, you won't!' I shouted back. 'I came to see Agnes, not to lose my vision permanently. Agnes, Agnes, wherefore art thou, Agnes?'

'Hark, tis my beloved Romeo,' Agnes sang, as she teetered in from the direction of her dining room. Agnes's perfectly round body is supported by matchstick ankles atop feet barely larger than chocolate eclairs. The latter she crams into six-inch high heels, in the misguided notion that flexed calf muscles miraculously make her look tall. Instead, she looks like a croquet ball that's been balanced on one of the wooden end stakes, and is just waiting to be knocked off. Don't get me wrong, though – appearances in this case are deceiving. This gal is not only sure-footed, but she has assisted me on many investigations which required the dexterity and stamina of an Olympic-winning gymnast. OK, perhaps that's a slight exaggeration.

'I assume that this is rather important,' she said when she stood directly in front of me, eyeball to collar bone level. 'Magdalena, from what I understood, you have important guests arriving this morning?'

I looked around her tastefully decorated living room. 'Is there anywhere we could sit? I mean, someplace that's off limit to your uncles.'

'Oh, you're so squeamish,' she said, but led me to a small

back porch which was shaded by a large, looming maple tree. 'They never sit on these wicker chairs,' she said. 'They find them uncomfortable.'

I got down to brass tacks. 'My important guests are now artfully arranged in Sam Yoder's dumpster bin.'

Agnes blinked. 'Come again?'

'They were murdered last night, and the killer has posed their corpses inside his garbage bin.'

Agnes gasped. '*Posed?* How?'

'Well, for one thing, they weren't just dumped; they were laid on their backs.'

'Poor Sam,' Agnes said. 'Imagine taking a bunch of wilted lettuce and some loaves of stale bread out to your dumpster bin and discovering a pair of corpses.'

'Ha,' I said. 'You know that my cousin would never throw away wilted lettuce or stale bread. The lettuce he would mark down and resell as rabbit food, and the bread he would try and market as a do-it-yourself crouton kit. Besides, it wasn't Sam who discovered the bodies; it was Monotone Mona.'

'Of course,' Agnes cried, 'who else? That makes perfect sense! Did Toy arrest her yet?'

'Calm down, dear,' I said. 'I don't think that she's even a suspect. Yet. Why should she be? Just because of that unfortunate event she experienced as a little girl?'

'*Unfortunate event?*' Agnes said. 'That event turned her into a cannibal, for goodness' sake!'

'That's not fair, Agnes. We don't know that for sure.'

'Well, I suppose her parents *could* have gnawed on each other,' Agnes said.

'Agnes!' I said sharply. 'Sarcasm does not become you. Besides, the primary reason that I'm here is to inform you that our annual Billy Goat Gruff celebration is still on, despite what rumours you may well hear in the near future. And since I'm the one calling the shots here, I'm determined that nothing is going to stop us, except for a genuine Act of God.'

EIGHT

My pal's petite hands flew to her pudgy cheeks. 'Golly, I hadn't even thought about cancelling the festival. About Sam warehousing all the candy, and some people thinking maybe Sam was somehow involved with the murders. You know how people talk in this town. It's like that game "telephone", but in this case it could have disastrous results.'

'That's where you come in,' I said.

'*Me?*' Agnes said.

'Gabe has foisted his cousin on me until after the celebration.'

'What cousin?'

'Get this: she's his mother's niece and has been estranged from the family for thirty-five years. And she lives in Australia!'

'Crikey,' Agnes said. She fancies herself an excellent mimic, especially of British accents. She'd be livid if I were to tell anyone that once, when she was attempting to speak with a brogue to one of my guests from Scotland, that guest said that he was sorry, but he didn't understand a word of Swedish.

'You've got to meet this gal,' I said. 'She does speak with an Australian accent – I think – but she's so pushy and manipulative, there's no doubting her American origins. Oh, and the most interesting thing is that she had a leg bitten off by a saltwater crocodile in Australia.'

'Double crikey,' Agnes said.

'My tale of woe gets better, dear, because this means I have to give up my downstairs bedroom suite. And all because my mother-in-law stole the election for Hernia Citizen of the Year.'

'Triple crikey,' Agnes said. 'Does this mean that you're going to stay in a hotel?'

'*What?*'

'Tell me that you're not planning to sleep in one of your own ill-appointed guest rooms,' Agnes said with a wry smile.

'I am,' I said. 'I'm also going to strike you from my will. Do you want to hear the piece de resistance, or not?'

'I do, I do,' she said, nodding vigorously. As a single woman who doesn't have many friends besides me, Agnes feeds on gossip like a vulture on roadkill.

'Well, this cousin, whose name is Miriam, by the way, brought her pet dingo all the way with her from the land down under.'

'That's terrible – wait, what's a dingo?'

'You don't know what a dingo is? Don't you watch the National Geographic channel on TV?'

'Remember Mags, if I wish to see wildlife, all that I have to do is look at my uncles. And speaking of whom, I've made arrangements for my uncles to spend a few days at a nudist camp for seniors so that they won't get into any trouble during the festival. I'm taking them there this afternoon.'

'Excellent idea. Anyway, a dingo is an Australian wild dog.'

'Quadruple crikey!'

'Lemon curd tarts!' I cursed. 'Stop saying "crikey" before I croak. You haven't even heard the worst. Cousin Miriam wanted to have that wild canine sleep in my bed with her. But I refused, of course. Instead, I'm making her put him in Little Jacob's old crib. She can keep that by her bed.'

Agnes laughed. 'You're a hoot, Mags. Thanks for coming over and brightening up my day – ooh, I don't mean that the double homicide is funny, just your ongoing travails with Gabe's relatives.'

'Well, I'm glad that I can amuse you, dear. But the whole point in my coming here was to let you, Madame Chairwoman, know what happened over at Sam's, so that you can get ahead of any rumours that the celebration will be cancelled.'

'One thing to bear in mind is that if you get any calls from the press that aren't related to the event, then just say "no comment". But no matter how tight-lipped you and I are about these murders, word is going to get out anyway. So, do you want me to tell Ida Rosen that two corpses were discovered in the bin of the biggest sponsor of her *parade*? Or do you think that you should handle it, because *you* volunteered to oversee this annual charity production?'

Agnes was no longer in a laughing mood. 'That is so unfair,' she said. 'I took this project on out of the kindness of my heart, because I knew how much you despise your mother-in-law, and that if you had to sing her praises to the entire village when she was awarded Hernia Citizen of the Year, you would choke on your own tongue. If not that, you would stab her with the commemorative brooch the officiant has to pin on her.'

'Stuff and nonsense,' I huffed. 'I don't despise Ida; I merely dislike her *intensely*.'

'I'm glad to hear that, Mags, because I just decided that I *do* despise the woman for the way that she's treated you all these years. Therefore I have decided not to deliver the tragic news of the double homicide to your husband's mother. I am also declining the opportunity to pin our village's tacky little medal to her much-inflated chest.'

'*What?*' I bleated. 'You can't back out on me now!'

Ever the good friend, Agnes reached over as far as her spherical body would allow, and patted the air, as her hand was still some inches from my arm. 'Don't worry, Mags, I'll still be working on publicity, but I can't be any part of further inflating her ego. Have you been keeping your ear to the ground lately?'

Before European immigrants slaughtered millions of native bison almost to the brink of extinction, Native Americans, by pressing their ears to the ground, could hear the thunder created by the hooves of these immense herds when they were still many miles away. As for *moi*, whenever I press one of my big ears to the ground, all I pick up is dirt – both literally and figuratively.

'No, dear,' I said. 'What's the scuttlebutt now?'

'Even though we have video proof that she stole the election – which we can't share with anyone else, or else your marriage will be over – someone has to crown her queen of the festival. But she wants to see the title of "queen" be extended to include a full year, not just a weekend, so to that end she's been campaigning for her cause at various churches and women's clubs.'

'Rough puff pastry!' I cried, so outraged was I that my cussing knew no bounds. Oh, shame on me and my wayward tongue.

'I'm surprised that you haven't heard about this,' Agnes said. I could tell that she was quite pleased with herself for getting the scoop on this bit of gossip.

'Agnes, you know quite well that I have little use for those other de— Well, I won't even say it, because that would be passing judgment.'

'Denominations? I believe you just *did* pass judgment,' Agnes said with a smirk.

'It's called discernment, dear, and there is a difference. But let's not quibble over the odd word here and there. What we need is a plan to stop that egomaniacal woman. The next thing you know she's going to demand that we furnish her with a crystal tiara that she can keep, instead of the cardboard crown which one of your uncles picked up at Burger King fifteen years ago.'

'She already has.'

'No way!'

'Yes, way.'

'O vey. When were you going to tell me about this?'

'When you saw her wearing her crown jewels, like at her coronation – I mean *installation*. Mags, what can I say? If you were me, wouldn't you want to put off facing the ire of someone like yourself for as long as possible?'

'I suppose that's true. But in this case, it's my mother-in-law with whom I'm angry, not you.'

'Yeah? Well, sometimes when you lose your temper there's collateral damage.'

'I never lose my temper!' I said hotly. 'Granted, there are times when I've expressed myself passionately, but that is a far cry from losing it.'

'If you insist,' Agnes said.

'I most certainly do! At any rate, what do you suggest that we do now?'

'Talk to Gabe,' Agnes said softly. 'Ida has already turned this year's Billy Goat Gruff Festival into a farce, and you are going to hate every minute of it. However, with a little legal pharmaceutical help, courtesy of your husband, you might be able to coast through the weekend feeling slightly less agitated.'

I stared at my dear friend for a long moment while the meaning of her words seeped slowly through my thick, but porous, skull. Then I clapped my cheeks in horror.

'You mean tranquilizers, don't you?'

'Just for one or two days – that's all. Not long enough to be addictive. Worst case scenario you'll get sleepy, so don't drive.'

'Why, I never!' I said. 'I'll have you know that I, Magdalena Portulacca Yoder Rosen, do not need drugs to help me deal with my obstreperous mother-in-law – not when I have the everlasting arms of the Lord to lean on.'

Agnes popped out of her wicker chair just as fast as a beach ball released under water. 'Well, I'm so sorry that you have to go now, Mags.'

'But actually I don't, dear,' I said. 'We've plenty of time for tea and those delightful little cakes that you make. What do you call them again?'

'Oh, you mean my store-bought cupcakes?' Agnes said drily. 'The ones that I buy from your cousin's corner grocery, and which you've described as tasting like sawdust?'

'There's no accounting for taste,' I said, 'is there, dear?' Then off I skedaddled while I still had a friend.

NINE

Thankfully, the rest of that day passed without another major crisis. The Hancocks disappeared until dinner, presumably to sightsee and antique shop in the surrounding towns of Bedford and Somerset. No doubt their destination also included the shop owned by Gabe's sister Cheryl, the retired psychiatrist from New York. Despite being a highly educated woman, she often has her head in the clouds. The cirrus clouds. How else can one explain Cheryl's decision to name her antique store Amish *Luxuries*? As for Cousin Miriam, she decided that she couldn't wait to spend time with her Aunt Ida, and off she went for the day. Even at dinner that night, everyone was well behaved.

It wasn't until the next day, which Agnes and I and two dozen volunteers spent putting together the finishing touches on the morrow's festivities, that storm clouds began to gather. Literally. The weather was seasonally hot and the forecast was for thunderstorms that evening and the entire day of the festival. The humidity was so unbearable that I said a prayer thanking the Good Lord for the birth of Willis Carrier, inventor of the modern air-conditioner.

When I got home, bone tired, I discovered that a storm of another kind had been brewing in my absence. Silly me – in order to work efficiently on the festival preparations, I'd turned off my phone. I wasn't being irresponsible, mind you. My husband is a doctor, and quite capable of caring for the five-year-old fruit of his loins, plus, Rebecca was home. And it wasn't like I was spending the day searching for rare marsupials in the highlands of Papua New Guinea, either; the village of Hernia is a mere four miles from the end of our driveway.

It wasn't until I was in my own driveway, and out of my car, that I remembered I'd turned off my phone. At that point the three urgent calls from Gabe (weren't they always urgent?) were a moot point, given that I would be seeing him face-to-face in the time it took to call him back. I fully expected to see a justifiably frustrated husband pacing the kitchen floor, or perhaps running his fingers through his still thick, dark hair. I was also bracing for a five-year-old boy to tackle me, while voicing loud complaints about boredom and hunger. Ditto for the Hancocks from Texas.

I certainly was not prepared to find the kitchen deserted, save for a solitary woman, who was utterly alien in appearance, while at the same time as familiar to me as the back of my right hand. Like me, she was tall and reed-thin, although her features were regular and thus far more attractive than mine. Also, I pegged her at being about a dozen years younger than me. This woman's hair was the same shade of mousey brown as mine, but she wore it in a buzz cut, whereas I wear mine in coiled braids, and it has never been cut, because the Bible states that a woman's hair is her glory. Now I ask you, how can a buzz cut possibly glorify any woman?

In our clothing choices we differed almost as much. I dress modestly, in a manner that Bible-believing Christians everywhere would do well to emulate, but the woman in my kitchen was dressed in skimpy attire more in keeping with that of a slovenly slattern – not that I'm judging, mind you. Her white shorts were filthy, as was her mustard-coloured tank top. In retrospect, I'm surprised that I even noticed all the stains on her clothing, given the copious amount of 'ink' that covered her body. 'Ink', by the way, is what our young people call tattoos. Perhaps this is their clever way of getting around the fact that in Leviticus 19:28, tattoos are unequivocally forbidden by God.

I had not spotted an additional vehicle parked anywhere near the inn, so surmised that the stranger might be a hitchhiker, or maybe a charity case who'd requested a ride to my door. Given that I am a wealthy, and with all due modesty, benevolent woman, my doorstep is often the dropping-off point for the chronically insolvent. As long as my first impressions of the stranger were things that one of my dresses and a straw hat could rectify, I could afford to be fairly tolerant of her. But when she reached into the pocket of her grungy shorts and pulled out a cigarette and lighter, I practically tackled her.

'There is no smoking in this establishment,' I barked.

'Well, fine then. I'll take it outside.'

'You do that, missy,' I said. I couldn't believe the woman's impertinence. 'Just so you know, dear, "outside" is entirely off my property – all twenty-two acres of pasture and woods.'

'Oh, Mags, you haven't changed a bit!' the woman said, and then proceeded to laugh so hard that she would have collapsed on the floor in a fit of hysteria, if it hadn't been for my kitchen island. This she managed to grab with both hands, including the one clutching that noxious cancer-causing stick.

'This can't be,' I squeaked. Fortunately the intruder was laughing so uproariously she probably couldn't have heard an elephant trumpet. This gave me time to rehearse my responses, so that by the time she'd wound down enough to focus, I was able to do so as well.

'Susannah Yoder Entwhistle Stoltzfus,' I said, my voice barely quavering, 'have you broken out of prison yet again?'

My sister started to howl once more, but I cut it short by wagging my index finger. And *scowling*. Now that I've begun my sixth decade, I've developed a crease across the bridge of my nose that is astonishingly deep. I live half in fear that Little Jacob, mischievous little boy that he is, might get it into his head to plant corn kernels in it one day while I nap. Normal sweat from my brow would be enough to germinate these seeds, and then soon I'd have corn stalks bobbing about in front of my eyes, impeding my vision. Although this might not be a very likely scenario, one must at least concede that a woman with an imagination as active as mine has a very difficult row to hoe, as we say out here in the country.

At long last my sister was able to hoist herself up on a kitchen stool. 'No, silly. I didn't break out *this* time; I've been paroled.'

I remained standing, knowing as I did that her stay would be short. 'Don't be ridiculous, dear. It was only five years ago that you broke out of prison and helped that murderous husband of yours escape from Hernia dressed as a nun – and this after he tried to kill me.'

'Oh, Mags, why is it that you can only remember negative stuff? Can't you at least compliment his ankles?'

'*What?*' I said incredulously.

'Surely you noticed how slim and white his ankles were, peeking out from beneath that long brown habit? They were like the ankles of a teenage girl.'

'Ugh.'

'Besides, it was your whackadoodle mother-in-law who supplied the habit and the bus.'

'Don't remind me,' I said. 'That doesn't change the fact that I still don't understand how a person who aided and abetted a convicted murderer gets out of the slammer in five years.'

'Overcrowding,' Susannah said. 'It's as simple as that. Yeah, I may have a lot of ink – I saw you judging me – but when push comes to shove, who do you think gets paroled, the nice-spoken Mennonite woman whose family has been in this country for almost three hundred years, or the woman who walked up from Honduras and entered the country without a visa?'

'Look,' I said, 'first off, we're not going to talk politics, and secondly, you haven't been a Mennonite since you were a teenager, and that was so long ago that even God doesn't remember it.' Then I slapped my mouth gently for having taken the Lord's name in vain.

Susannah grinned. 'Still feisty, eh? So, am I bunking with you, sis?'

'*What?*'

'Well, from what I understand, your Dearly Beloved took off

with my darling nephew in order to stash Fi-Fi in the bosom of his precious mama until the situation could be – uh – successfully resolved, seeing as how I am an ex-con.'

I staggered around in search of a kitchen stool of my own for support. 'You saw Gabe? He saw *you*? He recognized you?'

Susannah chortled. 'Gabe recognized me immediately. No offense, Mags, but your hubby's a bit weird. He doesn't have a clue who those Texans are, except that their name is Hancock and that they're super rich, yet he is willing to let my nephew sleep in the same house with them. Then I show up, and off he runs with my little nephew before I can get acquainted. Like I'm a piece of dirt.'

'If it walks like a duck, dear,' I said, not too unkindly. 'What about his cousin, Miriam, and her detestable dingo?'

'Good news on both counts. Miriam's in her room – no, your room – watching Gabe's massive TV. She's mesmerized by its size, so I don't think you'll be seeing much of her.'

'That's one bit of good news,' I said. 'What's the other?'

'That the dingo has turned out to be a Chihuahua mix and Miriam was only teasing you with the dingo story.'

'No way, Jose!'

My sister squealed with delight. 'Ooh, Mags, it gets me positively goose-pimply to see you all worked up like this again!'

'I'm glad to oblige you, sister dear. Just you wait and see what lies in store for Miriam.'

Susannah rubbed her hands together excitedly. 'Go Mags!'

'Yeah – hey, wait a minute. How is it that Little Jacob was able to take Miriam's mutt, Fi-Fi, with him to Ida's house, if that pitiful pooch suffers from separation anxiety?'

'Uh, what's that?' Susannah said.

'Pretty much what it says: that the dog and Miriam are so closely bonded that the dog becomes overly anxious when they are apart. In some cases the animal will chew up its bedding, chew on itself, or maybe howl constantly. In other words, they show signs of extreme distress.'

'Hmm, good point, Mags. I guess that was all just made up too. What kind of woman would try and torment her hostess with a cock-and-bull story about a fake dingo?'

'One who shares genetic material with my mother-in-law, Ida

Rosen? Say, Susannah, where are Freni and Rebecca? Were they here when you arrived? And how *did* you get here?'

Susannah cackled, as did a few hens out back in response. Perhaps they thought she was talking to them, or even a competitor laying an egg.

'What a silly question. I hitchhiked, of course.' She rotated her bony pelvis a few times. 'I've still got it, you know. As for Freni, our dear second cousin, once-removed, she took one look at me, and started praying. She thinks I'm the Whore of Babylon, you know.'

'Well,' I said with a sigh, 'she loves me. If Melvin Stoltzfus had been successful, I'd be pushing up daises right now, and you'd have been responsible for helping him getting away with my murder. Speaking of whom, where is Melvin?'

My sister sighed dramatically. 'How am I supposed to know? I've been locked in the slammer for five years. It's not like I've communicated with him after the second time he tried to off you and got away. For all I know, he's down in Florida, living in Key West, and taking tourists deep-sea fishing on his charter boat. Anyway, I told him I never want to see him again if I live to be a thousand!'

'Didn't you tell me once that Melvin gets seasick in a bathtub?'

Susannah scowled. 'That's only when I steal his rubber ducky and we splash around too much.'

'TMI!' I cried.

'Oh, Mags, you're such a prude. I swear, you're turning into a carbon copy of Freni.'

'Freni didn't sit by idly while someone tried to kill her sister, and then help that someone – her husband – escape.'

'If Freni is such an awesome woman, shouldn't she forgive me? I mean, doesn't the Bible say that one is supposed to forgive like a zillion times?'

'Cut Freni a break, will you?' I snapped. 'She practically raised you after Mama and Papa died in the Allegheny Tunnel, squished between a truck carrying milk and another carrying state-of-the-art running shoes. Let me guess, Rebecca volunteered to drive her home.'

'Yup. Now, *there's* an interesting woman.'

'How so?' I asked.

Susannah shrugged. 'There's just something really "off" about her. She gives me the creeps. Mags, what's her story?'

'Her story is exactly that, dear. It's *hers*.'

My sister rolled her eyes. 'Same old Mags; same old principles.' Then, without missing a beat, she said, 'Say, where do you want me to sleep? I prefer one of the en-suite rooms, if it's all the same to you.'

'What *chutzpah*!'

'Look at you! Your Yiddish has improved.'

'Susannah, I can't believe your insolence. Come on, I'm driving you into Bedford, and then I'm going to give you a little traveling money. You can take a bus from there to anywhere your heart desires. Just don't hitchhike; it's too dangerous.'

'Aw, sis, I promise to be good. You were like a mother to me after our own mother was killed. Maybe it's wrong for me to say this, but I love you more than I ever loved her. Pwease, Mags, pwease let me stay.' Susannah pulled the same pouty face she's been pulling on me since she was a year old.

'That was cute when you were "widdle",' I said. 'But now you're *middle*-aged! Hey, how about a plane ticket to Argentina instead? It will be spring there soon, and they have a history of welcoming criminals.'

My sister planted her feet about a meter apart and gripped the kitchen island with both hands. 'You can't make me leave. When our parents died, they left me half of the farm. Sure, you built the inn, but I can always go and live in the barn. Besides, if you let me stay, I think that I know how you can get back at Miriam in a wholesome, Christian sort of way. Please, Mags. I don't have anywhere else to go.'

I tapped one of my boat-size brogans on my oak plank floor. 'Vengeance is not a Christian sport, dear. On the other hand, I'm only human, which is to say, I'm willing to give your cockamamie idea a listen.'

Susannah relaxed her stance a skosh. 'Before he left to stay at his grandmother's, Little Jacob dragged me in to see his bedroom because, he said, I'm his favourite auntie.'

'Clearly the boy is no judge of character.'

'Anyway,' Susannah continued, 'it got me to thinking. Since

he won't be using his room, and since his room is connected to your room . . . do you see where I'm going with this?'

'You're leading me on a tour of my own house?'

'No. I'm suggesting that you let me stay in Little Jacob's room. His car-shaped bed is really cool.'

'Susannah, you're a pecan pie,' I said sweetly.

'You mean that I'm "nuts", don't you?'

'Let's put it this way,' I said. 'Gabe would go ballistic if I put you in Little Jacob's room. Miriam was once his favourite cousin, and he is really hoping to reconnect with her.'

'Did you invite her?'

'*What?*'

'It's a simple question. From the look on your face, and the fact that she's sleeping in your bed, I bet that you didn't even know that she was coming until the last minute.'

'Well, still, Hebrew chapter thirteen, verse two states: "Do not forget to entertain strangers, for by so doing some have unwittingly entertained angels."'

Susannah howled. At least Fi-Fi wasn't there to howl along with her.

'I can't believe how naïve you still are,' she said. 'Do you honestly believe there is the slightest chance that the woman sleeping in your bed is an *angel*? After what she said about you, I'd say that a Tasmanian devil is more like it.'

'What did she say about me?' I demanded.

'She called you a money-grubbing fake,' Susannah said with a smirk. 'She said that it broke her heart to see her poor cousin having to debase himself like a gigolo, dressing up in a cheap Halloween costume, just so his greedy wife could stuff her pockets with more money than she obviously knows what to do with, given that this place is a world-class dump.'

My ears burned: not with shame but with anger. 'That can't be true! Gabe would never put up with anyone saying anything disparaging about me. I mean, was he *there* when she said that?'

Susannah winked. 'Of course not, sis. He was off helping Little Jacob pack an overnight bag for his stay at his grandmother's.'

'*Dump?*' I repeated incredulously. 'Did she really say that?'

'Oh yeah, sis. And she said that quite frankly you were a "freakishly, frumpy, frowsy, flippant, fraud".'

'Why, the nerve of that Aussie hussy!' Everyone knows that alliteration is frowned upon these days, and for her to use a string of "F" words to describe *me*, in *my* house, why that just makes me flat-out furious!

'So I say we go for it! I'll put you in Little Jacob's room, and I don't care how much Gabe squawks. Our son's bedroom, and the master bedroom – which Miriam occupies now – function as a suite, but with only the one shared bathroom. So here's what you do: be the same old, slovenly Susannah that you used to be. Do you think that you can do that?'

Susannah wasn't offended in the least. 'You mean I can forget to drain the bathtub, dump wet towels and dirty clothes on the floor, smear toothpaste on the mirror and neglect to flush the commode? That kind of thing?'

'Absolutely,' I said.

My sister grinned broadly, revealing for the first time the effects of her prison dental care. 'Awesome,' she said. 'Believe me, Mags, I've got even more tricks up my sleeve than that.'

TEN

It turned out that my husband had some tricks up his sleeve as well. He stayed at his mother's the rest of the day, but when he returned, he was not alone. His mother was with him.

'Where's Little Jacob?' I hissed.

'At my sister's,' Gabe said.

'Susannah said you were taking him to his grandmother's.'

'*Nu?* She lives with my sister – her daughter – so what's your point?'

'Yah, *nu?*' my mother-in-law said. By then she had climbed out of Gabe's car and was finding her balance on her short, stumpy legs. The octogenarian is impressively top-heavy with a shockingly small noggin. If Ida Rosen was made of snack food, she'd be a quarter wheel of Gouda cheese standing on point, with pretzel limbs and a raisin for a head.

I ignored the woman from whose loins my lover sprang, but I couldn't ignore him for long. When Gabe learned that I'd billeted my criminal sister in the same suite of rooms as a whackadoodle cousin, he was indeed incensed.

'You will pay!' he said. Actually, he hissed those words without a single 'S'. Believe me, when a person can hiss without an 'S', that means that he, or she, is either the victim of a bad writer, or else they have something nefarious up their polyester blend sleeve.

I forced a smile. 'Loosen up, dear. Isn't that what you're always telling me? Besides, I think the two women might be good for each other.'

'Good for each other? *How?*'

'Well, Miriam is undoubtedly suffering from post-traumatic-stress syndrome, and of course, so is Susannah. Maybe they will bond over that, and give each other a measure of comfort and healing.'

Gabe stared at me. 'What traumatic stress did your sister ever experience that could compare to having one's leg eaten as lunch by the world's largest reptile?'

I stared back at him. 'Oh, so you don't think that having one's parents squished flatter than a pair of pancakes when you're just eleven counts? I've shared the gruesome details of that story with you more than once, so I'm not going to repeat them. But one of the tabloids got a photo of them and published it, along with the headline: *FARMER AND WIFE TURNED INTO FLAPJACKS*. What if that had happened to your precious ma, and your pa?'

A vein on Gabe's left temple began to twitch. 'Speaking of Ma,' he said, 'I've invited her to dinner tonight.'

'B-but, I thought you were going to keep Miriam as a surprise until her big day.'

'I was,' Gabe said, 'but plans can change.'

'Indeed, they can,' I said. 'Freni is feeling a little bit under the weather, so Rebecca drove her home. But I have a feeling that when dear Becca learns that she has to cook for the world's harshest critic, she might suddenly come down with a health issue of her own. That said, I think that you need to run down to Asian Sinsations and bring back a variety of dishes that will appeal to everyone's taste buds.'

'OK,' Gabe said.

'*OK?* Just like that?'

'Yup.'

'No fair,' I wailed. 'What am I going to do with my unused arguments?'

'Bank them in your memory for next time,' Gabe said, and kissed me on the end of my nose. 'Think of them like the Monopoly money that we used to tuck into books back when we played games that lasted all weekend.'

'I never did that,' I said ruefully. 'I never got to play games that lasted all weekend. Saturday was for chores, and Sunday was for church. "Idle hands are the Devil's playground", and Mama didn't want the Devil playing with me at all.'

Gabe bit his lower lip. 'Oops, my bad. Anyway, you get the picture. And yes, I'd be happy to pick up dinner.'

When one is in need of a hug, then giving a hug can be the next best thing. Also, if no suitable human being is around, a cow makes a perfectly suitable substitute. Of course, it can't be just any cow. She needs to have been bottle fed, hand-reared, and touched on a daily basis. Even stroked.

Miss Milchig and Miss Fleischig are two Jersey cows that fit the bill perfectly. When I was born my father raised Holstein cows here. I have always kept Holsteins as well, until four years ago when I quite suddenly decided that Jersey cows were the most beautiful creatures that the Good Lord ever created – other than my children and thirty-year-old men.

So, after my tense exchange with my fifty-two-year-old husband, I trudged out into the south pasture where my two cows were standing in the shade of a pin oak, chewing their cuds. I threw my gangly arms around Miss Milchig's tawny neck, and although she blinked and took a step or two back, she didn't really resist. After a few minutes I saw to it that Miss Fleischig also received a goodly amount of attention. Who knows how long I might have embraced my bovine friends, had it not been for the many flies one finds around livestock?

On my way back to the house I reflected on the last few days' bizarre events. The pair of bodies in the dumpster were, without a doubt, connected to the Billy Goat Gruff Festival. So was the arrival of the one-legged Aussie with her feral dog. As for

the odd Texan couple, that was all on me. Texans were known
to be cattle people. What were they *really* doing out here,
attending a festival honouring a goat, if they didn't have ulterior
motives? After all, weren't Texan cattle ranchers supposed to be
dead set against other ungulates? At least, that's how it was on
the old westerns on TV, like *Bonanza* and *The Big Valley*. Or so
I'd heard from my guests who watch TV. At any rate, shame on
me for being so tired of inn-keeping that I had gotten lax on
checking guests' backgrounds.

But now Susannah . . . how could the state prison system let
her out after just five years for aiding and abetting? Surely she
hadn't broken out again, or else the authorities would have called
me. In any case, the world didn't make sense to me anymore.

When I got back to the house, I was immediately drawn to
the sound of loud voices coming from my formal parlour. I've
deliberately furnished this room with uncomfortable furniture,
such as straight back chairs and benches with unpadded seats,
so that guests would rather do chores than sit on their derrieres.
Perhaps the most comfortable piece of furniture is an ancient
rocking chair that has been in the family for generations. Guests
usually shy away from the rocker for reasons that they can't
explain, but today was the exception.

'I'll sit anywhere I darn well please,' Delphia said, as she tried
to skirt around her behemoth of a husband.

'Dang it, dahlin',' Tiny drawled, 'you can't just sit on an old
lady's lap like she ain't even there!'

'Well, she ain't!' Delphia screamed. 'You've got eyes, don't
you? That chair's just as empty as your cousin Luanne's head
– bless her heart.'

'That's a low blow,' Tiny Hancock said. 'Cousin Luanne
suffered brain damage when a mechanical ride malfunctioned at
an amusement park.'

Delphia turned to address Susannah, who was the only other
person in the room at the time. 'Cousin Luanne Hancock and
her husband Jim-Bob had just gotten married that afternoon.
The accident happened when they tried to consummate their
marriage in the Haunted House. Not the Tunnel of Love, mind
you, but the *Haunted House*. What sane person would even
think of that?'

Susannah giggled. 'Speaking of haunted, wait until you sit in that chair.'

'I don't believe in ghosts,' Delphia said. 'It's just a bunch of nonsense. Anyone who believes in ghosts is an utter fool.'

'Boogers,' Granny Yoder said.

Susannah laughed. She can hear our great-grandmother but can't see her. I can do both. Over the years I've hosted a handful of guests who have the gift to tune in to one or both of those senses. Chief of Police Toy Graham can do both, and now, apparently, so could Tiny Hancock.

Just as petite Delphia managed to slip through Tiny's tree trunk legs, I found my outdoor voice.

'Stop right there, missy!' I roared. 'This is a formal parlour, not a gymnasium.'

Delphia froze in place, but her lips moved. 'A parlour? Who did the decorating? A lumberjack?'

I ignored her. 'Tiny, dear, please describe the occupant of the rocking chair.'

'Sure thing, ma'am,' he said. He turned to get a gander at Granny. 'Well, she looks to be a kindly lady of a certain age. She's wearing black – you know, widow's weeds – and this carved brooch on her right, uh, you know what I mean. And her hair's white as snow, and she wears it up in braids like you do. Also, she's wearing the same kind of white hat, except that hers is bigger, and has strings hanging down on the sides. Will that description do?'

I smiled. 'Tiny, that was an excellent description. However, please clarify something. What did you mean by a "lady of a certain age"? How old do you reckon her to be?'

Tiny rubbed his massive hands together. 'Now ma'am, it ain't right to be mentioning a woman's age, but—'

'She isn't a woman,' Susannah chortled. 'She's a spook. A ghost.'

Granny glared at her great-granddaughter. 'You hush your mouth, girlie, or I'll haunt you out of this house and right back to that prison where you still belong.'

'Prison, eh,' Tiny said, looking at Susannah, as if suddenly interested. 'Yeah, prison. Now, that makes sense. I was wondering about your cool tats.'

'*Prison?*' Delphia said. She turned to my sister. 'What did you do time for?'

I had to think fast on my globe-size feet. 'My people have a long history of volunteering,' I said. 'Prison ministry is one of them. I am so fortunate to have a sister like Susannah.'

OK, so I *implied* that my sister was in prison ministering to the inmates, not doing hard time for aiding and abetting a convicted murderer. Surely a lie by implication is not quite as bad as an out and out lie. Besides, I wasn't hurting anyone with my 'almost fib', was I?

Unfortunately, Delphia didn't buy my explanation. 'You look like an ex-con to me, sister.' She walked up to Susannah, and even sniffed her. 'And you smell like one too.'

'It might be me that you smell, girlie,' Granny said. 'I haven't had a bath in thirty-two years.'

Of course, Delphia couldn't hear that, but we other three living souls did and laughed. This so irritated Delphia that she strode out of the room on her stout little legs, which had come to remind me of turkey drumsticks, although perhaps a wee bit larger. She did, however, reappear at dinner, along with a double dose of attitude.

'I hope y'all don't eat "family style" here,' she said as she found her assigned seat. 'It's not that I'm afraid of germs, but I don't know where everyone's hands have been.'

'Oy vey,' my Jewish mother-in-law said.

At that moment Rebecca emerged from the kitchen bearing a massive platter which she set in front of Gabe. Mounded around the fifteen-pound pot roast in its centre were potatoes, carrots and onions. Next to come out of the kitchen were a pair of gravy boats, and then baskets of freshly baked bread to go with the home-churned butter. A variety of salads and Amish favourites had been placed on the table ahead of time. To be sure, these included pickled beets and pickled watermelon rinds.

Despite her reservations about handling dishes that others had touched, Delphia passed her plate up to Gabe for the entrée, and she didn't seem to mind helping herself to the salads when they were passed around. The one thing that she didn't do was wait until grace had been said before she dug into her dinner. She'd done the same thing the evening before, but then I'd managed to keep my liver-coloured lips closed in the interest of peace. On this occasion I was just too frazzled to 'put a sock in it,' as some have so rudely suggested I do at times.

'Hold your horses, dear,' I said, but not unkindly. 'We're a God-fearing household, so we thank the Good Lord for the fact that we're not starving to death like those poor children in China. If we forget—'

'Ahem,' Susannah said. 'That's what Mama used to say, like forty years ago. I bet there's another country now that needs our pity more.'

I frowned at her for interrupting my spiel of admonishment. 'I just had a thought, Susannah: why don't you say grace tonight?'

'Okey, dokey,' my sister said before closing her eyes and bowing her head reverently. The Hancocks followed suit. Gabe and his mother didn't bow their heads or close their eyes, since Jews normally pray with their eyes open. I, however, stared at my sister, because I knew exactly what she was up to, thanks to her sassy reply.

'Rub-a-dub dub,' Susannah practically shouted. 'Thanks for the grub. Yay, God!'

'A sacrilege, yah?' Ida said. Who was my mother-in-law to complain? Only four years ago she had been the Mother Superior of a fake convent.

'Well, I think that it was delightful,' Delphia said. 'Tiny and I are atheists – truly America's most hated minority – and the one thing I was dreading about this trip was having to listen to some long-winded, holier-than-thou, sanctimonious, hypocritical, chest-beating, Bible-thumping pedagogue, praying over my food before I had a chance to eat it before it got cold.'

'Harrumph,' I said. 'During your last sentence alone the pot roast not only got cold, it climbed back on the bone, and ambled back into the pasture.'

'Good one, sis,' my sister said.

Delphia shot Susannah daggers. 'Shouldn't the subject of last November's *Miss Prison* be eating in the kitchen with the help, and not out here amongst decent, God-fearing folk?'

'Hmm,' I said. 'You make a good point. Would all God-fearing people please remain seated, and all atheists, please pick up your plates and cutlery, and follow my sister to the kitchen?'

'Aw, come on, sis,' Susannah whined, but when she saw Miriam start to push her wheelchair back from the table, her attitude changed immediately. She even carried Miriam's place setting for her.

The Hancocks, however, didn't budge. It was my job as hostess to make them follow the rules – in this case, Delphia's rule. Of course, it came as no surprise when Ida butted into something that was none of her business.

'Nu, Magdalena,' she said. 'You will make the atheists go too?'

Delphia looked at Tiny, who shook his head. 'I would never believe in a God that I had to fear,' he said.

'He blasphemes,' Ida said.

'Do *you* believe in God, Mrs Rosen?' Tiny asked softly.

Ida shrugged. 'Sometimes yes and sometimes no. But when I do believe, then I am afraid.' She wagged a crooked, arthritic finger at the giant Texan. 'But you, young man, maybe you should be afraid all of the time. I only question God, but I do not reject him.'

'Oh, what a load of horse manure,' Delphia said. 'What is God going to do to someone who doesn't fear him? Huh? Will He strike me dead?'

ELEVEN

Delphia's answer was a crack of lightning that split one of a pair of two-hundred-year-old maple trees planted on the front lawn. The dining room has four, very tall, if somewhat narrow, windows. From my seat at the kitchen end of the table, I could see the majestic old tree be rent in twain, right down the middle. Everyone at the table at least heard the horrendously loud boom of thunder, and then the crash, as half of the tree landed on the front lawn. The top branches just brushed against the dining-room windows, even though the tree's base was some eighty feet away.

Susannah shrieked and dove under the table. Gabe and his mother both screamed; they can't deny it. As for the Hancocks, they hustled their heathen behinds post-haste into the kitchen, even shoving Susannah and Miriam along in front of them.

'Oh, crumpled crumpets,' I moaned. 'Now I have to remove the entire tree, and my landscape will look lopsided. Did you know that it was Granny's granddad who planted that tree?'

'B-b-babe,' Gabe said, 'how can you be so calm? That lightning strike could have killed us?'

'Oh, fiddlesticks,' I said. 'Lightning follows the path of least resistance and strikes the tallest object around. That tree was much taller than this house. Besides, if I die, I know I'm going straight up to Heaven to be with my Lord and Saviour Jesus Christ, and there I'll spend all eternity singing hymns of praise at the Throne of Grace.'

'That's it?' Ida said. 'Just singing for billions of years.'

'Ma,' Gabe said, 'don't start.'

But of course, my mother-in-law wasn't finished. 'As a Reform Jew I leave the afterlife up to God, but now I make a few suggestions, yah? For the first billion years, cruises. For the next billion years, Broadway shows. Then maybe Vegas—'

'Enough, Ma,' Gabe snapped.

'Thank you, dear,' I said, for I knew how hard it was for him to do, or say, anything that his mother could interpret as being critical of her.

But instead of being upset with her son, Ida continued to look at me. 'Nu, Magdalena, perhaps you are the right person to answer this question since you are *meshuggenah* too.'

'Wait a minute, Ma,' Gabe said. 'What do you mean that Magdalena is crazy too?'

'*Bubeleh*,' she said, using a Yiddish term of endearment, 'everyone knows that your wife is missing noodles in her kugel. That is no secret in this *fekakta* town. But your cousin Miriam, already? Now that was a surprise.'

'What's wrong with Cousin Miriam?' Gabe whispered, keeping an eye on the kitchen door.

'There's nothing wrong with my noodle,' I said tersely.

'Yah?' Ida said scornfully. 'Your noodle is like a strudel: flaky on the outside but soft in the middle.'

'Get back to Cousin Miriam,' Gabe said in what I can only describe as a shouted whisper.

'All right, all right, keep your britches on,' Ida said. She was clearly enjoying the catbird seat. 'This girl I have not seen for thirty years. Still, she is my flesh and blood, yah?'

'Then what is the problem, Mah?'

'She does not smell like a Finkleman.'

'*What?*'

'Like a Finkleman, like her mama and me. Or a Blumfield, like her father.'

'Ma,' Gabe said loud enough for his dead father to hear back in New York, '*that's* the craziest thing that I ever heard.'

I pointed with my chin at Ida. 'I hate to agree with this one, but I know what she means. If I were blindfolded, I could pick Little Jacob out of a room full of five-year-old boys just by his smell. A mother knows. Maybe an aunt knows as well. That thing about shared genes and all that.'

'But Ma isn't a bloodhound,' Gabe said, running his fingers through his still thick, dark hair.

'Just the same,' I said, 'when is the last time you gave your son a sniff? Appreciatively. Like after a bath – not right after he's been out playing and is sweaty and dirty.'

'Father's don't do such things,' Gabe said.

'Maybe they should,' I said.

Ida nodded. 'Yah, this one is right for a change. But another thing: I asked Miriam what she wanted me to do with the bar mitzvah present that her *bubbe*, my mother – may her memory be for a blessing – gave me to keep for Miriam until she got married. Do you know what she said?'

'What?' I said. 'Spit it out, dear. I hear voices approaching.'

'She said to me, she says, "Give it to someone who would have more use for it".'

Gabe turned a lighter shade of pale. 'Mags, that gift was bubbe's engagement ring. It had a flawless ten-carat blue diamond in it. That ring is worth a heap of money. It's even got a name in the biz: the Finkleman Blue. No one in their right mind would casually give that rock away.'

'Well,' I said, 'Gabe, how does it feel then to be one of the few sane people here tonight? We know that Susannah has a screw loose, or she wouldn't have aided and abetted a convicted murderer, so that leaves only you and the Hancocks. Frankly, I have my doubts about Delphia. I think she's got a burning ball of rage inside of her, and it's going to burst out of her chest at any minute.'

The door opened and in poured four sets of ears. 'What's this about my chest?' Delphia roared.

I prayed for guidance. Instead, the Good Lord opened the heavens and delivered a deluge the likes of which I had never seen in all my born days, bringing our conversation to an abrupt end. Truly, it was a sod-soaking, gully-washing, frog-strangling, duck-drowning, trash-moving, tree-falling, car-floating, bridge-flooding, coffin-popping event.

When the storm had passed Chief Toy called to report that two sets of remains had washed up onto the bridge that spans Slave Creek. It is the same bridge that Ida, as Hernia's honorary Citizen of the Year, was scheduled to cross the next day. I took the call in the parlour where, Granny notwithstanding, I had a modicum of privacy.

'Magdalena,' Toy said, 'have there been any instances in these parts when coffins popped out of the ground due to heavy rain?'

'I heard that it happened during the great Johnstown Flood,' I said. 'But in that case, it wasn't just rain; a dam broke, killing over two thousand people. Why do you ask?'

'Well,' Toy said, 'there's no way to put it delicately, but these remains have been dead a long time. One is a female in a very tattered yellow dress, and the other a male in trousers, and what might once have been a white shirt. But really, there's not much left of either of them but the skeletal remains and patches of hair on the skulls.'

I summoned my most sympathetic tone. 'Sounds like you really have your work cut out for you this evening, dear. No TV watching for you, I guess. Well, I have to get back out to the world of the living, to see if anyone needs me.'

'Boogers,' Granny said.

Toy laughed. 'Miz Yoder, is that you?'

'Is that the handsome chief of police that you are always pining after, Magdalena?' Granny had a loud voice when she was alive, and it was even louder when she was dead.

My cheeks burned with embarrassment. Perhaps the truth does hurt.

'Toy, she's just kidding. The dead don't joke very well. Besides, you know Granny, she's as thick as day-old cement.'

'Magdalena, I wish you wouldn't talk about your grandmother that way. I find her quite charming – like you, on your good days. And you two look enough alike to be mother and daughter.'

'Granny is really my great-grandmother,' I said tiredly. 'She's probably a hundred years older than I am.'

'Poopy-brains,' Granny said. 'I am not.'

'Listen Toy, I really have to go.'

'But Magdalena, I need a big favour.'

'Toy, I just gave you a big fat raise.'

'I know, and I appreciate that, but Magdalena, it will be dark soon and coyotes, foxes, and who knows what other kinds of scavengers will be out and about. So, I need you to please send Gabe down here to help me collect and bag up these remains. We can't expect any help from County because of the storm, which hit a lot harder in Bedford.'

'Where's your assistant? Officer Cakewalker?'

'She's working crowd control.'

'*What?*'

'It was Widow Detweiler, bless her lonely heart, who called me with the news, and then apparently she called everyone in the village with a phone. We've got sawhorses set up now to hold the crowd back, but we'd have to stay here all night to keep the remains from being molested. Really, Magdalena, we could use your husband's help as a physician with this – uh – unpleasant situation.'

'What do you expect him to do? Come and pick up the bones?'

There was a moment of silence. 'Yes, ma'am. I would be much obliged if he did. You come too.'

'Well, figgy pudding to you,' I said.

'Magdalena Portulacca Yoder Miller Rosen!' I heard Gabe say as he slipped between the pocket doors of the parlour. 'You just said the "F" word!'

'I *did*?' For the record, acting innocent is not the same as lying. Honestly, if you pray really hard about the issue of prevarication, I'm sure the Good Lord will eventually lead you to the same conclusion that I have reached. Or maybe not.

'It may not be my "F" word,' Gabe said, 'but it's in place of it, so it's the same thing.'

'It *is*?'

'Hon, if you'll stop trying to be evasive, and tell me what's going on, maybe I can help.'

'Yeah,' Toy said. 'I couldn't hear what Gabe said, but tell him that I agree, and then put your phone on speaker.'

That turned out to be an excellent idea because my Dearly Beloved was actually delighted when he learned that the much younger, and very charming, chief of police needed his help in gathering up two skeletonized corpses.

'Did Toy sound squeamish?' Gabe asked.

'Just overworked,' I said.

'No, wonder,' Gabe. 'You work him like a slave master.'

'I do not.'

'Do so,' Gabe said.

'Well, you sound jealous,' I said.

'Would that be so bad?'

I felt an unexpected surge of happiness. 'Every woman likes to know that her husband still desires her. Especially a tall, dark, handsome man like you.'

'Booger brains with poop sauce,' Granny said. 'I never liked that husband of yours. He parts his hair on the left. What kind of man does that?'

'A *live* man,' I said, and then felt guilty about my mean-spirited retorts all the evening – or at least all the way to the bridge where Toy was waiting impatiently for us. He hadn't been exaggerating about the crowd size, that's for sure. What he hadn't mentioned was its tenor.

When we stepped out of Gabe's car many in the crowd aimed their phones at us as they took pictures. A few even cheered. As we Mennonites are a reserved people, I assumed that the more boisterous of the onlookers were the Baptists, or Presbyterians. Perhaps even our few Methodists, because they were known to sip cocktails in the evenings.

It didn't take Gabe more than a few seconds to make a discovery that had Toy wishing that he had a cocktail to sip on. Thank heavens that Gabe had the presence of mind to act cool about it, and not embarrass the younger man in front of the crowd.

'These aren't skeletons,' my doctor husband whispered. 'Not real ones. These are high-quality resin fakes.'

'No way,' I said.

Gabe cleared his throat. 'You're the one who refuses to go into the Halloween stores with me that are set up at strip malls every year. You say that they are of the devil. Well, I'm telling you that this is what I see in them these days. They used to sell plastic skeletons – they still do, I'm sure – but you can get mighty realistic ones too. Last year I did a double-take on a couple of them.'

'And you had my precious son with you?' I cried, quite loudly too. 'In a store that celebrates demons and goblins?'

'He's my son too, hon.' Gabe was no longer whispering.

'Harrumph!'

'Cranberry sauce and turkey!' Toy said, also speaking in a loud voice. 'I can't believe that I was fooled so easily. If this gets back to Charlotte, I'm going to be the laughing stock of my old police academy.' Unfortunately, his voice was loud enough to be heard by everyone, and their amusement at Toy's mistake spread rapidly.

Before long, the assembled crowd was having themselves a merry old time. This did not sit well with me. Ninety-eight percent of us professed to be Christians, a people who are charged to live a life of compassion and empathy for the other. Isn't that what the parable of the Good Samaritan is all about? Yet here were my villagers, most of them local born, laughing away at a poor Southerner, Police Chief Toy Graham, who, as an Episcopalian, was a religious minority in our community. Even in the dying light I could see that the poor man's ears were flaming red with embarrassment. What must this member of the greater Anglican community think of us normal Protestants? We who eschew wine at communion, and whom, for the large part, believe that celebrating communion weekly is by far over-doing it?

In the deepest recesses of my mind, in my most private thoughts that I would never share with anyone, not even with my best friend Agnes, I have sometimes fantasized that I was a Joan of Arc type character. Well, a sort of Mennonite version of Joan who would never resort to violence, but who, I am quite certain, would fold in a second if threatened with as much as a hot curling iron pointed in her direction. Nonetheless, in my fantasy, I stick up for the underdogs of the world with my reputedly sharp tongue, one that is said to slice through cheese. Now it was time for me to show a little courage in real life.

'Shame on you, Good Citizens of Hernia,' I yelled, using my cupped hands as a megaphone. 'Police Chief Graham is the best thing to have ever happened to you since the invention of machine-sliced bread. Remember the nitwit we had before? Melvin Stoltzfus?'

The crowd groaned.

I smiled. 'Just so you folks know, that convicted murderer is still on the loose.'

'Hey, isn't he your half-brother?' Herman Neunschwander hollered from somewhere in the shadows.

'That's right, dear,' I said. 'But Herman, we don't choose our parents, do we?'

'That's a valid point,' said Frieda Bollinger, 'but what does that have to do with Chief Graham's competency? If he can't tell plastic bones from real ones, we might as well replace him with a bloodhound. Think of the money we'd save!'

Unfortunately, Frieda has a strong, clear voice that is perpetually tuned to 'wake the dead' volume. Everyone present, and at least two generations of their ancestors, heard her, and responded with uncharacteristic mirth. Even Gabe couldn't keep from smiling, for which he was later reprimanded by a loving female in his life.

But Magdalena of Arc would not let Frieda get the last word. 'Shame on you most of all, Frieda Bollinger! Don't you remember in May when you were positive that there was a terrorist hiding out in your attic because you heard someone speaking "foreign"? But it turned out to be Eric Schumacher's scarlet macaw that flew in through your broken window? It was Chief Graham who climbed up into your attic to fight the terrorist, and then later fixed the window for you. And you, Eric Schumacher got your "foreign" speaking bird back, for which you ought to be grateful, because I know that they don't grow on trees – at least not in Pennsylvania.'

The crowd twittered. OK, so maybe they were laughing at

Eric and Frieda – and that wasn't a good thing – but at least they were no longer laughing at Toy, the outsider, who had no support system. I know, two wrongs don't make a right, but sometimes a wrong is all that's left.

By then the fake bones had been bagged and there was nothing left for us to do but go home. Gabe appeared especially anxious to leave.

'I don't mean to be rude, Toy,' Gabe said, 'but I've got to get back to the inn and pick up Ma and take her back home for the night. Mags, you coming?'

I glanced at Toy, who seemed pretty spent. 'Sure. But Toy, I just want to say for the record that I think what we had here this evening wasn't just some high-school prank. I feel it in my bones – no pun intended – that whoever put those realistic-looking skeletons on the bridge was counting on us to cancel the festival day tomorrow.'

'What do you mean?' Gabe said. 'Ma will still be Queen, won't she?'

'Yes, your ma will still be Queen,' I said wearily. 'The question is whether or not she will still want to ride in a goat cart across the bridge when she hears about this? Because if not, she will have to abdicate.'

'Abdicate?'

'Yes. You do realize that the bridge is the central part of the celebration, don't you?'

'Yes, hon, I'm not deaf. You've been prattling on about that darn bridge ceremony for the past three months – well, the past four *years*, really. Ever since you thought up that *fekakta* festival.'

'*Fekakta* festival? Silly? That's what you call it. Let me remind you, sweetie-pot-pie, that the first of these *fekakta* festivals was to celebrate the fact that Gruff, a billy goat, saved my life by flinging our beloved son's soiled nappy into the face of a killer who had already successfully poisoned his wife.'

My husband threw up his beautiful surgeon's hands in a gesture of defence. 'Your sweetie-pot-pie surrenders. I remember. You were a hero then, and you remain a hero today. I just don't want Ma to be disappointed.'

Gabe didn't have to worry; given the events of the last twenty-four hours, I had a feeling his precious ma was in for the ride of her life.

TWELVE

There are days when that urge to stay curled up in a foetal position and never get out of bed might have been a wise one. But the success of the festival was my responsibility, and along with it my mother-in-law's pride, and my husband's happiness. Although I was able to throw off the guest sheet with ease, the feelings I had of impending dread did not leave. Shakespeare wrote: 'Uneasy lies the head that wears the crown'. In my case: uneasy was the head that wore coils of mousy brown braids topped with a white organza prayer cap.

In fact, before I could even plant one universe-size foot on the oak plank floor, my phone rang. Because I am the village mayor, a wife, a businesswoman, and a mother with a teenage daughter away at college, my phone is set up with several different ringtones.

'Good morning, Alison,' I said somewhat warily. By the way, when our daughter Alison was fifteen, she was our first Miss Hernia, and thus our first citizen to ride across the bridge in a goat cart on Billy Goat Gruff Festival. She wasn't elected to this honour; she was appointed by me. I chose her only because it was her little brother whose nappy had saved my life. It had nothing to do with the fact that already by that tender age, Alison was a buxom beauty who looked a full five years older than she was. But my, how I've digressed.

'M-mam-ma,' a nineteen-year-old Alison purred over the phone to me. (She usually calls me 'Mom'.)

'You're not coming, are you?' I said. 'You're supposed to crown the new Miss Hernia, you know. It's tradition. Except this year your Grandma Ida has forced me to change the title to Hernia's Citizen of the Year, because she's definitely not a *miss*. Of course, that concession wasn't enough for her, even though she stole the election. But, oh no, your Grandma Ida wants the title of *Queen* of Hernia. Can you imagine that? She should count herself lucky that she still gets a crown. So *you* have to put it on her head, because *I'm* definitely not doing it.'

'We-ellll, it's this, Mam-ma – but no, first, I want to know how you and Daddy are doing?'

'Who's your "daddy", Alison? If you're referring to the man with whom I have sexual relations, he's always been "dad" to you.'

'Ick, Mom! Don't say that stuff; it's gross.'

'Don't be silly, dear. Your dad and I are married. The two-sheet tango, the mattress mambo, the bedtime boogie-woogie, the pillowcase paso doble, the horizontal hula – they're all sanctioned by God and country, and we have the papers to prove it. And as you know quite well by now, those aren't real dances, so there is no sin involved. Those are just different terms to describe the glorious coming together of two naked bodies—'

'Mom! I *mean* it. *Stop*. You're grossing me out.'

'OK, I'll stop,' I said. 'But I was just starting to enjoy this call. I knew from the second that you referred to me as "Mama" that something was up. So spill it, dear.'

Alison sighed so hard that I could feel her breath tickle my ear through my cordless phone. What made this even more astonishing was that she was at the University of Pittsburgh, which was one hundred and fourteen miles away. After her world record sigh, she inhaled deeply and strove to spill her secret and her guts in a world record run-on sentence.

'You brought me up to care deeply about the plight of others who are less fortunate than I am, and I will always be grateful that you and Dad gave me a forever home and adopted me after my birth parents turned their backs on me, and that you showed me by your love how I could grow up to be a loving person too, and Mom, although your faith is mostly about saving sinners from Hell so that they get to go to Heaven to be with their Lord and Saviour Jesus Christ, and sure they do a ton of relief work overseas bringing food and medical supplies to people who desperately need it, and you know that Dad's and my faith is mostly about *Tikun Olam,* which means repairing the broken state of the world that we find ourselves in now, and since we don't believe in Hell and really don't give two figs about Heaven anyway, I decided to help suffering people now instead of waiting until after I graduated from college and then from medical school, so I'm taking what's called a gap year, and I'm going to Puerto Rico to do whatever I can because they are still rebuilding after

Hurricane Maria and the subsequent earthquakes, and people on the mainland seem to have forgotten about them, or else they no longer care, and if you want to blame anyone for me taking a gap year, then blame the Brits, because when I was a young girl I remember reading that Prince William took a gap year to go to Chile to do some volunteer work, and don't worry I won't be alone because I met this kindred soul, Alex, at Hillel when I went there for Shabbat services – oops they're calling my flight now! Love you, Mom! Give my love to Dad. *T'amo!*'

I was stunned. I was shocked. I was gobsmacked. Then I was outraged. It had been Gabe's older sister, a retired psychiatrist, who had urged us to let our nineteen-year-old daughter, along with her two best friends, attend Freshman Orientation at the University of Pittsburgh without parental supervision. 'They're adults now,' she kept saying.

Phooey on that! They're still teenagers. Even Gabe would agree that we humans aren't fully mature until somewhere in our mid-twenties. Just a week ago Alison was gung-ho about beginning the long but exciting road that would lead her to being a medical doctor. Now she was off to the Caribbean with a boy named Alex. And what is a nineteen-year-old male if not a walking, talking, breathing bundle of sex hormones! After all, the human male reaches his sexual peak at about age eighteen and thinks about sex almost constantly. But by age fifty this is no longer the case. At least that's the line my physician husband fed me when he had to start using little blue pills before we got intimate – not that this is anybody's business. My point is that without anyone to stop them, my precious daughter might that very night be doing the headboard hoedown, or even just the sleeping bag shuffle, but in the process creating an Alexander Jr. or mini-Alison. Oy Vey!

I could just wring Gabe's sister's scrawny neck. I could probably come close to doing it, too. After all, I was a country girl, and had wrung many a chicken's neck. Literally. Whereas Cheryl, the former New York psychiatrist, possessed a neck with hardly more girth than a chicken's neck. What's more, Cheryl's neck had been subjected to so many chemical peels, it was a wonder that it didn't just snap in two when she lifted her head from her down-filled pillow on any given morning. Of course, these thoughts weren't those of a good Christian, but I was feeling sinfully self-indulgent at the moment. Besides, what good is grace anyhow, if I can't get a much-needed dollop of it from time to time? Ergo, I dropped to my knees beside our California king-size bed to beg for some assistance.

'Dear Lord,' I whined, 'as thou didst send an angel to shut the mouths of the hungry lions so they would not eat thy prophet Daniel, wouldst thou please keep Alison's knees pressed tightly together until she returns home safely to my embrace, or until such time that she is old enough to be married – maybe ten years from now. And remember, Lord, the saying is: *Four on the floor*. That means that her and Alex *both* need to keep their feet on the floor at all times when they're in her room. Trust me, Lord, a lot of mischief can still be done with one pair of feet on the floor – not that you would know anything about that, of course. Anyway, if you would be so kind as to put that message in her head on sort of a revolving loop so that it doesn't go in one ear and out the other, I'll be—'

'A monkey's uncle!' Gabe said, and then rolled over to my side of the bed snorting with laughter. 'Oh, hon, I love you, you know that, and I mean no disrespect, but did I hear you giving God instructions on what to say to our daughter? Plus, what sort of omniscient God needs the meanings of words explained to him?'

I don't know which feeling was more intense: embarrassment or anger. I felt that my privacy had been violated, but of course it was my own fault. Any sane person whose aim it is to rant and rave aloud, and not be heard, would probably pick his, or her, automobile over their occupied bedroom. The key word being 'sane'. However, there are those who would say that ship for me sailed a long time ago.

My cheeks burned. 'You just interrupted a hotline to Heaven, buster.'

'Mags, I'm sorry that I hurt your feelings,' Gabe said, popping my balloon of bellicosity.

My bony knees had started to feel sore anyway, so I stood. 'Well, I'm done praying. How much of it did you hear?'

'Beginning with the fifth word into your prayer. Remember, that's how long it takes for a man to start listening. Even a sleeping man will begin to listen at that point if his wife prays as loudly as you do – no offense intended.'

'Nonetheless,' I said with a sniff, 'some offense was taken. I'll have you know that Heaven is a long ways off, so it doesn't hurt to pump up the volume. But what *you* really need to know is that tonight your daughter – our daughter – will become a woman in Puerto Rico, unless the Good Lord sends an angel to keep her legs as tightly closed as a clam at low tide, or else the Lord himself whispers that mantra "Four on the floor" into her ears all night.'

Gabe frowned. 'Mags, did Susannah offer you anything to eat or drink? Something that she brought into the house with her?'

'*What?* Do you think that I'm drunk? Or on drugs? You want to know what's what? I'll tell you, and it's all because of that sister of yours!'

'Cheryl?'

'No, your other one,' I said. Gabe doesn't have another sister, and I was being sarcastic. However, it could have been a reasonable question, because nothing surprises me about the Rosen family anymore.

'Oh, come on!' Gabe said.

'Cheryl convinced us that our dear, sweet daughter and her best friend could handle a few days unchaperoned in the Middle Apple.'

'The *Middle Apple*? What the heck does that mean?'

'Well, Pittsburgh isn't New York, is it? So it can't be the Big Apple, and it's certainly not Bedford, which is more cherry size than the smallest of apples. Not that it will do a lick of good at this point to say, but I was right: they *did* need supervision.'

Now Gabe was on his feet. 'Why? What happened to our little girl?'

'Our *little girl* just ran off to Puerto Rico with a man named Alexander who will despoil her before the village cocks crow tomorrow morning.'

'Come again?'

So I repeated what Alison had told me – give or take a few words. Well, maybe I gave more than I took, as I am wont to embellish stories in order to drive across salient points. To his credit, Gabe was properly outraged, but alas, clearly not entirely rational.

'Which airlines?' he yelled over his shoulder, as he raced to put on a pair of pants. 'And babe, grab my wallet, would you? Also, let me take your car; I don't have enough petrol to make it to the airport.'

'Stop!' I shouted. 'Freeze! It's too late.'

My Dearly Beloved had already thrust one well-muscled calf into a trouser leg before my words registered with him.

'But hon,' he protested, 'it's never too late.'

'She was boarding the plane when she hung up. On a good day you wouldn't be able to make it to her gate in less than two hours. She'll be halfway to San Juan in that time.'

Then the most surprising thing happened. My middle-aged, retired heart surgeon of a husband started bawling like a baby. He yanked his leg out of his trousers and, blinded by his tears, headed for me with open arms. I am not the most sentimental creature that the Dear Lord ever created, and I still blamed Gabe and his sister for Alison's predicament, but I am not altogether heartless. (Although your average stethoscope does have trouble locating my shrivelled ticker, eventually a good physician can find it.) That said, I found myself opening my arms as well, and eventually tear-blinded Gabe crashed into me and we tumbled back onto the bed. As for what happened next, it's nobody's business. Suffice it to say, that if I had read about a similar scene in one of Agnes Miller's romance novels, I would have laughed out loud before throwing the book across the room. How could so much external stress, and clashing approaches to parenting, ignite such intense passion? That was, by the way, a rhetorical question.

THIRTEEN

On my wedding day Cousin Freni had told me what sex was all about. 'About three minutes,' she'd said. Freni is Amish, and Mama, who had already passed, was

Mennonite, but their last-minute sex education sessions with me would have been virtually the same. 'The man will say, "brace yourself," Freni had continued. 'Then you must close your eyes and try to think happy thoughts. Maybe plan what you will cook him for supper.'

What Freni didn't tell me was that by a certain age the three-minute rule no longer applied, and that eventually an entire week's worth of supper menus could be planned during – well, let us call it 'the happy moments'. Suffice it to say, I have also memorized every hairline fracture in the plaster ceiling of our old farmhouse inn. Thus it was that Gabe and I were more than a wee bit late in leaving the PennDutch Inn for the festival. By then, even the Hancocks and Cousin Miriam had departed, presumably taking Susannah with them, as she couldn't be found either. As for Rebecca, she'd been given the morning off to attend as well.

Given our late start I was quite surprised that my phone hadn't been ringing constantly since the time I'd promised my team that I'd be there. I was even more surprised to discover that my phone had been turned off. But I was absolutely devastated to learn that my husband and I had gotten so much into the groove of things that he had been able to reach over and silence my phone during a moment of marital bliss. I felt used and betrayed.

'Babe, come on,' Gabe said when I complained. 'You needed cheering up, and that's always done the trick before.'

We were getting into his car then, and I slammed the door so hard that it undoubtedly rattled some of his fillings. I know that it did mine, as well as gave me a headache. And if he hadn't immediately started backing out of the driveway, I would have opened the door and slammed it again.

'Hey,' he said through clenched teeth, 'getting your knickers in a knot won't get us there any sooner.' Then perhaps realizing that my bloomers were indeed beginning to bunch he shifted tactics. 'You know, hon, what you've managed to achieve with this festival in just a few years is just astounding. I realize that the impetus was celebrating the fact that a goat saved our son's life, but now it's become much more than that. It brings the entire town together in a fun, silly way. Also, it's a perfect solution for those children who aren't allowed to celebrate Halloween.'

I smiled. 'You're forgiven.'

Gabe was right. The Fourth Annual Billy Goat Gruff Festival was much more than just about herbivores with disturbingly humanoid eyes. For instance, there was an Amish fresh market along Main Street in the morning where, in addition to produce, one could buy homemade cheeses and baked goods of many descriptions. There were numerous demonstrations of horses being shod. These were not contrived; they were Amish horses that really needed new shoes. There were buggy rides offered by enterprising Amish teenagers. In addition, there were at least fifty yard sales scattered throughout the village, some of them multi-family sales, and many of them featuring an antique piece or two.

The first year only villagers attended. The following year brought perhaps fifty outsiders to gawk at our quirky goings-on. The third year, we had hundreds of tourists show up, some from as far away as Pittsburgh. This year, we were prepared. Both Mennonite churches, the Baptist church, the Methodist church and the Presbyterian church had all agreed to lend us their parking lots for the occasion. The only church not cooperating used to be out by the turnpike and was known as the church with thirty-two words in its name. That was back when the Sausage Barn was still in operation. This church has since relocated within the village proper, and has been renamed The Only True, Two Testament Believing, Full-Faith Fellowship Practicing, Final Revelation Dispensing, Exclusive Righteous Interpretation of Scriptures, End Times Celebratory, Passport to Heaven Issuing, Welcoming Those Who Would Walk the Straight and Narrow Path that Leads to Salvation, and Shunning Those Who Meander Along the Broad Road that Leads to Damnation, Church of the One Holy God Who Lives Forever and Ever, Glory Hallelujah, Amen. The pastor of the renamed church, Reverend Gerald Splitfrock, said that his congregation would have nothing to do with a festival that featured a goat. They were satanic, he said. After all, when Jesus spoke of separating the sheep from the goats, it was the sheep who represented the redeemed, and the goats that were the condemned. We were to expect protesters from his church, Reverend Splitfrock said. And maybe 'something more'.

It was the 'something more' that was particularly troubling. This recently relocated church with sixty-six words in its name uses poisonous snakes in its worship services. New members are required to reach into a cardboard box and pull out a rattlesnake and hold it aloft while professing their faith. If they truly believe, the reptile will ignore them. If their faith is weak, they might get bitten and subsequently die.

The members base their belief on Mark 14:17-18:

> And these signs will follow those who believe: In my name they will cast out demons; they will speak with new tongues; (18) they will take up serpents; and if they drink anything deadly, it will by no means hurt them; they will lay their hand on the sick, and they will recover.

However, I had it on good authority that Rev. Splitfrock preached that Herniaites who did not attend his church were not true Christians, and thus would surely die if they tried handling the same serpents. He said that we 'so-called' Christians were vermin, nothing more than rodents that his snakes would be happy to dine on. By the way, this heresy isn't hearsay; I attended his four-hour-long preaching service one Sunday morning disguised as an old woman, which really wasn't much of a stretch. It occurred to me then, and many times since, that the bigoted man was capable of releasing his box of poisonous reptiles into the crowd at the Billy Goat Gruff Festival.

That threat was in February, and now it was August. Since then, the good reverend had been interviewed by Toy, the sheriff, and the FBI. Reverend Splitfrock was not a man who could be easily intimidated, but he finally confessed that the 'something more' would simply be spontaneous blessings bestowed on tourists by his members. Fine, Toy said, but he didn't want to hear any complaints from festival attendees about being harassed by religious extremists.

Much to my considerable relief, my Dearly Beloved got me into Hernia in plenty of time to do what I do best: boss people around. Before you judge me, I'm just being truthful. I know my strengths, as well as my weaknesses. I eschew committee work because I have no patience with folks who don't get right to the point or engage in crosstalk. May the Good Lord forgive me, but I was born to be a dictator – a good Christian one, to be sure. I believe that a lot could be accomplished if one person was in charge of everything, and she issued all the orders, and everyone else snapped to it and obeyed. Of course, 'dictator' is such an ugly word, don't you think? Therefore, I propose 'empress', and Empress Magdalena has such a lovely sound.

'Earth to Magdalena,' Chief Toy said about an hour after I arrived. 'It's still an hour until the festival is officially open, and already we have a problem.'

'Reverend Splitfrock and his gang of holy heavies?' I asked with a sinking heart. It's been said in jest, but in a good way, that Hernia has more churches per capita than Rome. I hated to think that the church that excelled in names was going to be the rotten apple in the barrel, the one that spoiled our town's reputation.

'No, ma'am,' Toy said. 'Our problem is – well, just look around, and what do you see?'

'Hundreds of tourists milling around, presumably waiting for something to happen. Although there seems to be a lot of angry buzz. They sound like a swarm of bees.'

'Exactly,' Toy said. 'And it's going to get worse. Both roads into Hernia are clogged and Route 94 is backed up as far as the Pennsylvania Turnpike. That's twelve miles of cars headed this way.'

I gasped so hard that I inhaled a gnat that had gotten too close to my face for its well-being. Small as it was, my visceral response was to try and hack the insect up.

'Are you all right?' Toy asked.

I forced a smile. 'I'm fine, dear. I was just taking a morning protein break.'

'Back to the problem at hand. Any ideas, Madam Mayor?'

'Count our blessings?' I said.

'Where are these people supposed to park?' Toy said. 'And what about security?'

'Well,' I said, 'we will just have to have someone stop them at this end of the bridge, and then inform them that they have to find a spot along one of our charming side streets. As to extra security, why don't I call up our volunteer fire and rescue members while you call the Somerset Police and see if they can spare a few officers today?'

We were having our conversation outside the Hernia police station, so that we could keep an eye on the crowd. Although I have told my children that I have an eye in the back of my head, one that can see what they're doing behind my back, that might not really be the case. At least that third eye wasn't functioning when the woman in the pink tennis visor and reflective sunglasses tapped me on the shoulder from behind.

I shrieked like a six-year-old boy. 'What the Victorian sponge cake!'

The tourist was unflappable, and she immediately thrust a newspaper advertisement in my face. The ad took up a full half page and bore the following title: FAIR OFFERS FREE FOOD AND FUN FOR THE ENTIRE FAMILY.

'I can't find any of what yinz promised. I drove all the way here from the Westwood neighbourhood in Pittsburgh with my three children, and my ninety-six-year-old mother-in-law, because of what it says right here in black and white.'

I snatched the paper from her hand. 'Toy, it says here that we have carnival rides, like a roller coaster called the Devil's Colon because of all its twists and turns. Also, a Ferris wheel with three rotating wheels. It's supposed to be the world's tallest. But get this, it says that we offer *free* food and drinks, including beer, all day and until ten o'clock tonight. Then at ten we're putting on a lollapalooza of a fireworks display to eclipse any ever put on in these United States of America.'

'Give me that,' Toy said, and snatched the ad from my bony hand.

Immediately someone poked my bony behind, causing me to shriek like a *nine*-year-old boy (I was not quite as startled this time). I even managed to compose myself a little before I turned to lecture the child who had assaulted my dignity. Needless to say, I was quite unprepared to have a second newspaper waved up at me by a nonagenarian in a wheelchair. There were three crabby looking children standing behind her.

'Here, lady,' she said, in the raspy voice of a smoker. 'You can have this. It's from Pittsburgh's other paper. The one that ain't partial to you-know-who.'

The second advertisement was identical to the first. That said, it had cost somebody, or some group, a sizable chunk of change to deceive a large number of people and wreak havoc on our peaceful village. I am most certainly not a betting woman (gambling is a sin), but if I were, I would bet my farm and the inn that Rev. Splitfrock and his bunch of snake-handlers were the guilty party. Well, I'd have to give him credit for thinking up a clever way to maximize the chance that at a least one 'so-called' Christian was bitten during our celebration to honour our quite elderly, 'satanic' billy goat named Gruff.

FOURTEEN

Toy and I didn't have any other option except to call in the big guns. I mean that literally. I called Sheriff Stodgewiggle up in Bedford, who thrives on confrontation, while Toy called the State Troopers. The latter blocked incoming traffic from the Turnpike, while the former brought four well-armed deputies wielding bullhorns.

At first there was mass confusion, and folks panicked. They initially thought that there had been a terrorist attack. Then when they realized that they had been duped into driving for over an hour under false pretences, they got angry. But frankly, who can blame them? If something comparable to that had happened to me, I'm sure that my sturdy Christian underwear would be tied in a knot – or at least in a pleasing bow.

At any rate, we did have one rather unpleasant incident. A heavily tattooed millennial kicked over a rubbish bin while taking the Lord's name in vain. However, a keen-eyed deputy yelled a sharp rebuke over his megaphone, and thereafter the only tantrums on display were from Pittsburgh residents under six years of age.

As much as I dislike Sheriff Stodgewiggle (I *love* him because the Bible says that I have to, but I *like* cockroaches better), I will admit that he and his men did an admirable job of clearing our village of all the folks who had invaded us because of the two erroneous newspaper ads. What's more, two of the deputies were off duty and volunteered to stay for the festival which had been delayed by only an hour.

And let me tell you, Deputy Hayes's megaphone was a godsend – a word I do not use lightly. Toy won't let me use his megaphone, because supposedly folks in China called in with noise complaints last time I did. Coach Listerbaum from the high school has said in the past that lending me his megaphone is tantamount to pouring kerosene on a fire – a metaphor that I'm still scratching my horsey head trying to figure out. As to why I don't purchase my own – well, I'm just too ding-dang parsimonious. Anyway, I was thrilled for the use of Deputy Hayes's instrument, and I put it to good use marshalling my many volunteers, plus managing our genuine record turnout.

Although the incoming traffic was still curtailed, practically every household in Hernia turned out for the first time, and in the end that is what made the event really special. Not that everything stayed hunky-dory, of course. I am speaking of my life, after all. You see, I still hadn't gotten up enough nerve to tell my mother-in-law that her title was *Hernia Citizen of the Year* and not *Queen of Hernia*.

I waited until the very last minute to break the news. We were standing in the shade of a large oak, next to the goat cart, on the starting side of the bridge, which is the opposite side from Hernia. Predictably, when the would-be blueblood learned that she would be 'installed' rather than 'crowned', she was not amused.

'*Vhat?* Zees eez a crime! To shteel a crown from an old lady is a crime und a dismal-wiener. I am vatching zee television, and I am knowing that for zees you can be inpreached, Magdalena. Den you vill be no more da mayor. Poof! All gone. Eez dat vhat you vant?'

'Uh, in a word: no. And for your information, dear, while a dismal wiener might be a good description of a hot dog left out in the rain, it is not a misdemeanour. It's merely poor judgment.'

'I *vant* my crown!' Ida hissed. OK, Ida is the one exception to the rule that no one can hiss without uttering an 'S'.

I politely slipped an embroidered hanky from its storage within my bony bosom and dabbed myself dry. 'I realize that being crowned queen is what you really want, dear. I can feel your angst to the tips of my surprisingly comely toes. But you see, whoever told you that there would be a crown was mistaken. There has never been a coronation in the history of this humble, but picturesque, little village.'

Ida's eyes narrowed. 'Yah? You are sure about dis?'

'Just as sure as the world is round.'

Ida recoiled. 'You tink I'm shtupid? The woild eez flat, you dummkopf! My precious Gabeleh take me on a cruise before he marry you, und zee whole time I see dat zee ocean is flat, yoost like your—'

'Don't say it, toots,' I said, not *too* unkindly. I try to turn the metaphorical other cheek from time to time. Really, I do.

'Mebbe I von't, und mebbe I vill,' Ida said. 'But you know vhat eez a landshlide?'

'Yes, dear,' I said tiredly. 'One kind involves dirt and rocks sliding down a mountain, and the other refers to an overwhelming victory in an election.'

'Yah, but I am shpeaking of zee foist one. Eef zee woild eez round, den zee dirt and rocks vould keep rolling around zee voild, and dey dun't, do dey?'

'Dey dun't,' I said uncharitably.

'So dere is your proof, dummkopf. Zee dirt and rocks go shliding off over the edge of the flat voild. End of shtory.'

'If you say so, dear.'

'Yah? Good. So now I want my crown,' my mother-in-law said in Standard English. I was surprised, but not shocked, by her linguistic transformation. Nothing about the crone without a crown will surprise me.

'Well, that's just too bad, sweetie,' I said, 'because we don't have one to give you. You will, however, be given a very handsome plaque made out of genuine walnut-coloured hard plastic, on which tightly glued, gold-coloured, plastic letters spell *Hernia's Citizen of the Yeer*. You are not to worry about the slight variation in spelling, because Mary Gill of our very own Crafty Mothers Club said that she can fix that with a razor knife and a little superglue. Mary Gill promised me that you will hardly know the difference, especially if you hang the plaque in a low-light area.'

Frankly, I don't blame Ida for being a mite disappointed in

learning about the spelling mistake (which was Mary Gill's fault, and not that of the nice lady in Beijing from whom she ordered it). However, I think that Ida was out of line for taking a swing at me with her purse. Like many women these days, her purse is large enough to cram a small turkey into, as she did last year when we took her home from a community Thanksgiving dinner.

'Ouch!' I cried out. 'What do you have in that thing? The Rock of Gibraltar?'

Her response was to open the bag and dump its contents on my feet. 'Ow,' I said, as I hopped away from the heap of detritus, holding my left foot in my hands.

It might not have been the Rock of Gibraltar, but there *was* an honest-to-goodness rock about the size of a croquet ball. As well as two honest-to-goodness croquet balls, a cracked snow globe, three hair-clogged combs, two boar bristle brushes, a stapler, a can opener, a tired-looking toothbrush, three tubes of toothpaste, a jumper (sweater), a pair of stretch yoga pants, a pair of sneakers, an address book, two cell phones, a very small, yellow rubber ducky, a package of cinnamon rolls, five ballpoint pens, seven pencils, seven envelopes, a tin of mints, a bottle of antacid and a small framed cartoon of a mermaid.

'Yah, I got rock,' Ida called after me. 'Dey not let me buy gun – say, I am more nuts den Hershey's bar with almonds. So how else to protect myself? With fancy talk like Magdalena? It not work for me, I promise. Den mebbe you vant arrest me now for litter? Old lady who no get crown, just cheap plastic trinket from China?'

'I don't want to arrest you, you tiresome old biddy,' I said. 'And I can't give you a crown, no matter how much you whine like a five-year-old. But I can promise you that I will make a big deal out of your installation as Hernia Citizen of the Year. I will use the megaphone that Deputy Hayes has let me borrow to announce to all of Hernia, and perhaps all of the known flat world – you know how loud I can be – that you are Hernia's *Unique* Citizen of the Year. This is the first time that we will be bestowing that title on someone.'

Ida blinked. 'Yah?'

'Indeed,' I said.

'Nu, vhy yoost "unique"? Vhy not "*most* unique"?'

I groaned. 'Because that's redundant. If someone is unique, then they are already one of a kind, and that is you, Ida. There isn't anyone in Hernia that compares with you.'

'Yah?'

'I'm positive.'

She nodded; that is to say, her head bobbled as much as she could force it to do so, given her lack of a neck.

'OK then,' I said, 'come along. It's time for you to take your ride of glory. Your triumphal procession into town, just like the Roman generals did when they returned to Rome from their military campaigns.'

'Are you daft?' Ida said, slipping into Standard English yet again. 'Titus entered Rome bearing the spoils of our temple in Jerusalem after he sacked it and burned it to the ground. If you don't believe me, then Google the Arch of Titus. Or better yet, visit it for yourself, like your Jewish husband and I did fifteen years ago.'

'Oy vey,' I said. 'Give me a moment while I take my foot out of my mouth.'

'Left foot, or right foot?' she said. 'And do you need my help, given how enormous your feet are?'

'What?' I said. 'Who *is* this new Ida Rosen? Have you been abducted by aliens and replaced by a lookalike? Not that this could happen, of course, because alien space beings can't exist, since they would have to have been created without sin, given that God had just one "only begotten Son" to offer Himself up as a sacrifice for our sin.'

Ida's head bobbled again. 'Magdalena, I honestly don't know what *my* son ever saw in you. It's not *just* your looks, or your lack of a decent education, but it's your paranoia, and your world view – which is simply bizarre, to say the least. To put it succinctly, you should be institutionalized. Just ask my daughter, Cheryl, a prominent psychiatrist. By the way, I'm a neurosurgeon. Allow me to translate that for a country bumpkin such as yourself – I'm a brain doctor. Capiche?'

I was flabbergasted. Nay, I was gobsmacked, a word which better describes the moment, for indeed, I felt like I'd been smacked in my gob. Talk about the pot calling the kettle black!

'You think that *I'm* crazy?' I said. 'What chutzpah! You're the one who spent four years leading a cult called the Sisters of Perpetual Apathy and dressing as a fake nun who self-styled herself Mother Malaise. You even turned the farmhouse across the road, the one that your son bought for you, into a convent for your followers. You can't tell me that those are the actions of a sane woman. And by the way, during those four years, the entire town was holding its breath waiting for you and your band of misfits to drink the Kool-Aid.'

Ida snorted. 'You want to know why I adopted the accent and acted like I did. To put you off guard, that's why. You're a religious woman. You know the story of Joshua and Caleb who were sent as spies to scope out the Promised Land. That's what I did. When my Gabe told me that he'd met a captivating woman out here in the sticks, I sent my spies here. They got your number so to speak and reported everything to me. Together we formulated a plan to—'

To what? Before she could finish her sentence, Agnes, my co-chair, sounded reveille on a beat-up old bugle loaned to her by Peter Gingerich, the Boy Scoutmaster. It was time for Ida to climb into the goat cart and the procession to begin.

'Hop in, toots,' I said, letting my temper get the best of me yet again. 'Think of the goat cart as a golden coach, and you're an English princess.'

'The cart is disgustingly filthy,' she said, 'and the goat stinks.'

'Ah, if only I had a magic wand, I would change a couple of things,' I said. 'Now, remember to smile, and do at least *try* to turn your head from side to side, once we cross the bridge, so that your many fans can get a glimpse of your unique face.'

Much to my surprise, Ida did board the cart without further ado, although it required me placing my gangly arms around her considerable midriff and heaving her into the cart as if she were a two-hundred-and-fifty-pound sack of potatoes. Then I had to climb aboard and help settle her in the middle of the wooden seat, which fortunately was made from a solid oak plank.

'Where are the reins?' she asked, while still trying to catch her breath.

'Ida, dear, you don't have to worry about steering the cart. This handsome young lad there, standing discreetly by the goat – neither of whom heard a word of our conversation – is Miguel

Yoder, the adopted son of third cousins, thrice removed. Miguel was born in Mexico, but he's the good kind of Mexican, *not* the bad kind that you may have heard so much about.'

Although in full disclosure, Miguel did cheat on an eighth-grade history test – or so I've been told. Not that I listen to gossip. And I heard that in church one Sunday he was seen checking his phone messages when he was supposed to be praying. 'Anyway, Miguel will have his strong brown hand on the Gruff's harness the entire time, so you are not to worry about running off the bridge or, heaven forfend, Gruff getting stung by a bee, in which case you might end up all the way down in the State of Maryland. Personally, I never travel there unless I'm carrying provisions because—'

'Magdalena,' Ida said, 'shut up, and let's get this circus on the road.'

'Hold your horses, toots. Lest you be unduly worried that this rickety old cart tip over on its way across this ancient bridge, I shall walk beside the cart with a steadying, liver-spotted hand clasped firmly on one of these rotting side boards. OK, Miguel,' I sang out in my not-so-melodious voice, 'take her away!'

Then the most astonishing thing happened. Billy Goat Gruff took two steps forward, just enough really to put tension on the traces, when there was a snapping sound. That's when Billy trotted to freedom, right out of his broken restraints, and straight across the bridge to uproarious laughter, followed by thunderous applause.

Miguel, who was just a teenager, and could be excused for his behaviour, slunk away with embarrassment.

At that point my mother-in-law swore like the proverbial sailor. But I can't be absolutely certain of it, because some of the words that issued from her mouth I'd never heard even Gabe use. I knew that a tea kettle left untended will eventually boil itself dry, so I waited a couple of minutes until she ran out of steam.

'Never fear, Ida, dear. I will pick up the traces myself, and whilst doing my inimitable imitation of a goat – baaing, of course – I shall hoof it across the bridge and deliver your exalted self to the award ceremony. Good baa.'

'You vill pay for dis!' she shouted at my back.

FIFTEEN

As per tradition, albeit one of only four years standing, as soon as the cart crossed the village side of Slave Creek, villagers showered the children with candy. Meanwhile I grabbed Agnes who was needlessly worrying about doing a sound check on the stage microphone. After all, I promised Ida that I'd use the megaphone, and to be completely honest, did anyone really want to hear what she had to say? I realize that doesn't sound very Christian of me, but Ida was an outsider, an over-educated New Yorker, a buttinsky, who'd admitted to having it in for me before she'd come to live in Hernia. Besides, she's been living a lie the entire time, with her fake accent, and her acquired persona, and that cult that had sucked in all our depressed Herniaites. The woman deserved to be ridden out of town on a rail, except that we didn't have one.

'So, Mags,' Agnes said, perhaps with a modicum of pain, 'please let up on the grip you have on my shoulder. I'm not old enough to qualify for Medicare, and my insurance policy doesn't cover physical therapy.'

First, I pulled her inside the police station which, I was glad to see, was empty at the moment. Then I gently massaged my best friend's shoulder as I spoke – or at least I tried to.

'Sorry about that, but she's a fraud, Agnes! She's a lying fraud.'

'All right, I'll buy that,' Agnes said, 'but given that you have the ability to – *uh* – not see the best in everybody, to whom are you referring now?'

'Ida!'

Agnes appeared taken aback. 'Ida? Isn't she old hat? I mean we've dissected that old biddy's bad habits until there's nothing left except for the actual habit that she used to wear when she was still a nun. Even then you called it the most disgusting shmatta you'd ever seen. "A burlap sack with four holes," you said.'

'This is much more than that! Her Yiddish accent is all put on. Agnes, she's a neurosurgeon, for crying out loud.'

Agnes reached up and placed a plump hand against my forehead. 'Mags, you don't feel hot. Don't get angry now, but have you been drinking?'

'Jam roly-poly!' I swore. 'Oops, pardon my foul mouth. My swearing has really gotten out of hand. Of course I haven't been drinking – you know me better than that. When Ida and I were on the other side of the bridge, she suddenly started speaking in perfect, unaccented, English. *Real* English. You know, *American* English – the kind without an accent. She said that this Yiddisher mama thing was all an act, as was the Mother Malaise shtick.'

Agnes's eyes were as big as dinner plates. 'Why would she do that? I mean, leave an exciting place like New York to walk around in a gunny sack for all those years to torture you – oh my goodness! That's exactly it, isn't it? That woman was determined to go to any length to get between you and Gabe. Magdalena, she's not only psychotic, but she's dangerous!'

'Exactly,' I said quietly, as the full meaning of Ida's revelation hit me. 'Agnes, this means that my husband, the one person who pledged before God to have my back until death do us part, has been a party to this deception all these years.'

'Huh?' Agnes said. 'But Mags, I was at your wedding; I don't remember any pledge about having each other's backs.'

'Oh, I could just strangle you now, Agnes, if I wasn't a pacifist,' I hissed, sounding like a bag full of angry snakes.

'S-s-sorry,' Agnes hissed back. 'You're absolutely right about Gabe. Why, I could just wring that scoundrel's neck – and I *am* a pacifist. What a horrible act of betrayal and deception. Oh Mags, my heart breaks for you.'

Then, because we were both Mennonites of Amish descent, who've been bred over the centuries to be even more stoic than the British, we each allowed six tears to fall – three from each eye – and then hugged each other – bosoms barely touching – while we slapped each other's backs in a contest to see who could get the other one to burp first. In a nutshell, that is what I call the 'Mennonite hug'.

'So, what are you going to do?' Agnes asked, after a long,

uncomfortable period of silence, during which we avoided making eye contact.

'I'm going to let him hang.'

'Pardon me?'

'Well, Ida's very last words to me were back in her shtetel accent. They were also a threat. She seems to think that I intended for Billy to break loose. That I planned it as a way to humiliate her. Anyway, if she continues to speak like the old Ida, I'm not going to say anything. *Yet.* I'm going to wait and see how the two Idas plan to resolve the dilemma they've gotten themselves into.'

'Good for you,' Agnes said, 'but consider this, if Ida Rosen is kookier than a room full of Black Forest clocks, and doesn't tell Gabe about her lapse into Standard English, then what?'

'Well then—'

Then the door to our small police station opened and Willie (short for Wilhelmina) Troyer literally flew in – well, not quite. Today, everyone and their uncle misuses the word *literally*, when they really mean to say *virtually*. But with a pair of balsa wood arm struts and enough feathers, Willie might be able to at least glide, if given a gentle push from a tall enough building.

The woman is petite. Not only is she short, but if she weighs more than eighty pounds, then I'll agree to give Ida Rosen a month of daily foot rubs. This year Willie was the festival's designated 'timekeeper'. It was her job to make sure that events began and ended on schedule, most especially the award ceremony.

'Ladies,' she chirped when she beheld us, 'It's ten minutes past noon. All of Hernia is looking for you!'

'Well, not all of Hernia,' I said. 'Patty King, who suffers from agoraphobia, hasn't put a toe across her threshold in thirty-five years.'

'This is not the time to be a smart mouth,' Agnes scolded me.

Thank goodness that Agnes is shaped like a wrecking ball, and I mean that both literally, and kindly. My bestie led the way through the teeming throng, with me following, and wee Willie bringing up the rear. Still, even with Agnes leading the way, there were so many large hats, parasols, and bobbing balloons to contend with, that I couldn't see the stage until we right in front of it. Then my jaw dropped so low in disbelief at what I saw, that I *virtually* dislocated it.

Enthroned in a crudely carved, gilded chair with cheap blue upholstery sat a very smug Ida Rosen. She was wearing a white taffeta gown that had probably been procured from a second-hand bridal shop. Long white satin gloves continued well past her elbows to her fleshy upper arms where they were filled beyond their capacity. That is putting it kindly, by the way.

On her head, Ida wore a ridiculously tall tiara, from which sparkled the finest bits of glass that one can purchase for under fifty dollars. I'd seen similar pieces of jewellery before on our more liberal teens on prom night. A massive glass necklace made to resemble tier upon tier of fake diamonds was spread across her behemoth of a bosom, and a bracelet comprised of many strands of glass encircled one gloved wrist.

The second that I saw Ida up there posing as a queen, I attempted to feint to the left of Agnes and put my God-given, long, spindly legs to good use by leaping on to the stage. I didn't even stop to think about the fact that by doing so, many men, and worse, impressionable young boys, might get a glimpse of my sturdy Christian underwear. Oh, the sins that I might have inadvertently caused them to commit!

But alas, Ida locked eyes with mine that same instant. She reached over to a small table beside her, picked up the megaphone and brought it to her bright red lips.

'Ladies und gentlemen off Hernia,' she blared into the machine. 'Dis eez your fees-tee-val queen, Her Majesty, Queen Ida Rosen. I am sanking you wery much for dis honour. I vill try to be a vize moan-ark und not to raise your taxes too mooch.'

Everyone laughed at the little joke. When Ida set the megaphone down and smiled regally, the crowd hooted and hollered their support. Oh, what loyal subjects. Even the Baptist minister, of all people, got into the act by bursting into a rousing, and rather moving, rendition of 'God Save the Queen'. Most unfortunate was the fact that a good deal more of our citizenry than I'd ever dreamed of not only knew the tune (which is the same as *our* patriotic song, 'My County T'is of Thee'), but they knew the words. Now *that* shocked me to the core. This could only mean that British television programs had infiltrated the heartland of God-fearing America.

Had the Brits been exporting their television shows to us as a propaganda tool? I'm not big on conspiracy theories, but let me just say this: our neighbour to the north is part of the British Commonwealth, so don't be surprised to wake up some fine morning to learn that Canada has invaded us. I'm just saying. And by the way, from that moment on, I promised myself I would stop using British baking terms as my preferred profanity.

At any rate, there in downtown Hernia, village of my birth, where I am the mayor and also, let's not forget, the village's chief benefactress, hundreds of my friends and relatives were serenading my nemesis. Oh, the humiliation! I felt like finding a crack in the pavement at my feet – of which there were plenty – and crawling into it. But when Agnes joined in the powerfully emotive anthem, I would have crawled out of my crack anyway and given her a very unchristian smack on her buttocks. Of course, the aforementioned assault would have been figurative, not literal. Actually, I would have just made a fool out of myself trying to shush a crowd of hundreds of emotional people, and then eject a popular octogenarian from the stage.

Now, I'm not saying that it was a miracle that saved me, because demons can't work miracles. But it was most definitely an unexpected turn of events that came from out of left field, and at just the right moment. Halfway through *our* anthem, the stench of rotten eggs suddenly became so overpowering that the festival attendees stopped singing, and stampeded hither and thither, as they charged in the various directions to where'd they'd parked their cars. In the blink of an eye, even 'Her Majesty' had vacated the stage. But that was by no means the end of the instantaneous evacuation. It was a wonder that no one was injured in the stampede. As it was, there were a few minor fender benders as our visitors tried to leave town simultaneously through just two exits.

I am by no means a hero, but I stood my ground. I did so only because I take my responsibilities as mayor seriously. That, and because I recognized the offensive odour as that of raw sewage. We in Hernia do not have a village sewer system. Instead, each residence has a septic tank buried at the rear of the house. Every five years or so, our septic tanks *must* be emptied by a professional waste removal company. Therefore, I was rather certain that a private residence was not involved.

But surely the source of this noxious odour was located somewhere here, on Main Street, in our little so-called commercial district. Trust me, my probing proboscis is the envy of many a bloodhound owner, so I was able to locate the origin of the revolting stench merely by turning my head slightly to the right.

The stage was set in front of Sam Yoder's Corner Market, the first business one comes to on Main Street after crossing the bridge. Adjacent to Sam's, in a separate brick building, is Cheryl Rosen's bizarrely named antique shop: Amish Luxuries. Between the two buildings a thick hose was pumping raw sewage *out* at an astonishing rate. Clearly someone had sabotaged the festival, and someone was going to answer for their crime.

I may be over half a century old, but I am still capable of running. I dropped my purse and ran like a girl – that is to say, fearlessly and fast. I hoofed it around Sam Yoder's store and immediately I spotted the culprit. A sewage disposal truck was parked in the narrow alley that runs behind Sam and Cheryl's store, and its engine was running. A hose connected to it snaked through their two buildings. Foolishly, perhaps, I continued running until I reached the truck. What I planned to do with the person, or persons, I hadn't the foggiest idea. I wouldn't have used a firearm, even if I had had one, and I didn't have my purse to swing at the culprit (that I might have done). All I had as a weapon was my big fat mouth with its liver-coloured lips.

Fortunately, when I reached the truck there was no one anywhere to be seen. There was, however, a placard laying on the driver's seat with the following words inscribed on it in gothic lettering: *This is just a warm-up.*

I dialled Toy, like I should have in the first place. 'Where the clanger are you in Bedfordshire?' I shouted.

'I'm at Primrose and Main, Magdalena, regulating traffic flow on the bridge. I've got Deputy Hayes answering accident reports. Unless there's been an injury, they're just to exchange information. As for those two deputies that Bedford loaned me – well, I guess that they drove off holding their noses. So tell me, what's up, and where are you?'

After I filled him in Toy was silent for far longer than I expected him to be. I knew that he'd be angry at me for being so impetuous, but I didn't think he'd give me the silent treatment.

'What in tarnation is a "clanger", if not the metal thing inside a bell that strikes against the sides?'

'That's a "clangor" with an "O". The former is a British suet pastry that has a savoury filling at one end, and a sweet filling at the other. A meal in one item, so to speak. And I didn't mean to cuss British, it just sort of slipped out.'

'OK then, now that my education is complete, we can move on. Magdalena, I don't care what they say, you are both the gutsiest, and most foolhardy, woman that I've ever met. But if you keep acting on impulse, one of these days Gabe is going to be called into the Bedford morgue and asked to identify you on a slab.'

'Uh-huh,' I said. 'So what do *they* say about me? If it's Miranda Speicher who is spreading rumours, I didn't mean to push her off the monkey bars in second grade. And Noah Webber totally had what I did coming to him; he sat on my pack lunch on the bus and squished it flatter than a pancake.'

'I don't mean to be rude,' Toy said, 'but it isn't easy talking with you, while at the same time preventing impatient people from ramming tons of steel into each other. So do me a favour, will you? See what you can find out about that waste disposal truck. Like who rented it, and when.'

'Yes, boss.'

'*You're* the boss, Magdalena. I work for the Village of Hernia, and essentially, you *are* the village. Keep that in mind if anyone gives you grief about this entire fiasco of a day, because it wasn't your fault. OK, gotta go.'

Scottish shortbread fingers! That was a mixed message if ever I heard one. The day had been a complete failure, but it wasn't my fault, despite the fact that I ran the village with the power of an autocrat. That's how I interpreted his statement, and boy, did that ever rub me the wrong way. Just for the record, I'd decided to go back to swearing with British baking terms, on the off-chance that I was right about the impending Canadian invasion.

At any rate, I will admit in the privacy of my heart that I've always had a soft spot for Toy. He is, after all, quite easy on the eyes, and his slow Southern drawl has a way of pulling you into his conversations and having you hanging on to every word that falls from his young, full lips. Agnes, who isn't married, and who is far too liberal for her own good, once confided to me that he was her romantic fantasy. Her 'boy toy' Toy, she called him. I giggled politely at the time, but felt more like slapping her (gently, mind you) for stealing something from me. I realize that just thinking along those lines is a sin, but we can't help our thoughts, even though the Bible says otherwise – oh my gracious, I'd better change subjects right now.

The best way to get my mind off the question of whether or not Toy had insulted me – or maybe even given me a left-handed compliment – was to get the particulars on the waste disposal truck as per his request. Funny, but what I hadn't even noticed before was the peculiar name of the truck: *Six Feet Under*.

The tiny blond hairs on my arms stood at attention. Some person, or persons, had gone to considerable effort to ruin our festivities. Well, at least a bag of angry snakes hadn't been let loose – not that I was aware of. So far. Nonetheless, when my phone rang, I virtually jumped out of my best black brogans.

'Rough puff pastry!' I cursed into the phone. Sadly, I was becoming a real British potty mouth.

'Magdalena, this is your sister-in-law, Cheryl. You need to come over. I have something very important to tell you.'

'Not now, Cheryl. I'm in the middle of an investigation, and for another thing, I don't think that I'm ever speaking to you again, given all the lies and deception that you—'

'I know about the truck.'

SIXTEEN

'Excuse me?'

'The waste disposal truck.'

'I'll be there in a minute.'

It didn't take me much longer than that. Cheryl lives two houses behind her shop. Like many others in the historical district of Hernia, her house is a large Victorian, with a wraparound veranda and white gingerbread trim. There are the requisite rocking chairs out front, and a white wicker table topped by a monstrously large Boston fern. The interior of her house is overly decorated with early Americana of all descriptions. In other words, Cheryl's house is crammed with old stuff that people inherited from dead relatives, but didn't want.

Cheryl, like many antique dealers, buys items that appeal to her at estate sales, and then she enjoys these things in her own home, before she resells them. Not only is there no such thing as an 'Amish luxury', there is really no theme to what Cheryl actually sells, except that each piece has to be one hundred years old, or over, to be considered a genuine antique. Cheryl does employ a cleaning woman, but with so many 'finds' displayed higgledy-piggledy, her house is impossible to keep dust and pollen free. But the main reason that I didn't want to go inside was that Hernia's self-styled Queen of the Year lived there, and she was undoubtedly inside reigning over some dust bunnies. On that account alone I was relieved to find Cheryl waiting for me on her veranda.

'Have a seat,' she said, gesturing to a white wicker rocking chair. Wicker and I have never been friends. It always looks good in the store, or in someone else's house, but it doesn't look good on me. Sure, a pad placed on the seat, and even one against the back, will take the 'bite' out of wicker. But what about my poor forearms? At the end of the visit, my arms always look like long, thin waffles.

'No, thanks, dear,' I said. 'I prefer to stand.'

'Because of waffle arms?'

'*What?* Can you read my mind?'

'Of course I can't read your mind, not with a skull as thick as yours. But when I sit out here in shorts, I get waffle thighs like any other middle-aged woman. I was extrapolating from my own experience, sitting on these chairs. I much prefer the sensual smoothness of my Italian leather sofa.'

'Harrumph,' I said. 'Tell me about the truck.'

'Yes, the truck. Well, I was working late in my shop last night, getting ready for this morning – Magdalena, you wouldn't believe how inconsiderate some customers can be. They'll pick up an item from one corner of my shop, and then drop if off in another aisle where the merchandise is totally unrelated to it. And you wouldn't believe how messy they can be. I've finally hung a sign on the toilet door that says that it's out of order. What do you think of that?'

'I think that you still haven't told me about the truck,' I said. '*Tempest fugits* whilst the temperamental fidget.'

Cheryl, a licenced psychiatrist, scrunched up her face in what I took to be annoyance. 'I think that you could benefit from meditation, Magdalena. I'm speaking as a doctor, not as your sister-in-law.'

I attempted a wan smile, which was meant to be insincere. 'And speaking as your mayor, and not your sister-in-law, I've been thinking about widening this portion of Main Street so that we can have a special lane – no make that two lanes – just for horses and buggies. Of course, since your shop is built on land leased to you by the village—'

'You can't do that, Magdalena! I'll sue!'

'The truck, dear? Tell me about the Victoria wedding cake truck!'

'Is *that* all? Well, there really isn't much to tell, except that it pulled up behind my shop last night around nine. Just about twilight. Then a man and a woman jumped out and started to connect this long hose to the rear of the vehicle.'

'Did you see what they were wearing?' I asked excitedly. Finally, I seemed to be getting somewhere with the investigation.

'Jumpsuits – I think. Dark jumpsuits. Like magenta. Or maybe black. I don't know, because it was starting to get really dark.'

'There is a big difference between magenta and black,' I said. 'Magenta is a proper colour.'

'OK, so then they were magenta. But you're not going to be using my name in any official report, are you? I want to be a responsible citizen, but as a single businesswoman I feel especially vulnerable to reprisals.'

'You're preaching to the choir, dear,' I said.

'Excuse me?' Cheryl said.

'It means that I know exactly how you feel. I was a single businesswoman for most of my career.'

'Yes, of course,' she said. 'Until you turned my brother's head with your considerable feminine wiles.'

'Ahem. What did you just say?'

'Oh, Magdalena, don't be so vain; you know exactly what I said. Gabe tells me about how you go on about how ugly you think that you are. About your body dysmorphia, when you're really this stunning beauty. Give me a break. Now, do you want to hear about what was really so odd about this couple in the magenta bodysuits, or not?'

'Spill it, toots!'

'They were wearing masks.'

'*Masks?*' I said. 'What sort of masks?'

'Duck masks,' Cheryl said with a laugh. 'Donald and Daisy Duck masks. You *do* know who those two cartoon characters are, don't you?'

'Hmm,' I said, rather than admit that I did not. 'If it was so dark, then how could you tell what the masks were?'

'Now that's the craziest thing,' she said. 'They both had flashlights and shone them on each other's faces – well their masks – that is. Then they laughed and went about running the hose between my shop and Sam's grocery store.'

I sighed and plopped my bony bottom into her wicker chair after all. My modest gabardine skirt was guaranteed to protect my thighs, but it was going to be a losing struggle to keep my hands folded in my lap and my arms away from wicker.

I sighed. 'Waffle arms, here I come.'

'There's always that smooth Italian leather couch. It's the next best thing to sex.'

'But isn't your mother inside?'

She nodded.

'So tell me,' I said, 'why didn't you call the police when you saw two people in duck masks running a hose past your shop last night? Or at least call me? Didn't you think that was extremely out of the ordinary?'

Cheryl shrugged. 'Frankly, I thought that they had something to do with this whacky goat festival you Mennonites put on every year. Besides, like I said, my shop was in disarray, and today was supposed to be my busiest sales day of the year. I sold five times more last year during that one day of festival than I did in the four months after that leading up to Christmas.'

I prayed for patience; it is my least answered prayer. 'Look, this "whacky goat festival" has nothing to do with Mennonites, but everything to do with the fact that a goat saved the life of your only nephew. You've lived here long enough to know that masked strangers and sewage-pumping trucks are never part of the festivities. If you had spoken up, then today *could* have been a banner sales day for you.'

'OK, OK,' Cheryl said, 'you don't have to bite my head off. I'm just a single woman, trying to get along the best that I can. I don't have the emotional support system that you have. I don't have any friends out here in the sticks. Sometimes I get caught up in my work – now, that's my shop – as a way to cope.' She sucked air between her teeth. 'And there is Ma.'

'Ah, yes. Your ma. We had quite the illuminating conversation earlier today. Heretofore I had no idea that she was a neurosurgeon.'

'She's not.'

'Please, Cheryl. It's time that the three of you – Ida, you, and especially, Gabe – stopped lying to me. I mean it when I say that I *can't take it anymore.*'

Then Cheryl lunged at me and grabbed my clasped hands. Had she been a blood relative, that move would have been taboo, and never would have happened. As it was, I squawked in alarm like a hen, one that had been pounced upon by the farmer's wife fetching the evening's dinner.

'Magdalena, relax,' she said as she tightened her grip. 'I'm not going to hurt you; I just want your undivided attention for the next few minutes.'

I tried not to grimace, but the woman was squeezing my bony hands like a vise. 'Is this when you tell me about your third career shelling walnuts with your bare hands?'

Cheryl shook her well-coifed head. 'Always joking, aren't you, Magdalena. That's a symptom of deep-seated insecurity. At what age did your mother begin toilet-training?'

'We began potty-training when I was two, but she died when I was nineteen. But bless her heart, she still hadn't gotten the hang of it by then.'

'Magdalena! That is the most disgusting, disrespectful, and—'

'Well deserved,' I said.

Cheryl sighed. 'Touché. But what you need to know is that Ma is not a neurosurgeon; our father was. And the accented

English that you've heard her speak ever since you've known her – that's our maternal grandmother, Hannah Abrams.'

I ripped my hands from hers and jumped to my feet. 'That's ridiculous! Ida told me herself that she put on the accent as a way to keep me off guard. That's a quote. Her plan all along has been to come between me and Gabe.'

'Oh, I'm sure that's been part of it, but that's by no means the gist of the story. You see, we grew up on Long Island, where we lived the American dream. Both sets of grandparents had emigrated from Europe absolutely penniless. Anyway, Pop was extremely successful, and Ma was . . . well, she was a socialite. I know that's hard to believe seeing her now.'

'I can only imagine,' I said as I resumed sitting.

'Then the unthinkable happened. It was our grandparents' sixtieth wedding anniversary. There was a big reception planned, but our parents took them out for a private dinner the night before. Gabe and I were both away at school. Anyway, Pop had drunk a little too much at dinner, so Ma volunteered to drive them all home. Actually, Pop wanted to take a cab, but Ma *insisted* on driving, because she hadn't been drinking, and she didn't see why they should spend any money when they didn't need to. Can you imagine that?'

'A penny saved is a penny earned,' I said, and then felt like slapping my tongue.

Thank goodness Cheryl didn't appear to hear me. 'My grand-mother had a thick Yiddish accent, and she was in the back seat with my father, trying to feed him some gossip she'd overhead at the next table concerning someone they all knew. My grandfather was riding in front. At any rate, Ma was straining to hear the gossip more than she was paying attention to the road. She ran through a stop sign and they were hit head-on by a semi-trailer truck.'

'Oh no,' I said when she paused.

'Both passengers on the right died immediately, and my grand-mother, who was seated behind Ma, and who wasn't wearing a seatbelt, was thrown out of the car when her door flew open. She was pronounced dead at the hospital. Ma, who'd been buckled securely in, survived with a plethora of bruises and multiple broken ribs from the steering wheel. Inside, however, she was totally destroyed.'

'Of course,' I said. It was a shocking story, but was it true? Why hadn't my husband shared this with me before we tied the knot and became one?

'Magdalena,' she said, 'I can tell by your expression that you don't believe me. But call your husband right now and ask him.'

I threw up my hands, resigned to the fact that my life was stranger than fiction. 'No, that's OK. Whatever he'd say now, he'd say the same thing when I got home. Look, I can't deal with this right now,' I said, changing the subject. 'So tell me, these masked people in the dark jumpsuits, did you see them leave on foot? Or did a car come along and pick them up?'

My sister-in-law shrugged. 'I haven't a clue. Like I said, I was engrossed in my work. I noticed them, thought they were part of your team, and didn't give them another thought – well, not until Main Street became a cesspool. What are you going to do about that?'

'*Oy vey*,' I said.

'Well, you're still the mayor, aren't you? Or have the people revolted already and taken away your badge?'

'No, dear,' I said with a forced smile. 'The badge is solid, twenty-four-karat gold, so I keep it at home in my dresser drawer, hidden beneath my sturdy Christian underwear. Say, you haven't found any poisonous snakes in your house today, have you?'

'*Excuse* me?'

'Perhaps I shouldn't be worrying you – aw, tea and crumpets, why not? You are a psychiatrist after all; you can talk yourself out of panicking. It's just we were worried that this one rather disapproving church in town was going to release a bag of rattle-snakes on Main Street during the height of the festival. So far there haven't been any reports of sightings. Now, snakes generally avoid busy places and confrontation, so if they were released, they might have immediately slithered away to the side lines, and into the nearest yards. And you, my dear, live right behind your shop, as close to Main Street as one can get.'

Although everything that I had just said was true, I had said it out of spite, because she'd asked me if I was still mayor. Yes, that was quite un-Christian of me, but I'm not perfect. What's more, I took great pleasure in noticing that she had drawn her feet up off the floor.

'Magdalena, you're mean!'

'I'm sorry, dear. I really am. The Devil made me do it.'

Cheryl laughed. 'I thought you didn't watch stand-up comedy.'

'What does that have to do with my apology?'

She wagged a finger at me. 'Oh, you're priceless. Just how you manage to keep that placid, bovine look on that long horsey face of yours, while saying all those hysterically funny things is beyond me. You should have been a stand-up comic. Really, Magdalena, you missed your calling.'

'*What?* You just said that I was a stunning beauty, for crying out loud. Which am I? A raving beauty, or a hideous beast?'

'You're definitely raving, I'll grant you that.'

'Grr. You Rosens have a knack for driving me up a wall. Tell me, Cheryl, was it you who outfitted your mother with that cheesy tiara and cheap glass necklace?'

She wagged her finger again. 'Yes, and those weren't as cheesy as you think. Those weren't glass pieces; those were vintage rhinestone pieces from the 1950s. I had them on display in my shop. I knew you weren't going to come through with a crown, and I wasn't going to let Ma be disappointed.'

'I see,' I said. It was all I could do to resist wagging a finger in return. 'So you supplied your own *Amish* rhinestone jewellery.'

'Magdalena, *dear*,' Cheryl said, 'sarcasm does not become you.'

'I'll own that,' I said and popped to my feet again. 'Toodles, as they say in the land of Big Ben. I'll see you whenever. And seriously – do keep at least one eye open for slithering serpents.'

'Ha, ha. I'll see you tonight at dinner. Toodles.'

I'd already turned and, given the size of my feet, I was halfway to the front steps. I pivoted, always a dangerous thing when I'm concerned.

'I don't remember inviting you, dear.'

Cheryl smiled. 'My sweet, long-lost cousin, Miriam did. Ma and I will be there at six o'clock sharp. As promised.'

'That's what you think,' I said with a smirk. If only I'd been a better Christian and been nicer. Or at least believed in karma – well, then again, is anything that straightforward?

SEVENTEEN

Car theft is virtually unknown here in bucolic Hernia. Murder, you betcha. As mayor, and the one who hires the police force, I have given this matter some thought. So this is what I have come up with: no one in Hernia drives a car that anyone else could possibly *want*.

For starters, *most* of us are modest people, of modest means. I am one of the few wealthy people in town, and I no longer care a hoot about cars, except as a means of getting from point A to point B. Secondly, our winters are snowy, and we salt the roads. The result is that our cars turn into rust-buckets before our very eyes. So there really is no point in getting a fancy, schmancy model with all the latest technology. No, siree, we Herniaites believe that as long as you can't see the street, or the highway, through the car floor, it's still a keeper. Even then, a sizable hole in the floorboard does come in handy on slippery roads, especially if one is wearing hobnail boots and has sturdy legs. And nothing beats a generous hole in the floor to address nausea or emergency bathroom issues.

Of course, no one even thinks about locking their car doors. Why should they? I trotted down Cheryl's walk with zero concern for my safety. Instead, I congratulated myself for having gotten the last word. When I plopped my pitiful patooty down on the driver's seat of my car, it was with a sigh of relief. But a nanosecond later I screamed so loudly that I put Bob Neubrander's cows off milking, and he lives two counties over.

Something beneath my bony bottom was moving. I was wearing a heavy gabardine skirt, and a cotton broadcloth slip, plus my sturdy Christian underwear, mind you, and I could still feel movement – vigorous movement, in fact – under my derriere. One might be surprised as to what goes on in the mind of one Magdalena Portulacca Yoder Rosen at a time like that. Or maybe not.

My third grade Sunday school teacher, Miss Esch, related the time she awoke to the sound of breathing under her bed. Somehow, she knew that it was the Devil. Well, Miss Esch was a spiritual warrior. After a fervent prayer, she reached under the bed, grabbed old Lucifer, and flung him across the room. She told our terrified class of mini-believers that the Devil had felt for all the world like a rubber mat.

'What sort of rubber mat?' I'd asked. The question earned me a whack with Miss Esch's yardstick, but it was worth knowing the answer.

'The kind of rubber mat one puts in the bottom of the bathtub so as not to slip. Exactly like that.'

'He even had *suction* cups?' Billy Wharton asked. That earned Billy two whacks, the second of which broke the yardstick. There was only a month to go until the end of the term, and so Miss Esch didn't bother to replace the broken stick.

Anyway, you can bet your bippy that the Devil was the *first* explanation I thought of for my undulating underparts. After all, I was raised to believe what I was taught, and to take the Bible literally, like every good Christian should. Never mind the many apparent contradictions in it, for they will be explained to us when we get to Heaven. Miss Esch's encounter with the Devil made an enormous impression on my young psyche, one which I never really outgrew. The reason is that for me, and many conservative Christians like me, the Devil is a real, and sometimes physical, presence is this world.

'Get behind me, Satan!' I cried.

Of course that didn't do any good. Satan wasn't behind me; Satan was squirming beneath my bony bottom.

'Get from beneath me, Satan!' I screamed.

It felt like the Devil was not in the least bit affected by my fervent prayer. Perhaps I was meant to reach beneath my buttocks, grab Satan by the horns, so to speak, and fling him into the rear seat. The problem with that scenario is that I am not the spiritual warrior that dear Miss Esch was – may she rest in peace. Instead, as casually as I could, I opened the car door, jumped out and hightailed it three houses down the street to my best friend Agnes's house.

Now, Agnes may not be a Conservative Mennonite, but she is a good Christian, and even she believes that the Devil can be a shape-shifter (as Gabe calls him in jest). I didn't even knock;

I just burst into her house and headed straight for her kitchen where there was a ninety-nine percent chance of finding her while she was awake at home.

Sure enough, my bestie was sitting at her dinette table, eating a bowl of cereal and watching a popular talk show on TV. I recognized the program immediately as the one on which four, or maybe five, ladies interrupt each other for an hour. Sometimes they discuss topics that are so filthy, that I'm tempted to hop on a bus to New York and wash their mouths out with soap.

'Agnes! The Prince of Darkness hath assailed me,' I wailed.

'That's nice,' she said, without glancing away from her boob tube. 'You can tell me about that book when this is over.'

'It's not a book,' I wailed. 'It's Lucifer – the fallen angel.'

'Shh, Mags, *please!* Darn, now you made me miss the name of the woman who claims to have slept with the vice pres—'

'I sat on Satan!' I shrieked. 'Satan, I tell.'

'What in the blue blazes?'

'The Devil, Agnes, and I'm not making this up. I got into my car and plopped my patooty right on top of the Devil himself.'

'No way!'

'Way! Of course, first I prayed for Satan to go away, but he didn't. Agnes, remember Miss Esch back in third grade Sunday school? Well, I wasn't brave enough to yank the Devil out from beneath my buttocks, so I ran like a coward. That's why I'm here. Oh, Agnes, I'm not a spiritual warrior – I'm just a coward and a failure.'

I don't have a single drop of British blood running through my veins. The only stiff upper lip I've ever had was the result of a bee sting. That said, I turned my back to my friend so that she couldn't see the tear that I felt rolling down my left cheek. I am not one given to hyperbole, but it is only a slight exaggeration to say that when I again beheld Agnes's face, each of her eyes was as large, and round, as a child's backyard wading pool.

'M-m-mags,' she stuttered. 'You didn't sit on Satan.'

'Are you calling me a liar? You're supposed to be my best friend, for heaven's sake! I did so sit on Satan, and I can still feel him twitching about my hind parts.'

'N-no,' Agnes protested, 'I'm not calling you a liar. Now, just keep calm.'

'And *what*? Carry on?'

From the way Agnes giggled, I could tell she was extremely nervous. 'Good one, Mags, but you're far too restrained to ever pass for British.'

'Sarcasm does not become you, dear. What in a buttercream-filled, triple-layered Genoese sponge cake is going on? I demand to know immediately!'

'OK, I'll tell you,' my best friend said, 'but first you have to promise – on a stack of genuine English muffins – to not freak out. If you break your promise, I'm going to tell your Reverend Diffledorf that you said his sermons were so dull that, if you could get away with it, you would pay someone to poke you with something sharp to keep you from falling asleep.'

'Why, I never!' I said indignantly.

'Now you are lying,' Agnes said.

'OK,' I said. 'I promise not to freak out.'

'You sat on a garter snake,' Agnes said.

'*I what?*'

'Relax,' she said. 'They're harmless garden variety snakes. We're both country gals. We've run into them oodles of times while weeding our vegetable gardens. Besides, this is just a little fellow.'

How was I supposed to relax? Didn't Satan appear to Adam and Eve in the guise of a serpent in the Garden of Eden? Also, the Bible didn't specify which species of snake, so Satan *could* have been a garter snake. But then an even more important question occurred to me.

'Agnes! How do you know I sat on a snake?'

By then Agnes was up on her undersized feet and had grabbed my massive mitts in her pudgy little hands. She is deceptively strong. If I was a betting woman, I'd wager that she could milk a steel cow.

'This is when the keeping calm part is really important,' she whispered. 'At the count of three, I'm going to tell you something very upsetting, and then I'm going to give you a solution to the problem. Do you understand? Nod slowly if you do.'

I nodded.

'Good. Mags, the reason I know that you sat on a little garter snake is that it is still clinging to the back of your skirt. Apparently

you sat down so fast that you didn't see it, and the snake didn't
have time to properly strike. Its fangs appear to be embedded in
that wide elastic waistband of your denim skirt. That's what you
feel whipping around your thighs, not Satan.'

My knees felt like wet noodles – well, I can only imagine that
they did, having never actually had pasta for legs. The only thing
that kept me erect was the thought that if I fainted, or sank to my
knees, the snake would be closer to my head and face. Who cared
if it was supposedly just a garden snake? Anyway that was just
Agnes's assessment. She once mistook her neighbour's stallion for
a mare, and trust me, even a city girl can tell the difference between
those two animals. In any case, how in tarnation was I supposed
to rid myself of the reptile? I certainly wasn't going to reach behind
me and grab it. Perhaps my bestie would.

'If it's only a harmless garter snake,' I said weakly, 'then be
a doll and remove the poor thing.'

'First I'm calling Toy,' Agnes said, and clutching her cell phone
scampered from the room on her elfin feet. It is plum amazing
how fast a woman her shape can move when properly motivated.
Given my excessive height, I would be flat on my back from
wind resistance if I attempted to accelerate like that.

Frankly, I was surprised when she returned just a minute or
two later. 'It's going to sound preposterous, but Toy said it could
work, so we have to trust him. OK?'

'OK, *what*?' I demanded. 'I don't know what it is?'

'You'll see soon enough. Just try to stand absolutely still in
the meantime.'

'Do I *have* to? I was thinking of going into Bedford to do a
little shopping. You know, buy a snakeskin purse, and a pair of
snakeskin shoes, to go with my snakeskin tail.'

But Agnes hadn't heard a word of my brave banter. She was
too busy tossing frozen food items from her freezer into a humon-
gous ice chest. It both astounded and surprised me to see that
almost everything that my friend was tossing into her cooler was
a single portion frozen dinner. Truly, there, but for the grace of
God went I. Agnes had a much more pleasing personality than
I did, and when it came to dancing the headboard-hora, what
man wouldn't prefer the well-upholstered woman to a bag of
bones? Finally, after several weeks' worth of single portion frozen

meals (of the weight conscious sort), had been dumped into her giant ice chest, Agnes called to me.

'Now, walk here slowly,' she said.

I did as she directed.

'Now sit in the ice chest. And do it quickly.'

'*What?*'

'Toy said that the cold will inactivate your cute little buddie. To quote Toy, "By the time I get there that fella will be right sluggish." So now sit.'

'I don't want to sit on your frozen dinners,' I wailed. 'Can't I just pass gas instead? That's been known to clear a room.'

Without further ado, Agnes punched me in the solar plexus, and when I was hunched over, gasping for air, she pushed me down into her wallopalooza of an ice chest. Although I landed hard, the snake not only survived me falling on top of it, but it started squirming immediately.

'How long does it take for this thing to settle down?' I whispered hoarsely. If there was any chance that my 'cute little buddie', as Toy put it, was going to nod off in a cold-induced slumberland, I wasn't about to disturb him.

Agnes shrugged. 'How should I know? I'm not a herpetologist. But while we're waiting for Police Chief Toy to show up, why don't we two girlfriends make idle chit-chat. Let's talk about stuff that has nothing to do with today and the weeks leading up to it. I'll go first, if you want.'

'Sure,' I said, 'but keep your voice down.'

Agnes giggled. 'Well, you're never going to believe this, but I joined an internet dating site for singles called Bodaciously Buxom Broads with Curves.'

'You didn't!'

'Now you go,' she said beaming happily.

'Mine is horrible news – but then again, aren't all my news flashes awful?'

My dear, loyal friend shook her head. 'In May you drove all the way down here to show me the new toenail that was growing back in after you dropped a log on your foot last winter.'

'Well, how about that! I can be a basket of cheer, after all.'

So my bestie and I gabbed. Rather, I pumped her for details on the men who'd responded to her profile on that ridiculous dating website. I thought the idea of an innocent Mennonite woman like Agnes labelling herself a 'bodaciously buxom broad' was incredibly foolish. The poor dear had all the worldly acumen of a poached egg. Even a man in a medically induced coma could take advantage of my gal pal.

At least all my stewing over my friend's innocence and vulnerability took my mind off the reptile beneath me. Or could it possibly be that, true to Toy's prediction, the snake had been rendered inactive by Agnes's frozen dinners? Had lemon grass chicken really done the trick? After all, snakes were cold-blooded creatures, and their body temperatures reflect their environments.

Agnes read my mind. 'It's stopped squirming, hasn't it?'

'Yes,' I said. 'At least I'm pretty sure that it has. On the other hand, my bottom is frozen. Be a dear and reach under me; see if you can feel any movement.'

Agnes recoiled like a snake preparing to strike. 'Are you nuts?'

Just then Toy burst through the side kitchen door. 'Hey, ladies. How're you doing, Magdalena?'

'I'm fine as frog's hair,' I replied, using one of Toy's Southernisms. 'However, I think that my backside might have gone into hibernation.'

'Good,' Toy said. 'That means our little fellow has as well.'

'Agnes, where do you keep your oven mitts?'

After he'd donned a pair of red-and-white checked oven mitts, and propped open the kitchen door, Toy exhaled deeply. Then he turned to me.

'OK, at the count of three, I'm going to hoist you out of there by your armpits. Then I'm going to yank that critter off your skirt and toss him out the door. Agnes, your job is to slam the door shut after him. You both got that?'

'Aw, that's so cute,' I said. 'You called that snake a "him" and not an "it" like we did.'

'I'm all kinds of polite,' Toy said. 'Now, here we go. One. Two. Three.'

It was that fast. He had me on my feet, snake free, and the critter out the door, all in the same amount of time that it takes Toy to pronounce his own three letter name.

Agnes clapped. 'That was awesome!'

'Oh, Toy,' I said. 'Thank you, thank you! But if it was just a harmless little garter snake, weren't you a bit rough on him?'

Toy and Agnes exchanged glances. 'Do you want to tell her, or should I?' Toy said.

'Mags,' Agnes said, 'it wasn't a harmless little garter snake. It was a medium size Eastern Diamond-Back Rattlesnake. It's a good thing that you were wearing your thick denim skirt. When I saw the rattles—'

But I didn't hear the rest of her sentence just then because I fainted dead away into Toy's strong, young arms.

EIGHTEEN

I came to my senses in Toy's strong young arms just seconds later, but of course I didn't let on right away. I'm only half as stupid as I look, if I do say so myself. Toy was born to be a hero and raised to be a gentleman. He scooped me off my feet and carried me into Agnes's living room (I made sure that my head was resting against his shoulder), where he laid me gently on her sofa. Then he patted me ever softly on my cheeks with hands that were both manly, and well-manicured.

'Magdalena,' he practically cooed, 'Magdalena, are you in there?'

'Of course she's in there,' Agnes said. 'Maybe she really did faint, but she's faking it now. You can always tell by her breath.'

'Her breath?'

'Yeah. When she pretends to be asleep, or unconscious – which happens more than you think – her breath smells like rotten pumpkins.'

'It does not,' I said, and sat up so quickly that I bumped heads with poor Chief Toy.

'You see,' Agnes chortled. 'I told you she was faking.'

'I was not.'

Toy's blue eyes twinkled as he rubbed his forehead. 'Actually, I can detect the faint odour of last year's jack-o-lantern.'

'Very funny. But seriously, am I remembering correctly – before I fainted dead away – that the snake was a rattler?'

'That's right,' Toy said. 'A rather large one at that. Nice and fat. Agnes here is quite a brave little trooper, a real hero in my book. She needs to be given some sort of award. I don't know of any other woman who would have remained as calm and collected under those circumstances as she did. Why, when she called me—'

'What about *me*?' I said.

'You fainted,' Agnes said. '*Dead* away. And you were so terrified from just hearing the word "rattlesnake" that you remained passed out until after Toy carried you in from the kitchen.'

'Well, the snake was attached to my waistband. I ought to get some credit for that.'

'Ladies,' Toy said gently, 'I do believe that we have lost sight of what's most important here.'

'That I saved her life?' Agnes said.

'That I ruined her TV dinners?' I said, and then slapped my mouth. 'Oops, that just slipped out. I'm sorry, Agnes.'

Agnes smiled. 'Did the Devil make you say that?'

I smiled back. 'No, those *particular* thoughts I'm keeping to myself.'

Toy cleared his throat loudly. 'Ahem. We've lost sight of the fact that even the most intelligent rattlesnake is incapable of opening and closing a car door. Therefore, one can safely surmise that the snake in question was placed in Magdalena's car by someone who wished to do her harm.

'Also, I think that it's possible there could be a link to the snake and the three previous acts of vandalism within the last twelve hours. It's pretty clear to me that someone, or some party of persons, was not happy with Hernia's Fourth Annual Billy Goat Gruff Festival.'

'What about the bodies found in my cousin Sam's dumpster?' I said. 'Do you think that there's a connection there?'

Toy cocked his head. 'Maybe. But why start off by playing your highest trump card first?'

'What?' I said.

'Card games, at least the ones in which the cards have faces, are against her faith,' Agnes said.

I felt my cheeks colour. 'He already knows that, dear.'

'Yes, of course. What I meant was that if someone simply wanted to ruin this festival, all they had to do was start off with the release of the sewage into Main Street. Killing two tourists was totally unnecessary. The only person affected by it, and then indirectly, was you.'

'Yes, *me*,' I said. 'That's exactly it, isn't it? Someone is targeting me!'

'Wait a minute,' Agnes said, sounding mildly irritated. 'Why does everything have to be about *you*? Where was your old jalopy when you sat on the snake? You never did tell us? And I want to hear what the third act of vandalism is. So far, all I know about is the broken traces on the goat wagon, and the sewage released into the street. I was never any good at maths, but I'll clean your inn for a month, if those two acts of mischief add up to more than three minus one.'

For some inexplicable reason Toy found her pitiful attempt at humour worthy of a chuckle. 'Agnes, the missing piece to your puzzle occurred last evening. Just after that frog-strangler of rain we had last evening, someone reported seeing two skeletons washed up on the bridge. We might have had to shut the bridge down for an investigation while we sorted out their origin had not Magdalena's husband, Gabe, immediately recognized what they were.'

'Halloween skeletons,' I added. 'Made out of resin.'

Agnes shivered dramatically. 'Those things give me the creeps. I backed into one at Walmart last year. I thought someone was tapping me on the shoulder, and then I nearly jumped out of my penny loafers.'

Toy sighed as he put his handsome head in his hands. 'I wish we could stick to the point. We could accomplish so much more, so much more quickly that way. Instead the two of you dart this way and that in a conversation – I swear, y'all remind me exactly like my mother and sister.'

'Oh, really?' I said archly. 'Which of us would be your mother, pray tell? We're both the same age, you know.'

'That's right.' Agnes sniffed. 'Our mothers were best friends. We were bathed together in the same tub as infants, and we shared the same playpen until Magdalena started hogging all the toys.'

'It was *my* playpen, dear, and they were *my* toys!'

Toy threw his hands in the air. 'Stop! Listen to yourselves. You sound like you should both still be in that playpen. And how old are the two of you, anyway? Sixty?'

'Why, I never!' Agnes and I shrieked in one voice.

Toy smiled slyly. 'Apologies to you both. I know that you are a decade younger than sixty, but it shut y'all up, didn't it?'

'We're actually fifty-four,' Agnes said.

'Maybe *she* is,' I said. 'But since you said that you *know* that I'm a decade younger than sixty, that's the age that I'm choosing. I'm only fifty.'

Toy grinned. 'OK, now moving on. We all know who at least some of the snake owners are in this town, and they were dead set against our so-called heathen festival. I'll be heading right over to pay Reverend Splitfrock a visit.'

I popped to my feet so fast that I left my good sense behind. 'I'm going too!'

'Please, Magdalena,' Toy said, 'you're not a police officer. If I feel the need for back up, I'll take Officer Cakewalker with me.'

'Oh, I have no doubt that she is excellent at her job, but she doesn't know these fanatics like I do.'

'Magdalena speaks from a lifetime of experience,' Agnes said drily.

'What is that supposed to mean?' I said.

'Just that your congregation, Beechy Grove Mennonite Church, has rubbed shoulders with those fanatics since before you were born. Maybe sometimes literally. That was inevitable, given that their old location was adjacent to your building. My comment wasn't meant to be offensive.'

'No, of course not, dear. You see,' I said, practically wagging a long, thin finger in our poor chief's face, 'even Agnes agrees that I understand the snake-handlers of the church with sixty-six words in its name.'

'Maybe you could be an observer,' Toy said. 'But that's it. You'd have to promise to keep your . . . well, just don't say a word.'

'But first, what was it that you wanted me to promise?'

'To keep your big mouth shut,' Agnes said.

I glared at Agnes lovingly. Yes, such a thing is possible; it just takes a little practice, and a lifelong friend who can irritate you to no end from time to time.

'Well, I did stop myself from saying it,' Toy said. 'OK, we're off then.'

'No,' Agnes said. 'You can't just leave me. Whoever put the snake in Magdalena's car while she was out of it was most likely watching her return to sit on it. Then they would have followed her back here, and watch you pull up, siren wailing, and lights flashing. How safe does that make me when you drive away? Huh? On a scale of one to ten?'

My poor buddy was genuinely terrified. I was reminded of the time when we were ten and Jimmy Wenger talked us into climbing with him into the belfry of an abandoned church building on Schantz Road. He said he wanted to see if there really were a few bats up there. He made us go first because we were girls, and Jimmy wanted to be polite. Well, there weren't just a few bats in that old belfry; there were close to a hundred.

'Agnes is right,' I said. 'She has to come with us. Besides, she might even know more about how to handle the snake-handlers than I do. You see, Agnes used to date one of Reverend Splitfrock's misguided flock.'

'I *did*?' Agnes said.

'Tut, tut, Agnes,' I said, 'how can you have forgotten Gilroy Snipps? The two of you used to be absolutely inseparable.'

'Oh, yes, Gil,' Agnes said, and pressed her hands over her heart. 'He was my first love. But when one has had so many loves, as have I, one tends to forget a few.'

For the record, Agnes and Gilroy were inseparable in Kindergarten. The fact that they refused to stop holding hands was a bone of contention for both me, and our teacher, Miss Kurtz. I will admit to the fact that, technically, what I referred to as 'dating' was stretching the truth, but it was for a good cause, wasn't it? It wasn't like I was lying to benefit myself. Also for the record, Agnes's real dating history can be counted on a single finger, and I mean that kindly. I needed her to put a cork in it, so to speak, before she blew her chance to tag along with us.

Toy might have been born yesterday, relatively speaking, but his mama didn't raise no fool – to borrow a phrase from his lexicon. He appeared amused by our shenanigans and ushered us out the door with a chuckle.

'Just be careful where y'all step, ladies,' he said. 'Snakes are hard to kill, and all I did was toss that sucker out in the yard. I reckon it's had time to thaw out by now, and slither around to this side of the house.'

Agnes and I both screeched. Silly me. I bolted for Toy's police cruiser and hopped up on the bonnet. Meanwhile Agnes, who weighs twice as much as I do, attempted to jump into Toy's muscular arms. Poor Agnes was unable to achieve lift-off, but instead managed to bowl him over and pin him to the walk. In the process every molecule of oxygen seemed to have been squeezed from Toy's lungs and his face turned blue, while Agnes's face turned chalky white.

I am no hero, mind you. All I can say is that I love Agnes, and I care deeply about Toy. They both needed assistance, so I leaped off the car bonnet without a second's thought. One heel of my clodhoppers struck driveway asphalt, while the other had a somewhat softer landing, accompanied by a soft crunching sound. At the same time, something smooth and scaly whipped around my ankles. I didn't have to lift my heavy denim skirt to know what it was upon which I had landed.

'Timber!' I rasped, as I pitched face forward into the lush grass of Agnes's seldom mown lawn that bordered her drive.

NINETEEN

'It was no accident that I didn't break any bones,' I said. 'It's all because I drink two glasses of milk every day. Cow's milk.'

'You should try almond milk instead,' Toy said. 'It's healthier.'

'Pshaw! If God wanted us to drink something called almond milk, he would have given almonds little udders.'

Agnes giggled. 'You're being udderly ridiculous.'

'At any rate,' Tory said, 'I will admit that it is plum amazing that a woman your age – uh, I mean any person of any age, could fall flat on their face and not even break their nose.'

'Especially a beak like yours,' Agnes said. 'If you made a divot in my lawn, you *will* replace it.'

'Ha, ha,' I said. Of course Agnes was only joking, but her japes embarrassed me in front of Toy.

'So how did the snake fare?' I asked.

'Our hero Magdalena dispatched it with one step,' Toy said.

'Just like you told her three times before on the way over here,' Agnes said. 'Maybe Magdalena does need to see a doctor after all.'

'Nope,' I said. 'Because that little white house with the dirty vinyl siding, and the broken screen door, that's Reverend Splitfrock's.'

'Hmm,' Toy said. 'I knew he lived around here, but I didn't know that he was that hard up. His flock must not pay him very much.'

'They don't pay him,' I said. 'The church is too small to give him a salary. Instead they pass the offering plate around; God gets ten percent of that, and the rest is his.'

'Then how does he earn a living wage?'

'He cleans toilets and mops floors. He's a janitor over at Autumn Days Retirement Home in Bedford. I'm not saying that's a living wage, but it's considerably more than his congregation pays him.'

Toy parked the car in the shade of a silver maple and we trooped up the walk to the reverend's front door. Toy took the lead, I lumbered along in second place, and dear, bulky Agnes bounced along behind us on feet as tiny as a newborn goat's hooves.

If the president of the United States ever awards a medal to the most pessimistic citizen in this country, then surely he would have to pin it to my scrawny chest. But where to pin it – now that would indeed be a challenge. At any rate, I wasn't in the least bit surprised when no one answered Reverend Splitfrock's door; I was merely annoyed. I was, however, pleasantly surprised when a woman identifying herself as Viola Taylor came scurrying over from one of the houses next door to inform us that Reverend Splitfrock was out of town and that he would not return for three days. If she were to be believed, the congregation had left en masse two days ago.

They had travelled south to Tennessee, in a caravan, to participate in a large, inter-church baptism of likeminded believers. While they were in the south, they planned to collect more snakes before they went dormant for the winter.

'Well, there goes that theory,' Toy muttered on our way back to the car. 'I should have known that it was too tidy a theory.'

'I was almost positive that I saw some of the church members in the crowd,' Agnes said. 'They're the unhappiest-looking bunch of Christians that you can imagine.'

'Dodging fangs will do that,' is what I was *going* to say, but I got a call from Gabe, so I trailed behind a few steps.

'Husband dearest, what's up?'

'What's up, babe, is that we're all worried sick about you?'

'Who's we?'

'Well, your son and I, for starters.'

'For *starters*? Someone else misses me as well?'

'Ma.'

'*Right.*'

'And your sister. Susannah and Cousin Miriam just got back. They've been riding around looking for you.'

'Well then, why didn't they just call me? I've been right here the entire time.'

'Where's that, hon?'

'What did you say?' I asked needlessly.

'I asked—'

'I'll have to call you back, dear. But don't worry, I'm fine.'

Once back in the car with the others, I told them what Cheryl had seen the night before. There may have been a few occasions in my life when I've embellished stories to make them sound more interesting, but this one needed no help from me. A man and a woman in magenta jumpsuits, at dusk, wearing cartoon duck masks – why, even my fertile imagination couldn't make that stuff up!

'Holy guacamole!' Toy said. 'Magdalena, now that one takes the cake.'

'You've got to hand it to our Mags,' Agnes said, beaming. 'In our high school's Speech and Creative Writing class, Magdalena made the highest grades. In fact, she was the teacher's pet.'

'Well, *somebody* had to be,' I said. 'But the duck masks and magenta jumpsuits – that's straight from Cheryl's lips. Although, she also said that the suits may have been black. How does one confuse magenta and black?'

'Perhaps they were a very *dark* magenta,' Toy said. 'I've seen cars that colour, and you did say that it was dusk. Besides, Cheryl Rosen has always struck me as being a level-headed businesswoman.'

'*Ex-cu-u-suh* me,' Agnes said. 'Are you forgetting that she used to be a psychiatrist? They're nuttier than a PayDay bar.'

'I don't mean to be rude, Agnes,' Toy said, 'but have you ever seen a psychiatrist? I mean as a patient.'

'No,' Agnes said, 'but I have seen them portrayed on television. They're all very controlling and have lots of torrid extra-marital affairs.'

'How very interesting,' Toy said. 'My mother must be the exception to the rule.'

Agnes gasped. 'I am so sorry. I had no idea. I am sure that your mother is a wonderful woman. Yes, she must be the exception to the rule, or maybe the TV writers don't know a thing about what they're writing, or maybe I'm just babbling too much—'

'Which you are,' I said kindly.

We rode in silence until we got back to Agnes's house. Agnes and I had both been sitting in the rear of the squad car, like prisoners, behind the bulletproof partition. However, a state-of-the-art sound system between the two compartments allowed us to communicate easily. Toy had no compunctions about either of us riding 'shotgun' as he called it – that is to say, sitting up front. Unfortunately, Agnes and I could not agree on who the lucky woman would be. Therefore, we both lost out.

'Here we are,' Toy said cheerfully as we pulled into Agnes's drive. 'Agnes, while I run Magdalena back to her car, why don't you run in and pack a few things in a small bag. I'd feel better if you bunked with me for a day or two.'

I gasped in dismay. 'You needn't be worried about her being alone,' I said. 'Her two nude uncles can protect her.'

Agnes shot me a look that could have frozen over a pot of hot fudge. 'Ha! Protect me, how? Uncle Fred is eighty-one, and Uncle Ned is eighty-three. Anyway, as you well know, Magdalena, the young man who usually minds them when I work, took them back to his family's farm for the weekend.' She smiled at Toy. 'Those dear, sweet men can no longer handle all the stress there is to be felt in Hernia these days.'

'Toy,' I said, 'how many times have Amish called to complain about the sight of naked men walking down the streets of our village?'

Toy ignored me. 'So, Agnes, how about coming over to stay for a couple of days? That is, if you don't mind.'

Agnes practically chortled her answer. 'Why should I mind?'

'Well, you know how tongues can wag in this village,' Toy said.

'Wiggle woggle waggle, and *how* our village tongues will wag!' I said naughtily, for I could not believe my friend's astonishingly good fortune. 'Toy, doesn't Periscope Pam live directly behind you?'

The poor man couldn't help but laugh. 'Yes, she does. But after the second time that I caught her rising from behind the bushes, with a pair of binoculars pressed to her eyes, she has pretty much stopped spying on me. That is – I think that she has. Or it could be that now I just tune out Pam Olsen rising out of a sea of green, like a submarine periscope.'

'*Eee*,' Agnes squealed. 'What fun these sleepovers are going to be! Do you like old movies? Cary Grant and Katherine Hepburn? Or Doris Day and Rock Hudson? I adore Doris Day.'

'So do I,' Toy said, still maddeningly cheerful. 'What's your favourite movie of hers?'

'*Pillow Talk*,' Agnes said, her voice suddenly husky. 'Yours?'

'*Lover Come Back*,' Toy said.

'Enough of this nonsense!' I cried. 'It's starting to sound like Sodom and Gomorrah in here.'

'Well in that case I'll hop out and get my overnight bag.' Agnes made a point of looking me directly in the eye. 'Or, just to be on the safe side, Toy, should I plan to stay longer?'

Then Toy had the temerity to look back at me through the bullet-proof glass and grin. 'Maybe pack a *small* suitcase. Also, Agnes, do you have any snacks that you could bring? Like maybe popcorn?'

'Oodles,' she said to him. 'Toodles,' she said to me, and then she did hop out, and off she went to pack for her life as Periscope Pam's newest victim.

'So that's what it's come down to,' I said.

'I beg your pardon?' Chief Toy said.

'Nothing,' I said, although I really meant 'something, and you should figure it out on your own, so that I won't have to embarrass myself'. But he was clueless, so we rode to Cheryl's house in silence. He did, however, invite me to sit up front. I accepted the invitation of course – I'm not a complete idiot – but if Toy thought it was going to compensate for a sleepover with popcorn, he had another think coming. As for watching a movie titled *Lover Come Back*? I don't think that I could bend my morals that far, even for a man like Chief Toy.

Anyway, how could I be so stupid, and so sinful, as to be envious of Agnes? So what if she got to be the guest of our young, handsome, and charismatic Chief of Police? Here was a man who watched what he ate and bothered to stay in shape. Never mind that Agnes was old enough to be his mother, and that she too had a reputation to protect. Did either of them even ask if *she* could come home with *me*? I was a professional innkeeper and staying with me would have been beyond reproach.

Also, since I was the one most in danger, wouldn't it have made sense if *both* Toy and Agnes came back to the inn with me? Of course space was an issue, what with Cousin Miriam having been sprung on me at the last moment, but Alison's room was free now, and so was that of the poor deceased couple, Gerald and Tanya Morris, whose mutilated bodies had been discovered in a dumpster behind Yoder's Corner Market earlier in the week.

As newly minted Apparition-Americans, the Morris's were most unlikely to be using their room again. In my many years as an innkeeper, and an amateur sleuth, it is folks who die tragic and sudden deaths who hang around after they pass because they have unfinished business. But almost to a corpse, they stay within fifty feet of where they died. My point is, I had room, even if that weird Texas couple, big Tiny and loudmouth Delphia, insisted on being selfish and hogging most of them.

We pulled into my sister-in-law's driveway alongside my car. Before I could draw another breath, Toy had flipped on the flashing red lights atop the cruiser.

'What's going on?' I said.

'Call Cheryl,' he ordered. 'And you both stay put.'

I called Cheryl, but no one answered. I tried again, still with no luck.

'Toy, what *is* it?'

'Someone has slashed your tyres, Magdalena,' he said. 'I'm calling Officer Cakewalker for backup, and then I'm going in to check on Cheryl and her mother.'

But Officer Lucinda Cakewalker was at the corner of Juniper and Tulip Streets, involved in a rather serious accident. More specifically, it was she who had run a stop sign whilst texting, hitting an SUV broadside. As Toy was still getting details from her, she passed out, and the call was dropped.

'Holy guacamole!' Toy swore. Then he just sat there beside me in the driver's seat of his cruiser, motionless, like a pillar of salt.

'Call the ambulance for her,' I said. 'You know where she is. Then press the pedal to the medal, and let's get over there and see if we can help. We're a whole lot closer than anyone in Bedford.'

'Right,' Toy said, 'but I need to check on Cheryl and her mother first. About your slashed tires – that's a crime scene. I will admit that I didn't see it at first, but someone is clearly out to get . . . well, at least to scare the dickens out of you. So sit tight while I run in.'

So that's what Toy did, while I called the ambulance for Lucinda Cakewalker. He jumped out of the cruiser, ran up her walk, and then leaped up her front steps two at a time. Cheryl didn't answer her door, and it appeared to be locked from the way Toy acted. Next he appeared to be talking to someone on the phone for far too long, given that his sergeant might have been lying in the street at the corner of Juniper and Tulip. Officer Cakewalker might even have been dying of mortal injuries for all Toy knew. Frankly, I was mighty irritated by his behaviour.

When he finally returned, I started in on the third degree before he'd had the chance to say anything. Over the years I've learned that the person asking the questions is less likely to be interrupted than the one who is put in the position of having to answer them.

'Who were you talking to?' I said.

'Cheryl,' he said.

'Why didn't you just go in?' I asked.

'Because she's at *your* house.'

'What?' I said.

'Following your visit,' he said 'after she'd learned what the couple in the magenta jumpsuits and duck masks had been up to, she had second thoughts about sleeping in town. She's decided that she'd be safer a few miles out, at the inn, and with her brother.'

I sighed so hard that Toy's cruiser was flooded with dust motes. 'I suppose that she took my beloved mother-in-law with her.'

Toy reached over and patted my knee gently. Confidentially, under normal circumstances, such a gesture might have sent teensy-weensy sparks of pleasure to my lady parts. Then after a microsecond of bliss, I'd spend days, if not weeks, wallowing in shame and guilt. I might even feel a strong desire to convert to a faith where private confession of sin was one of the services offered. On this occasion, however, I felt nothing other than a hand on my knee. It might have been Gabe's hand, or a monkey's hand, for all the difference it made.

'Yes,' Toy said. 'Both Cheryl and Ida Rosen will be bunking at the inn tonight, so it's a good thing that Agnes won't be going back with you.'

'Oh, really?' I said. 'I thought there was supposed to be safety in numbers.'

Toy laughed. 'You know the thing that I like best about you is that you're a real trooper. Always making jokes, even when you've had a really lousy day. When danger comes your way, you keep calm and carry on. Are you sure that you're not British?'

I shook my horsey head vigorously. 'No way!' I neighed. 'I'm *never* calm. I lurch from crisis to crisis like a Soviet era lorry on a rutted dirt road, and with each new spot of trouble I wail like a banshee on the Scottish moors. I mix my metaphors as frequently as you mix your cocktails, but one thing is for sure, I am never, *ever* calm. And for the record, about half the time that you think that I'm joking, I am not. Conversely, half the time that you think that I'm being serious, I am not.'

Toy nodded sombrely. 'Which is it now?'

'At the moment I'm so scared that I don't know,' I wailed.

'Then change of plans,' Toy said firmly. 'We're collecting Agnes on the way to Juniper and Tulip. It won't take but a minute. She's spending the night with you – and so am I. I'll drop the two of you off at the PennDutch, but I should be back to stay about nine.'

'I don't think we have room,' I said.

'Oh yes, you do,' he said. 'Agnes and I—'

Toy was interrupted by an ambulance dispatcher telling him that EMTS had arrived at the accident scene and were already loading Lucinda Cakewalker and a thirty-six-year-old man with life-threatening injuries into their vehicles for the trip into Bedford. Toy changed his plans again and we drove straight to the scene of the accident. We arrived to find a crowd of gawking neighbours, and the damaged vehicles still in the intersection, but the injured parties had already departed. With the help of volunteers, Toy managed to relocate both cars to one side of Tulip Street, where he also wrote down the names of three people who claimed to have seen the accident, and one who had merely heard it.

After that, siren wailing (even louder than I can), lights flashing yet again, we sped back to pick up Agnes. Toy broke the law by not even fastening his seatbelt, shame on him. Although he is neither Superman, nor an angel, I would swear (if it weren't against my beliefs) that he flew to my best friend's door. She didn't answer either, so he paused to call her, and when that proved fruitless, he raced around to the back of the house. A moment later he was back at the car, breathless, and practically witless.

'She's *gone*! Agnes has gone missing!'

TWENTY

'Calm down, dear,' I said, 'so that you can carry on.'

Toy pulled himself together a tad as he slid back into his seat. 'You don't understand. Her back door is wide open, and two of her patio chairs are overturned. I'm calling Sheriff Stodgewiggle so he can issue an all-points bulletin.'

'Think carefully, Toy,' I said. 'For one thing, Sheriff Stodgewiggle is your arch-nemesis. Second, Agnes is an adult, fully in charge of her faculties, and can't be classified as a missing person for forty-eight hours, and even then there needs to be just cause. Have you considered calling Esther Sweetgrass?'

'Her next-door neighbour?'

'Yeah. Esther is Agnes's SBFF.'

'Second best female friend?'

'Yup. She grew up with us and goes to Agnes's church. She's also a dynamite baker, which Agnes isn't. From what I hear, when Agnes is finished eating her single portion frozen dinners, she heads over to Esther's house for pie or cake. Maybe both. Not that this is gossip, mind you; it's police business.'

'Gotcha,' Toy said. He jumped out of the cruiser once more, and this time sprinted to the lovely little Cape Cod owned by Esther Sweetgrass. As soon as he disappeared inside, I called Gabe to give him an update.

'Oh, babe,' he said, 'I was just about to call you!'

'What is it, dear?' I said. 'Did you hear from Alison? You sound distressed.'

'No, hon, no word from our daughter. And we probably won't for a while; she'll need time to settle in.'

'Crushed crumpet crumbs! With all the *tsuris* I've been having today, I've managed to put her dancing out of my mind.'

'Dancing? What are you talking about?'

'By now our beautiful, innocent daughter has most assuredly done the bedspring bossa nova with her boyfriend Alex, that's what. There can only be one "first time", you know.'

'*Oy veys Meer*,' Gabe moaned. 'I can just see the two of them, having just arrived in this strange place, taking time off from their orientation program to dance the pillow sham shimmy.'

'But theoretically, it's possible! And here I thought that fathers were especially protective of their daughters.'

'Who says that we're not? You stopped me from racing to the airport like an idiot after she'd already boarded her plane. What is it that you expect me to do now? Anyway, at least you had the all-important sex talk with her. Didn't you?'

'You bet your bippy,' I said. 'I told her that the act should last five minutes these days and not three like it did for me the first time. I also told her that if she and her husband had been arguing prior to their love-making, and she hadn't quite gotten over her negative feelings, that it shouldn't stop her from the proceeding. She need only grit her teeth and think about England.'

'*England?* Why England?'

'Or Italy, or Greece, or Australia. Just any place that she'd like to visit and then blurt it out at the last minute. Sooner or later her husband will get the hint; it worked for me.'

'Why, you little minx. I'm glad you've regained your sense of humour, because we don't even know *if* it's happened. Anyway, it is, or was, bound to happen sometime. She wasn't born with a chastity belt.'

'*I* was her chastity belt!'

'Oh, you religious types! You slay me. You know that even some Amish girls don't remain virgins until their wedding day, and how much stricter can you get than that?'

I had plenty to say about Amish girls during *rumschpringe*. That's the period when Amish parents look the other way as their children in their late teens experiment with a few of the world's temptations. Boys are generally given more latitude than girls and may go so far as to leave the Amish community for a year or to two and immerse themselves into a secular society. Girls will usually restrict themselves to riding around in their boyfriends' newly acquired cars, and applying previously forbidden make-up, drinking alcohol, and smoking. Both sexes might engage in *actual* dancing, something that *I*, as a Conservative Mennonite, was forbidden to do by my parents.

If Mama had caught *me* drinking and smoking, she might well have broken her hairbrush on my backside. Also, as a good Christian daughter, I would have obeyed her when she told me to bend over, and stayed in that position no matter how many whacks she delivered to my stinging bum. I'm just saying that in my opinion Amish girls had it easier than I did in some ways, even though I didn't have to spend my early years listening to sermons in German, or riding to church in a buggy on cold winter days like the Amish did.

'Magdalena!' Gabe was shouting into my ear. 'Have you heard a word I said?'

'Of course, dear,' I cooed soothingly. 'It was about Amish virgins on their wedding nights.'

Gabe swore so long and hard that even my phone blushed. 'So you haven't! I said that the Texan woman and her husband just came through the front door, and she's covered in blood. Oh – gotta go.' He hung up.

In a way his timing was good, because I would have been interrupted anyway by Toy's laughter, and Agnes's high-pitched, unseemly squeals. I looked over to see the young police chief striding to the car, with my rotund friend riding piggyback. All I can say, and with upmost Christian charity, is that Toy must have a spine made of steel and spend every off-duty hour working out in a gym. Agnes had her feet hooked in front of Toy's slim waist, and her tiny hands were grasping his bulging pectoral muscles, but Toy was, of course, doing most of the work, holding Agnes's nearly three hundred pounds aloft. I was gobsmacked. When they got to the car Toy set her down gently, as if she were a life-size porcelain statue.

'Open up, Magdalena,' Toy said, 'and let Agnes in. I've got to run back into her house and grab her suitcase.'

'And lock up for me,' Agnes said. 'And don't forget to water my plants – sugar.' Then she giggled for absolutely no reason.

'Yeah, that too,' Toy said. Then off he ran, like Agnes's obedient manservant.

'Well, well, well,' I said, as Agnes slid into the back seat.

'A well is a deep hole in the ground,' Agnes said, 'and I already have one. What would I do with two more?'

I turned around to face her. 'What about you and Toy? Don't you know how ridiculous you look riding on his back piggyback style like a small child? What was that about, anyway?'

'Expediency. Toy said to move fast, and since I don't have long, giraffe legs like *someone* I know, he squatted, and told me to hop on his back. But since we're playing Twenty Questions, how about being honest with your best friend from birth and sharing with her the reason that your face looks like a travel poster for Ireland.'

'I beg your pardon!'

'You know – fifty shades of green.'

'Why I never!'

'Mags, you do realize, that when an unmarried woman lusts in her heart, it's not considered spiritual adultery – even by Jimmy Carter standards.'

'What? You're wrong!'

'No, adultery has to have at least one married person involved.'

'But that's so unfair!'

'Aha, so you *do* lust after Toy; I knew it.'

'Maybe just a wee bit. But you can't say anything to anyone, because if Gabe finds out, it could ruin my marriage, which has always been on shaky ground. Agnes, I'm fighting a constant battle against the Devil; He keeps popping naked pictures of Toy into my mind.'

'Did you just say *naked*?'

I nodded grimly. 'As mayor I have keys to the police station, both front door and back. Anyway, one time I came in unannounced through the back door to deliver a dinner to our one prisoner. It was Easter, so I also brought some leftover hot cross buns that I meant to drop off for Toy. This was three years ago. You remember the drunk tourist who tried to steal our village sign because he thought the name Hernia was so funny?'

'Yes!' she practically screamed in my face. 'Get on with it. Lover Boy will be back here any second.'

I recoiled in horror. '*Lover Boy?*'

'What else *should* I call a virile young man who tells me to hop on his back? Mags, I had no choice but to press my bodacious bosom against his muscular scapulae and press my womanhood against the small of his back so that my slim ankles might meet against his glistening eight pack.'

'Clean my ears out with cotton swabs,' I cried, 'and then wash them with a disinfecting soap and hot water. That is unmitigatedly pornographic.'

'Oh, Mags,' my bestie said, 'you're such a prude. Besides, if you're going to be an anglophile, then perhaps you should know that the UK dictionary on some word processors doesn't even contain the word "unmitigatedly".'

'Do you want to nitpick,' I said, 'or do you wish to learn about the nude photos that I saw of Toy's lap – I mean, on his laptop?'

'Get on with your story,' Agnes barked. Honestly, that woman can sound like a trained seal at times.

'OK, OK. Anyway, I went straight to Toy's office to let him know that I was there, but soon figured out that he was in the bathroom. Then I set his buns on his desk next to his computer, and because the Good Lord gave me an active and curious mind, I glanced at the lit screen. Well, it's a good thing that I had a tight grip on the prisoner's dinner tray, because your virile, young Lover Boy, and some equally young woman, with a truly bodaciously large bosom, were lying together on a bed, face up, and grinning lasciviously at a camera that was obviously mounted on the ceiling. It was Sodom and Gomorrah on steroids.'

'I don't believe it,' Agnes said.

'Ask him when he gets back.'

'Well, if it's true, then why didn't you fire him?'

'First of all, the photo was on Toy's personal laptop. Second, I'd given him Easter Sunday off, so he wasn't on duty. And third, Toy is the best chief of police that Hernia has ever had. Wouldn't you agree?'

Agnes looked absolutely crestfallen. So much so that I abandoned my plans to point out to her that, unlike Toy's woman, her bosom is anything but bodacious. If it wasn't for her excess weight, she wouldn't have any at all. What I didn't do, and maybe should have done, is to inform Agnes that it was around this day that Toy received a 'Dear John' letter from a woman named Autumn Tartt. I know this because, not only did I discover him red-eyed on numerous occasions in the next couple of weeks, but one afternoon he actually blurted out the entire sad saga of his sordid love life, and then sobbed on my shoulder.

'Hmm,' Agnes said, 'I'm not sure that I believe you, Mags. Toy is an Episcopalian. They're laxer in their beliefs than we Mennonites, but they're not altogether godless.'

I was about to be a good friend and inform her that Toy and the aptly named Miss Tartt were no longer an item, but Toy had suddenly reappeared, carrying a paper gift bag. He let himself in and handed the bag back to Agnes.

'There wasn't a suitcase to be seen in any of the bedrooms,' he said, with a wry smile. 'Only this bag containing a couple of negligees and some silky under things.'

'Shame on you, Toy Graham!' I admonished our chief of police. 'You said the "N" word!'

Toy turned the colour of farmers' cheese. '*What?* I did not! I said *neg*-ligees. Not what you thought that you heard.'

Agnes snickered. 'To Magdalena, negligee is also a forbidden word.'

'Well, you won't find either of those "N" words in the Bible,' I said. 'And about the contents of that bag, Agnes, is that what you consider decent nightwear for the house of a gentleman? And for heaven's sake, don't you have a decent suitcase?'

Agnes stuck her tongue out at me – but just a quick flick, mind you. 'Maybe I do, and maybe I don't. And as you well know, Miss-Holier-Than-Thou, there are a lot of words that aren't mentioned in the Bible. Are roller skates mentioned in the Bible? Or trampolines? Ha, so there!'

'How would you even know?' I said. 'Have you read yours all the way through?'

Now Agnes snorted, which I found doubly irritating, as I lay claim to that equine sound. 'Of course I don't read it through from cover to cover every year like you do,' she said. 'I give myself permission to skip the boring books.'

'Of the sixty-six books in the King James Bible, how many does that leave you?' I asked.

'I read the Gospels and the Book of Psalms,' Agnes said.

'So five books,' I said.

'Don't judge me, Magdalena,' Agnes snapped. 'I'll tell you another thing that you won't find in the Bible, and that's any mention of your so-called sturdy Christian underwear. Do you know if anyone even *wore* underwear back in those days? Huh? Do you? Maybe they all walked around, in biblical times, dressed commando-style.'

If my blood pressure got any higher, the bun atop my head would start to bob. 'What does commando-style mean?' I demanded of Toy.

'It means without underpants,' Toy said. 'But hey ladies, let's lighten up, shall we? I don't even *own* a Bible,' Toy said.

Surely he was joking. If so, neither Agnes nor I found it worthy of the smallest chuckle. If Toy's comment was sincere, well then one, or both of us, had our work cut out for us. Biblical illiteracy is a serious problem in this country. How can we answer the questions of unbelievers, if we haven't read the material that is being tested? And what about the dozens of inconsistencies in the scriptures for which there are no answers? We need to have *our* lists of questions drawn up, so that we can present them to the Almighty when we meet Him.

Neither Agnes nor I responded to Toy's shocking admission. Agnes's sacrilegious suggestion that our Lord might have wandered around the Holy Land clad only in a robe and tunic was what shut me up. If I opened my mouth to speak, there was no telling what words the Devil might force out between my withered, unpainted lips. Of course, I could only guess at Agnes's motive for remaining mum on the ride to the PennDutch. I rather doubted that she was quite as concerned as I was with spiritual welfare. Although it was a long shot, I was hoping that she was feeling remorseful for causing me so much emotional distress. Then maybe after inwardly repenting of having intimated that Jesus wore neither briefs nor boxers, she would then make a pledge to the Lord to cease being a trollop, open the car window, and toss the bag of scandalous merchandise into a drainage ditch.

After all, I am a legally married woman. If I, perchance, should choose to retrieve that paper bag of silky, scarlet, see-through unmentionables in hopes of using them in Operation Restore the Rosen Marriage, then that is my business. A married woman could even don such shudder-inducing duds just to lollygag about in bed by herself, if she so chose, just as long as her thoughts never strayed to a man other than her husband. But since the Devil kept pushing Toy into my thoughts, I'd be wearing cotton flannel nightgowns to bed for the foreseeable future. Frankly I was relieved that Agnes hugged the paper bag the entire trip as if it contained the Crown Jewels, and she was the Queen's lady-in-waiting.

Well, so what if it had been one of the worst days of my life? At least I was home! Home, sweet home, and where my heart lay. I knew that Little Jacob would hug me, maybe even smother me with kisses. That's all a mother really needs, after all, isn't it? Or, so I guess. Although a working marriage as well would be ideal. But beyond that, what can one really expect of marriage after the initial bloom of exciting has worn off, and there have been so many arguments, and angry words spoken that can never be taken back?

But the marriage could wait. I was equally at fault for that, me and my spiritual adultery. In the meantime, there was a five-year-old boy to hug and kiss. Before the car had hardly come to a stop, I jumped out and ran to the kitchen door. As it turns out, I ran from one problem straight into a host of problems, beyond anything that I ever have imagined. I walked into a living nightmare that made the beginning of the day seem like naptime at my son's former preschool.

TWENTY-ONE

The first thing that I noticed was that everyone and their uncle seemed to be gathered around my kitchen table, which is reserved for immediate family. No heads turned my way, except for the youngest one, and since his was the one that mattered most, I wasn't too disappointed.

'Mama!' he exclaimed, as he threw his arms around me, and hugged me tightly. 'Where have you been?'

'I had to find out what was causing that bad smell. What's going on here?'

'The really short woman fell in a pit?'

'Her name is Mrs Hancock, dear. But a pit, yes?'

'Yes, Mama.'

Even though Little Jacob is already half my size, I hoisted him up to sit on my hip. He's already too big for that, but next year he'll be *way* too big. Then I staggered over to see what the fuss was about, and had to set him down.

'What's this I hear about a pit?'

The huddle of bodies that had been shielding Delphia Hancock from view broke apart. Gabe, Susannah and Cousin Miriam stepped to the right; Tiny Hancock, Dr Cheryl Rosen and her mother Ida Rosen moved slowly to the left. That left the obstreperous little Delphia sitting in *my* chair, on *my* special cushion, for crying out loud!

The second Delphia saw me, her eyes emitted a greenish glint. She pointed to a clean white bandage that had been expertly wound, just twice, around her lower leg.

'I'm going to sue you,' the tiny Texan said in her gravelly voice. She didn't sound like she was in the least bit of pain. Instead, she sounded happy, as if she had found a new way to amuse herself.

'Now Mother,' her not-so-tiny husband, Tiny, said, 'I'm sure that the trap was set by a prankster, and not this quaint, conscientious objector.'

I turned to Gabe. 'Now it's a trap, and not a pit? Have you been out there to inspect whatever it is?'

Gabe frowned. 'Of course not. I've had to hold down the fort here. Besides, you know that our woods are full of poison ivy, and that I don't go near them until after a hard frost.'

'Then maybe you should describe what you mean a little better,' I said to Tiny. 'Here, draw on this.' I thrust a small paper pad and pen at him. Just so you know, in my opinion every kitchen needs at least *three* pads of paper, in different colours, and a jar full of writing implements for jotting down to-do lists and various notes, to pin to a cork board, or fasten to the fridge with magnets.

What Tiny drew looked like nothing that I could identify for certain, but what did come to mind was a strip of Agnes's back lawn in autumn when she neglects to rake the leaves from beneath her towering maple. That, and a dead cat I once saw that had rigor mortis. Well, it sort of looked like those two things if I *had* to say that it looked like *something*. I mean, it looked messy, and fluffy, with sharp things poking out of the fluff. Tiny used a black marker, whereas the maple by Agnes's back porch has orange, yellow, and red litter.

'Was there a dead cat in the trap?' I asked.

The man named Tiny roared with laughter, whereas his truly tiny wife roared with indignation. It was clear that Delphia's baritone voice startled Agnes, Cheryl, and Ida. Little Jacob watched their reaction with glee.

'She's twansgendoh,' he said by way of explanation. Having just turned five, he's still incapable of pronouncing 'R's, especially at the end of words, which means that he sounds delightfully British in my book.

'I am *not* transgender,' growled Delphia.

'Wait a minute,' Cheryl, our family shrink said. 'My nephew isn't judging you. Are you, Little Jacob?'

Little Jacob shrugged. 'I don't even know what it means. I just huhd Mama say it.'

'I said that I was totally accepting of transgender women.' I turned to my son. '"Transgender" is another word for "special".'

Delphia snorted. 'What are you? Some kind of bleeding heart liberal? I thought your kind were supposed to be conservative like scriptures command us to be.'

'So *was* there a dead cat?' Agnes said. Bless her heart for noticing the steam escaping from beneath my white organza prayer cap.

'Dead cat?' Delphia roared again. 'It was a pit, with sharpened stakes in it. I could have fallen in and died. Or worse yet, broken a leg, and then suffered a cruel death while being eaten alive by wolves and vultures. Oh, I know that y'all are thinking that my big strong husband would have come to my defence, but he's afraid of everything, even squirrels.'

'Squirrels can have rabies,' Tiny said. His face was bright red.

'Yeah,' his wife sneered, 'but at one point, when we were in the woods, you were convinced that you saw a pair of giant magenta-coloured ducks. Was Big Foot leading them, or following them?'

Poor Little Jacob buried his head in my voluminous skirts. 'Shame on you, Mrs Hamhocks,' I said angrily, 'for frightening this impressionable young child.' I could have said a lot more, and perhaps I should have. For it had occurred to me that the Hancocks could not possibly be the duo in the magenta jumpsuits – Delphia was far too short and squat for that. And if the jumpsuit wearers had been responsible for the bodies in the dumpster, then the Hancocks could have been murdered right here in my very own woods.

'It's Hancock, you blithering fool!' Delphia retorted.

Those who know me well may find it hard to believe that I did not intend to get her name wrong, I honestly didn't. For one thing, she was such a wisp of a thing, there would have been no sense in referring to pig parts. For another, calling her a name other than her own only diverted attention from what she had done, which was to scare the daylights out of my son.

I chose to end our confrontation. '*Mr* Hancock, may I please speak with you alone? We can retire to the parlour for privacy.'

'I won't stand for this,' Delphia said, stamping a miniscule foot on my tile floor. She may as well have been tapping a potato puff against a dinner plate.

I never thought I would say this but thank heavens for my sister-in-law. Cheryl proved herself to be both perceptive and mildly manipulative.

'I'll go with them, Mrs Hancock,' she said. 'I know from first-hand experience how wily your innkeeper can be—'

'Yah,' Ida interjected. 'Like a coyote.'

'Hush, Ma,' Cheryl said. 'This is important.'

'Yah, und I'm not?'

Little Jacob tugged on one of my three-quarters length sleeves. 'Mama, why are you like a coyote?'

'Only that she's smart like a coyote,' Cheryl said, and winked at me. 'Come with us, Mr Hancock. I'll make sure nothing bad happens to you; I promise that.'

Tiny had every reason to be embarrassed, but he played gamely along. 'Sure thing, ma'am. I can't wait to talk to your great-grandmother again.'

'Claptrap,' Delphia snapped. 'There's no such thing as ghosts.'

'No, ma'am,' Little Jacob said passionately. 'Just 'cause you can't see her don't mean nothing. You can't see Jesus, germs, and Santa Claus neither, and they's all real!'

'OK then,' Cheryl said brightly, 'off we go!' She grabbed big Tiny's arm and steered him around my massive kitchen island and through the dining room door. Later I remembered that the woman had taken ballroom dance lessons.

First, I made sure to close the parlour door tightly behind us. Then as Tiny lumbered to a seat, I managed to grab Cheryl by a designer sleeve with one of my prematurely liver-spotted hands.

'Just so you know, dear, Mr Hancock both saw, and heard, my great-granny before I even said a word about her to him.'

As a psychiatrist, Cheryl has an irrational fear of anything that isn't rational. She refuses to believe in ghosts, no matter how much evidence I can provide to support their existence.

'Then maybe someone else in your household filled his head with that nonsense,' she said.

'That would have to be your much-loved nephew, Little Jacob,'

I whispered. 'He's the only other person in the family who can see her.'

Tiny cleared his throat. 'Excuse me, ladies. Why are we ignoring the lovely lady sitting in the rocking chair? Where I come from, turning your backs on an elderly person – especially a woman – is the height of impoliteness.'

'Now *that's* a proper gentleman,' Granny said, 'unlike that other fellow who's always causing you so much heartache that you can barely eat. I mean look at you: you look like a single strand of unravelled string.'

'That other fellow is my husband, Granny, and the father of your great-great-grandchild.'

'Are you quite sure, child?'

'Yes, I'm sure!' My cheeks felt as hot as waffle irons so I turned to Tiny, despite being red-faced. 'I'm not sure that you believed me when I first told you that this so-called "lovely lady" really is a ghost, but she is. And I can prove it.'

'We prefer to be called Apparition-Americans now,' Granny snapped.

Tiny laughed, and then he must have noticed the grim expression on Granny's face because he bit his lip. 'Prove it, how?'

'Go over to the rocking chair and try to sit in her lap.'

Tiny was horrified. 'No, ma'am! That wouldn't be right.'

'Why, I wouldn't mind at all,' Granny said. 'Come on, sonny. Come on over here, and let this old granny give you a ride.'

It was Tiny now who turned red. 'What in tarnation?'

'Then watch me,' I said. I hopped over to Granny's rocker and plopped my bony patooty down on its hard, wooden surface.

Tiny gasped. 'What in the world?'

'You see,' I said. 'I'm sitting right inside that lovely old lady, as if she wasn't even there. That's because she's not – well not physically, at any rate.'

'How dare you,' Granny rasped. 'Then again, why am I not surprised? Magdalena, you were always a nuisance. You were forever ruining my fun at family gatherings when I was alive.'

'Granny,' I wailed, 'you died and were supposed to have passed on when I was only three years old. How much of a nuisance could I have been to you? And besides that, your marriage vows were "to death do us part", and you have yet to totally depart. Are you sure that you have the right to flirt with a man other than your fully departed former husband? Especially to ask one who is very much alive to sit in your lap?'

'You big doo-doo head,' Granny said angrily. 'If I could, I'd wash your mouth out with soap. Shame on you for trying to confuse an old woman like me with facts.'

I popped back to my original seat. 'OK folks, enough digression. I'll get right down to what I wanted to speak to you about in private, Mr Hancock.'

'It's about time!' Cheryl said. 'But just so you know, Magdalena, I insist on looking at a list of your medications later.'

I shot her a look that could start a fire without the use of flint. Then I turned to Tiny with a warm, encouraging smile.

'Mr Hancock, I want you to understand that I, for one, believe that you saw a pair of giant magenta-coloured ducks in my woods today.'

'Boogers,' Granny said.

'Just ignore her,' I said. 'Dr Rosen, here, also believes you, and she's a psychiatrist. Aren't you, Dr Rosen?'

'Yes, I am, but I didn't see an actual pair of giant ducks; I saw Donald Duck and Daisy Duck.'

'You head doctors are all quacks,' Granny said.

'What Dr Rosen means,' I said, 'is that she saw people wearing masks of those two comic book characters. They also happened to be wearing magenta jumpsuits.'

'Yes, yes!' Tiny said. 'That's it, exactly. I know that I should have clarified what I said before to my wife out in the woods, but she's so – uh – what's the word I'm looking for?'

'Critical?' I said. 'Exasperating? Infuriating?'

'Belittling?' Cheryl said. 'And emasculating?'

'All that,' Tiny said. 'I know that it must look terrible, the way that she treats me, but you have to understand that everything that we own is in her name: our ranch, our private plane, even our vacation homes in Hawaii and Montana.'

'Aw, you poor man,' Granny said. 'If you sit on my lap, I'll comfort you.'

'Miss Yoder,' Tiny said, 'can a ghost really be horny, or is this

some kind of an elaborate practical joke after all. Because I ain't
in the mood right now.'

'That does it,' Cheryl said in a huff. 'If it's a practical joke,
then you're in on it, Mr Handcuffs – or whatever your name is.
I was going to corroborate your testimony, because I too saw
those horrible people dressed up like comic book characters.
Except that I saw them in town, and apparently getting things
ready to dump sewage into our streets today. But now that you
and my sister-in-law are playing this game in which the two of
you pretend to speak with one of Magdalena's long dead ancestors, I'm out of here.'

'Then *you're* a big doo-doo head too,' Granny said.

After the no-nonsense Dr Rosen slammed the parlour door
behind her, I smiled reassuringly at Tiny Hancock. The poor man
looked as if he'd awakened and found himself a character in a
work of bizarre, psycho-sexual fiction.

'Pay no attention to Granny,' I said. 'She's been lonely ever
since Great-grandpapa died, which was more than seventy years
ago. As for her swearing, I'm afraid that's all Little Jacob's fault.
He heard boys calling other boys "boogers" and "doo-doo head"
at preschool. Then he thought it would be fun to teach those
words to Granny, and she took to them like ticks to a Mexican
hairless dog.'

Tiny nodded. 'Thanks for the explanation.'

'Booger buns,' Granny said, and howled with laughter.

'Mr Hancock, tell me the truth about your wife's mishap. Is
there really a pit in my woods, and if so, where is it? I frequently
walk the trail to make sure that it's safe for my guests. I can't
imagine a real pit being dug so suddenly.'

Tiny cracked a few knuckles before answering. 'Well, uh,
maybe the word "pit" was a slight exaggeration. I think that
"shallow trench" might be a more accurate description.'

'Oh goody, I adore trenches!' I said, just to keep him off guard.
'How deep a trench is it? Can an armoured tank hide in it? Let's
say that I had fallen into it. After standing, would my knobby
knees protrude over the front edge? If so, is it at least deep enough
to lay a row of tin cans, end to end, and not have them touch a
ruler laid across the top? An inquiring mind wants to know.'

Tony smiled wearily. Or was it warily?

'Your knobby knees would definitely have been exposed, because it's only a foot deep at the most.'

'Aha!' I said. 'Finally we're getting somewhere, and the "where" doesn't seem all that big of a deal. Now tell me about the sharpened stakes that lined the trench.'

'They were shish kabob skewers.'

'I beg your pardon?'

'You know, like for barbecuing chunks of meat and vegetables. They were pushed into the ground to make them stand on end. Then leaves and long grass were fluffed over the top to disguise the skewers and the pit. It was supposed to be a trap, you see. On TV I saw a documentary where natives in the Congo dug a real pit and lined it with sharpened logs. They caught an elephant to feed their village, but I fail to see what sort of animal this trap was intended to catch.'

'Tourists,' I said.

'Beg your pardon, ma'am?' Tiny said.

'It was a tourist trap,' I said, 'and it caught your wife. How badly hurt is she? I mean, *really* hurt?'

He laughed with embarrassment. 'It's barely a scratch, but Delphia loves to make a scene. The path was muddy from all that rain, and most of the skewers were flattened into the ooze when Delphia stomped on them. I guess one skewer gave a little resistance on the way down and grazed her shin.'

'Wait a minute,' I said. 'Are you telling me that your wife purposely stomped on the trap?'

TWENTY-TWO

The poor man groaned. 'Miss Yoder, you may have noticed that my wife is a cantankerous and contrary woman. When we encountered this strange mound of vegetation bisecting the path, I told Delphia to step over it, or else walk around. She immediately jumped right on it with both feet and started stamping as if she was putting out a fire. That's just the kind of woman my wife is – she *hates* being told what to do.'

'Imagine that,' I said. 'At long last I've discovered my much older, very much shorter, identical twin sister from another mister.'

Tiny was not amused. 'Miss Yoder, please don't be so hard on yourself. You're nothing like my wife. You, I could live with happily.'

'Magdalena already has at *least* one husband,' Granny snapped.

'Don't start, Granny,' I said. 'I was an *inadvertent* adulteress, and you know it. But if you want to bring that subject up with a perfect stranger, then I'd be happy to resurrect the rumour that Great-aunt Pearl told me about what you and Ned Kershbaum did on that infamous hayride of 1912.'

Granny didn't *say* anything in return, but trust me, there's nothing quite so chilling as the glare of a blue-eyed ghost. The temperature in the parlour plummeted. I shivered. Big Tiny rubbed his biceps.

'Tell me,' I said to Tiny, 'why do you let Mrs Hancock treat you the way she does?'

Tiny chewed his lip before answering. 'Frankly, Miss Yoder, it's because she holds the purse strings. In the beginning it was her father, Big Daddy Joe-Bob, as everyone called him, although he never scraped together enough flesh and bones to even touch five-foot two. He was the richest man in Southwest Texas bar two counties, and when he died he left everything to Delphia. By then we'd already been married twenty-nine years, and I was used to the good life. Just be a "yes man" and you get taken care of right nice. So why rock the boat, right?'

'What about your self-respect?' I said.

'I don't have any ma'am,' he said, 'but I have my own little plane, six cars, and a righteous little speed boat for weekend trips to the lake. Then there's Delphia's yacht down in Galveston, which I get to use from time to time.'

'Is all that worth your self-respect?' I said.

'Well, it's a sight more than your husband gets, ain't it? No offense, ma'am, but he has to live in an old farmhouse in a backwater town, and among a bunch of religious types. I been looking around, and I don't see a plane in your garage, or no six cars, or no speedboat. Now, you are better looking than Delphia, I'll give you that, but still, I reckon that he still loses were we to compare our assets.'

Not only was I so mad that I could spit cotton, but the cotton had been spun into thread, and the thread had been knit into a dress. I rose shakily to my feet.

'You, sir,' I said, 'are a loathsome coward.'

Tiny appeared genuinely confused. 'Miss Yoder, I didn't mean to offend you. One of the things that I liked about you was your directness. I honestly believed that we could share our inner truths, and not have the other judge us. I wouldn't have opened up to you if I thought you were going to turn on me! You tricked me into exposing my true self. You beguiled me with your feminine wiles.'

'I don't have any wiles,' I hissed.

'Booger-filled buns,' Granny said.

'Careful, Granny,' I said, 'or I'll sit on you again.'

'Case in point,' Tiny said. 'You mince no words. I found that very refreshing.'

'Your wife certainly doesn't hold back,' I said.

'Ha! Not with her words, that's for sure, but with her money. Do you know how many times I've thought about . . . never mind.'

'Don't stop venting now, Mr Hancock,' I said.

'Are you being sarcastic, Miss Yoder?'

'No, I'm speaking from experience,' I said.

'Maybe from her experience with two husbands at the same time,' Granny said.

'Granny did the rumpy-pumpy with Ned Kershbaum under the hay,' I said.

Granny's look was one of surprise. 'Yah – maybe. What does this lumpy-dumpy mean, Magdalena?'

'It's an English expression, Granny, and according to the rumour, it's what you did with Ned. Now please be quiet like a good Apparition-American.'

Tiny cleared his throat loudly. 'Miss Yoder, if you don't mind some friendly advice—'

'Which I very much do, dear.'

'But you might appreciate this,' Tiny said.

'I doubt if I will.'

'But just listen for a moment. A commonly held belief is that Apparition-Americans are souls of the dead who haven't

completed their transition out of this world, because they don't
realize that they are, in fact, dead.'

'Now you're dead to me,' Granny said vehemently.

'Far be it for me to defend this old battleaxe,' I said, 'but in
this case I think that you're full of prunes, Mr Hancock. You
don't think that during all the decades that she's been occupying
that rocker, scaring the living daylights out of folks who can only
hear her but not see her, she hasn't been able to figure things
out? Of course she has!'

Tiny shook his head vigorously. 'Miss Yoder, have you, or
anyone, ever told her directly: "You are dead?" That it is time
to move on. Time to pass into the afterlife. Time to go home to
God. Have you ever said those exact words? Because I have
said those exact words to numerous ghosts when we've travelled,
and when I've inquired later, invariably the reports are that the
hauntings ceased abruptly after our departure.'

'Tell that man he's a charlatan,' Granny said, sounding
panicked. 'I want him out of my house. Now!'

'Yes, go!' I said.

Tiny laughed. 'But don't you see? She has nothing to worry
about if she's going to Heaven.'

'Leave now, or I'm coming over there – and I'll momentarily
suspend my pacifist beliefs – and I don't know what I'll do.
Maybe kick you in the shins. But you're leaving this room right
now!'

'Yes, ma'am,' Tiny said and flashed me a big ole Texas grin.
But then just as he got even with the rocking chair, he paused
and loomed over it like a redwood just beginning to topple. 'You
are dead,' he said to Granny. 'Go home to spend eternity with
God.'

I was furious with what he did. I was so angry that I sat open-
mouthed and watched him as he strode to the door and threw it
open. When I thought to turn back to look at Granny, well, she
wasn't there! I couldn't believe my faded blue eyes.

'Granny!' I hollered. 'Come back! Granny don't go! Don't
listen to that big lummox from Texas. I need you. You weren't
exactly a paragon of virtue, Granny. How do I know if you're
headed up, or down?'

That might sound like a stupid question for me, a 'born again'

Christian to ask, because having been 'born again', the Bible
assures me that I am headed up. Granny, however, never discussed
her spiritual life with me. I know, there are folks who say that
once you are dead it's too late to repent of one's sins, but I say,
how do those people know this for a fact? That is, unless these
same people are speaking from experience, in which case that
would make them spirits – and evil spirits at that.

At any rate, my hollering sent the big Texan on his way and
brought everyone else running to the scene of his crime.
Immediately my precious, and precocious, male progeny pointed
at the empty rocking chair.

'Where's Granny?' he said.

I choked back a sob. 'She's gone, dear.'

'Where'd she go, Mommy?'

'Heaven,' I said. OK, so I couldn't be sure, but there was a
fifty/fifty chance that I was right, so in the event that I was wrong,
it was only half of a lie.

'How'd she go, Mommy?'

'She was exorcized, dear.'

'But Granny didn't like no exercise. Just sitting.'

'Excuse me,' said Cheryl, Miss Know-it-All Psychiatrist from
New York City, 'but it isn't healthy to encourage these sorts of
dark fantasies in young children.'

'You're excused, dear,' I said, and not exactly kindly either,
mind you.

'Gabe,' Cheryl said quite sharply, 'say something to your
stubborn wife. That boy is your son as well.'

'Und my grandson,' Ida said.

'Maybe both of you should butt out and leave Magdalena
alone,' Agnes said. 'I've never seen Granny, and I know that the
two of you have never seen her either. Nor has Gabe. But Little
Jacob has acknowledged her since the day that he could talk. I
know this for a fact because I was babysitting for him, right here
in this room, when he pointed at her chair, and said, "Ga-ga".'

Cheryl's face went white with rage. 'How dare you, an interloper, tell me to butt out? For all you know he'd heard Lady
Gaga mentioned on my brother's TV.'

'Enough,' Gabe said softly. 'Agnes is the best friend our family
has ever had – and that includes the two of you.'

Ida pounded her ample bosom with a jewel-encrusted fist. 'Oy, such pain dis son gives to his poor mama's heart.'

'So, Mags,' Agnes said, 'now that she's gone, is that like *forever* gone? I mean, can she at least come back to irritate you on your birthday and holidays?'

I shrugged and turned away because I was tearing up. If folks want to see Magdalena cry, they better be prepared to pay big bucks for a private showing – either that or bury me up to my neck in peeled onions. Ida, on the other hand, having received no response to her little outburst, resumed attacking her bosom.

'What tanks does a mudder get?' she moaned.

'What's a "mudder"?' Little Jacob asked.

'It's the voman who married your daddy's fadder,' I said.

'Mags, was that kind?' Agnes said, as she placed a pudgy hand on my bony hip and attempted to steer me to a chair.

I shook my head. 'No. I'm sorry, Ida, for making fun of your fake accent. There's no excuse for my bad behaviour. None at all. *Except*, that it's been the absolute worst day of my entire life. While I know you will all expect to be fed dinner in an hour or two, I'm afraid you will either have to fend for yourselves, or have someone run into Bedford and get carry-out.'

'Even me, Mommy?' My son's clear, high-pitched voice made me feel even worse than I was already feeling.

'No, not you, dear,' I hastened to say. 'Daddy, or one of the ladies, will take care of you. Won't you, Gabe? Agnes?'

'Sure thing, hon,' Gabe said. 'But no need to worry about anything; supper has already been taken care of.'

'It has?'

'Yup. While we were all at the festival this morning, my cousin Miriam and your sister Susannah hightailed it into Bedford and did a little grocery shopping, and guess what?'

'This is all a dream, or else I've been pranked, because Susannah wouldn't hightail it out of a burning building, even if she was wearing a paper dress, and had just washed her hair in gasoline.'

Gabe put a loving arm around my shoulder and gently moved me toward the door. 'It's not a dream, babe. And not only that, they've already made dinner. It's a scrumptious-looking Australian seafood salad. They even made the dressing for it.'

I stopped abruptly. 'Does it contain shellfish? Gabe, you know that Little Jacob is allergic to shellfish.'

He nodded. 'No worries, mate,' he said to our son. 'I remembered seeing a pizza in the freezer with just your name on it. How does that sound?'

'Awesome,' Little Jacob said.

Then after we'd trooped out and had dispersed into various rooms, I cornered Gabe alone in the upstairs bedroom that we were temporarily occupying. Frankly, the behaviour he'd exhibited in the parlour was uncharacteristic of him. My husband is not fond of Susannah, whom he refers to as 'the felon'. Wasn't he worried that my shiftless sister would be a bad influence on his precious cousin?

'Darling,' I said sweetly, 'how wonderful of the girls to make dinner for us. But speaking of whom, where are they now?'

'Oh that,' Gabe said, and then chuckled. He might even have casually tossed a string of connected chuckles over his left shoulder. 'Ha-ha-ha-ha-ha-ha.'

'Yes, *that*, ha ha!'

'Mags, I've been sworn to secrecy. You don't want to make a liar out of me, do you?'

'Perhaps I didn't yet tell you that Toy insists on spending the night until he discovers who put the snake in my car and slashed Agnes's tyres. This means that we're out of guest rooms. It looks like I'll be sleeping with Little Jacob, and you'll be spending the night bunking with your ma – unless I can be coaxed into making other arrangements for some of our guests.' I gave him a knowing smile.

'They went to a club in Pittsburgh,' Gabe said. He couldn't have spoken any faster if he'd been an auctioneer at an estate sale.

'Like a book club? That's wonderful! But, dear, we have book clubs right here in Hernia, and I'm sure Bedford has oodles of them. Why go all the way to Pittsburgh?

'It's not a book club, hon; it's a gay nightclub.'

'Oh.' I prayed for guidance. 'How do you feel about Miriam being gay?'

'*What?* It's not Miriam, Babe, its Susannah.'

'Don't be silly, Gabe, my sister is madly in love with that

convicted murderer, Melvin Stoltzfus. I know that I call him a praying mantis, but he is decidedly male.'

'Yes, but Susannah was in prison,' Gabe said. 'You know what they say that does to a person.'

'That's a stereotype,' I snapped. 'I know Susannah. She loves men like I love cinnamon rolls. Neither of us are prepared to give them up. Did my sister say that she was a lesbian?'

'No. They just said that they're headed into the city to spend the evening at a gay bar, and I just assumed.'

'Darling,' I said. 'I think it would be wise not to say anything to your mother; let Miriam come out to her, if that's what she wants to do.'

'Absolutely. Just like I haven't told her that the murderer with whom your sister is in love, and who escaped from prison five years ago, *still* hasn't been caught.'

I couldn't help but giggle. 'Can you imagine what would happen if you *did* tell your mother, and then you went on to tell her that this sociopathic killer was also my half-brother? What do you think her reaction would be?'

Gabe laughed heartedly. 'She'd *plotz*. She'd faint dead away.'

That's when the devil firmly fixed that wicked thought in my head. 'Oh, let's tell her,' I said.

TWENTY-THREE

Take it from me, as a world-class sinner (I am not bragging, mind you), we do not have control over the thoughts that just flit into our brains. I am confident that even many Christian psychologists will agree with me on that score – although sadly, I fear, those psychologists will not agree with me on much else. But if we dwell on these evil thoughts, and especially if we follow through on them, *then* we are surely sinning. By the way, we are *all* a bunch of sinners, not just Yours Truly. If you doubt *my* word, then see what the Apostle Paul had to say in Romans 3:32.

So I listened to the Devil, and not my God-given conscience

and chose a moment when everyone was schmoozing around my spacious dining-room table indulging in afternoon snacks. Little Jacob had already wolfed his snack down and was upstairs in our temporary quarters watching 'caw-toons' on a small television that Gabe had taken from Alison's now acquisitioned room.

'Agnes,' I said loud enough for everyone to hear, 'do you remember Melvin Stoltzfus?'

My friend dropped a macaroon that was an inch from her mouth. '*What?* Is this some kind of a joke? How many times did that man try to kill you? Three times? Four?'

'Only two times, dear,' I said. 'But I survived Melvin's attempts to murder me, and that's what counts. What's more—'

'Mags,' Gabe said sternly, 'I wasn't serious in the parlour. You know, about having this conversation.'

'Well, you could have fooled me,' I said crisply.

Delphia swallowed a gulp of tea. 'Where Tiny and I come from, it's the height of bad manners to argue in front of your guests. Since y'all have brought up a subject that is obviously important enough to generate some pretty strong emotions, then I believe we, the victims of your negative energy, have the right to know what's going on.'

'I concur with this rather odd woman,' Cheryl said.

My blabbermouth husband needed no further encouragement. 'I was going to add that at least three other people *did* die. Plus, authorities are guessing that there are more victims in other states.' He sighed dramatically. 'Also, to be perfectly honest, I worry about the issue of so-called "bad blood".'

That's when I dropped a carrot stick. '*Bad blood?*' I said. 'I can't believe you, a doctor, just said that!'

'I don't mean it literally, hon, but since this convicted murderer is your half-brother, that makes him my son's half-uncle. The jury is not completely out yet about what sort of emotional and mental tendencies can be inherited.'

'Just shut up, Gabe,' Cheryl said. 'You know there's no such thing as "bad blood".'

Even at that point I could see Ida swaying. The short woman had been headed back to the buffet for more noshes when our conversation had made her pause in her elfin tracks. Given that

her weight distribution is skewed almost entirely to the top front
of her frame, the odds were good that she would plotz face down
on my hardwood floor. At least she wouldn't leave any dents,
unlike me, with my ice-pick of a nose.

'Magdalena,' she managed to croak. 'Eez dis evil man really
your brooder?'

'Yes,' I said.

Then plotz Ida did. Fortunately for her, Tiny Hancock was
sitting at the end of the table nearest to where she was standing,
and he was able to reach out with a gargantuan arm and stop her
fall. Perhaps the most distressing aspect of the moment was that
his outstretched gargantuan hand made contact with Ida's most
downward-facing body part, which was by far her enormous
bosom.

This spontaneous action by Tiny elicited three quite unexpected
responses: Ida regained consciousness and shrieked like a banshee
on steroids; Tiny's jealous wife Delphia joined in the din with
her basso profundo voice; and the Babester began hollering at
me for subjecting his poor mother to humiliation.

I felt my face turn fifty shades of white. Nonetheless, I rushed
over to support my teetering mother-in-law. Because Ida is so
top-heavy, and has such tiny tootsies, standing her upright was
like balancing a bowling pin on its head. Throughout the ordeal,
her stubby arms whirled like hummingbird wings, and I was
struck repeatedly about my head and shoulders.

'Now how do you feel?' Cheryl said to me.

'Like a punching bag,' I said.

'I meant,' Cheryl said, reprovingly, 'do you feel proud of
yourself?'

'Leave her alone,' Agnes said. 'You have no idea how much
ts-ts – what's that word, Mags?'

'Tsuris?'

'Yes, that's the one,' Agnes said, continuing to address Cheryl.
'Your mother did everything that she could to make my friend's
life miserable before you came to town, and even since then.
Besides, Magdalena wasn't the one who spilled the beans about
her half-brother being a convicted murderer; it was your brother
who did that. So you need to apologize to Magdalena.'

'Ha! I'll do no such thing.'

'Nor should you,' Delphia said. She turned to me. 'Since your one-woman fan club stopped you from answering this woman's question, I'm going to ask you the same question a second time. Miss Yoder, are you proud of yourself for causing an old woman so much distress?'

'No,' I said, 'but to be completely honest, I do feel rather satisfied.'

Delphia snorted. 'And here I thought you were supposed to be a good Christian woman.'

'*Oy vey*,' I said, and rolled my eyes so far back into my head I could see just how pitifully small my brain really was.

'Enough!' Cheryl said in a commanding tone. 'Look, lady, you asked Magdalena how she felt about herself, and she gave you an honest answer. I am not a Christian, and I assume that you are, but I would think that a good Christian is supposed to be honest. That is exactly what Magdalena was. She was honest.'

'Hear, hear,' Tiny said.

'Where, where?' Agnes said and winked at me, for that used to be my line.

'Why I never!' Delphia said.

'Then maybe you should,' Agnes said, and smiled slyly.

As for me, I was gobsmacked that Cheryl would do such a quick about-face and stick up for me, her mere sister-in-law. They say that blood is thicker than water, and although Cheryl and I weren't 'blood' we were still family, so I guess that made our relationship thicker than water – perhaps akin to low-fat milk. Delphia, however, was a true outsider, and as objectionable as I was to Cheryl, it was heart-warming to know that in her mind I took precedence over my guest from the great state of Texas.

Gabe smiled, so I decided to cut my losses then and go for a walk. Perhaps it was too early to mourn the loss of Granny. I'd grown up with the sarcastic spectre and had never contemplated life without her. I hadn't even considered if such a thing was possible. Perhaps she would show up on the morrow, just like the sun sometimes does in Pennsylvania (I've heard that it almost always does so in Southern California). In the meantime exercise, fresh air, and solitude were what I needed, so I headed out towards my patch of woods.

After my parents died in that horrible accident, squashed as they were between two trucks in a tunnel, I sold off all of their dairy farm except for twenty-eight acres with the house and the barn. Seven of these acres are in pasture, and twenty are in woods. The house and surrounding lawns make up the twenty-eighth.

To reach the woods, one must walk (or skip gaily) through the pasture (avoiding the cow pies if desired), where one is sure to encounter my pair of resident bovines. As I have mentioned before, one is a Jersey milk cow named Milchig, and the other an Angus beef calf named Fleischig. This particular afternoon found them on the far side of a small, spring-fed pond that sits approximately in the middle of the pasture.

My intention was to head over to them to say 'hello' before my walk in the woods. With few exceptions, I find animals to be far less annoying than people. Perhaps I should never have sold off my father's dairy herd and stayed out of the people-pleasing business. But I was just a young woman of twenty-two when my parents died, and when I dove head-first into the inn-keeping business just eight years later, I was a good deal more tolerant of everyone else's shortcomings than I am now.

I was halfway around the pond when I heard my name being called. In the Bible, there is the true story of Balaam's ass speaking to him. By that, I mean his donkey, not his hindquarters. Because neither Fleischig nor Milchig had spoken to me, it was only natural that I assumed that the voice I heard out in my open field was the voice of the Lord. I'm sure you agree.

'Here I am,' I trilled. However, I didn't stop walking. I've always fancied a late-afternoon stroll with the Lord, the two of us ambling across rolling green meadows that are punctuated by drifts of wildflowers. Perhaps a cow pasture dotted with clumps of manure doesn't quite compare with the former, but one can't always be too picky, can one?

'I know where you are, Magdalena,' the voice called to me. 'Stand still and let me catch up.'

Now that was a bit odd, even for God. I don't mean to be disrespectful, but just that so much of His ways are hard for us mere mortals to understand. Now, I've been accused of walking fast when I get a bee in my bonnet, both literally and figuratively, but surely I couldn't outwalk the Good Lord. So why did God need me to wait for Him to catch up?

'If you like, Lord,' I hollered through cupped hands at the sky, 'why don't you just zap me up to Heaven and we can do our chatting up there. I'm positive I'll be sliding all over those slippery golden streets mentioned in the Book of Revelation. You can be sure I'll be taking baby steps up there. But when we're done talking, please zap me back down here again because I have to feed this ungrateful bunch supper, and I have more worrying to do about Alison. Worrying is one of the few talents that you gave me – not that I'm complaining, mind you. *Sir.*'

The next vocalizations I heard were definitely not the Lord's; they came from Chief of Police Toy Graham. They started out as a series of pants, and then pants alternating with guffaws. I had no idea that Toy had been following me, and I was not amused that he had been witness to my desire to have an actual, Old Testament-style religious experience. Just because I believe that every word in the Bible is literally true, does not make me foolish or ignorant. There are plenty of other things that I do, and believe, that qualify me for those labels.

'Don't *even* start with me,' I said. 'I'm not in the mood.'

'OK,' Toy said. 'Who am I to judge. But just so you know, I have an aunt in Melbourne, Australia who believes that Heaven is located straight up in the sky somewhere directly above her house.'

'Get out of town and back!' I cried. 'That's fascinating; I've been puzzling over that same question all my life. I mean, when the Rapture happens, we Christians can't take off in all directions, given that there's a billion of us worldwide. Some of us are bound to get lost in space – wait a minute! You're mocking me, aren't you?'

'Absolutely not,' Toy said. 'You never fail to charm me, Magdalena.'

'Really?' My high-pitched squeak sent a family of field mice scampering back to their burrow.

'Really, but that's not why I want to talk to you. We tried to trace the sewage truck, but still no hits. Now about that snake: apparently you were lied to this morning by a Miss Viola Taylor. Reverend Splitfrock did not leave town with his flock. He was actually inside Miss Taylor's house at the time, possibly even in her bed.'

'No way! I mean, how do you know?'

'His wife was inside the parsonage when you stopped by earlier; she just didn't want to get involved. That is until after she saw Miss Viola Taylor run out and talk to you. She waited a while and called me. She said she'd been watching her husband sneak in and out of Miss Taylor's house for the last three weeks, but this is the first time that he's done it in broad daylight. She finally worked up the nerve to call him on it and threatened him with a nasty divorce. It turns out that Reverend Splitfrock was rather surprised by that. He'd reckoned that as head of the church he could get away with just about anything.'

'As it says in the Book of Numbers 32:23: "Be sure your sins will find you out".'

'Amen to that,' Toy said agreeably, 'whatever that means.'

'It means that sooner or later you're going to get caught,' I said, 'and that there will be consequences.'

'Oh yeah?' Toy said. 'Then you're going to like this. About an hour after Mrs Splitfrock laid into her husband, one of the church deacons called the reverend to report that the church with sixty-six names had been broken into during the night and burgled. Can you guess what was taken?'

'Collection plate money?' I said. It was a solid guess.

'Come on, Magdalena, you can do better than that. Use your imagination.'

'Seven cherry pies and an albino giraffe?' I said wearily.

Toy laughed. 'You're warmer this time, even though they are not warm-blooded. The answer is a rather large terrarium containing a dozen rattlesnakes.'

'Get out of town and back!'

'Magdalena, where did you learn to talk like that? No other Mennonite I know uses those expressions.'

'I'm not like any other Mennonite.'

'I'm glad of that,' Toy said. 'I didn't mean that to sound bad. Anyway, the reverend called me, and he asked me to help him find his missing snakes, so I told him the approximate location of at least one of them. Or what I assumed was one of them.'

'What was his reaction?' I said.

'He was surprised that it appeared that just a single snake had been set loose. He would have expected the vandals to dump out the contents of the entire terrarium and then run, leaving the ground crawling with the serpents. He didn't think that a sane person would be brave enough to reach into the glass tank to extract a single snake by hand.' Toy chuckled. 'That's a bit ironic, don't you think?'

'Now, now, we mustn't judge,' I said. 'To paraphrase an old Quaker saying: everyone's looney but thee and me, and sometimes I wonder about thee.' (But mostly *me*, I added under my breath.)

'Besides,' I continued, 'what made Reverend Splitfrock think that it was vandals, and *not* run-of-the-mill thieves who swiped the slimy serpents?'

'You've obviously never held a snake, Magdalena; they are *not* slimy. Anyway, when you mentioned the collection plates a minute ago, you were sort of on the right track. These people don't believe in banks, so they keep the weekly offerings in a locked wooden box in the pastor's office until disbursements are needed. Virtually all the members know where it is. Magdalena, I know that you've had a really rotten day—'

'You don't know the half of it.'

'But if I were to string together a theory now, I'd have to say, and forgive me for saying this, but it's clear that some person, or persons, has gone to a lot of trouble to ruin this day in particular for *you* in particular, including murdering two of your intended guests. We're not talking about a random killer here – I reckon they know you, Mags. Someone who wishes you harm . . .'

I batted at a fly as I stood and digested what Toy had said. That stupid fly kept trying to land at the corners of my mouth. Few things are more disgusting than flies when one is standing in a cow pasture. At last my brain sorted it all out, connected all the dots, and formed a very detailed but horrifying picture.

'Come on, let's go back to the house,' I said quietly. 'On the way there, I'll tell you who killed the couple that Monotone Mona discovered in Sam Yoder's dumpster bin, and why their killer is torturing me. I have it all figured out now.'

TWENTY-FOUR

Toy grabbed my arm. '*Who*? Who murdered that couple who were scheduled to be your guests?'

'Someone who hates me more than anyone else?' I said.

'Oh, Magdalena,' Toy said. 'Did you just hear yourself? How sad that there is even *one* person that hates you.'

'Yes,' I said, 'but when you've solved as many crimes as I have, and been responsible for those folks doing time in prison, then it is inevitable that some of them will hate you – even want you dead.'

'So who is it now?' he asked. 'Because I know for a fact that Wanda Hemphopple is still locked up. She's not even eligible for parole for another ten years.'

'It's Melvin Stoltzfus.'

'*Our* Melvin Stoltzfus? Hernia's ex-chief of police? That scrawny little ninety-pound weakling with the bobbly head and the googly eyes?'

'*Tch, tch*, it's not nice to judge someone on their physical appearance. You're a better man that. However, you've described him perfectly, except that I would have added that he looks like a praying mantis. But those are all things that could be disguised by a magenta jumpsuit with the collar turned up, and a duck mask.'

Toy's hands are slightly smaller than mine, a fact which annoys me, but they are much quicker. He managed to catch that pesky fly on the wing and throw it with enough force on the surface of the pond that it broke the tension of the water. A second later a sunfish gulped it down.

I offered Toy some hand sanitizer from a small bottle that I keep in my skirt pocket, but he refused. 'Nah, I'll just wash back at your house. I don't mean to cast shade on your theory from the get-go, but bear in mind that Cheryl saw two people in disguise operating the sewage truck hose.'

Then I told Toy that the Hancocks had seen the same magenta ducks in my woods, and that Delphia had stumbled into a twelve-inch-deep trough lined with bamboo kabob skewers. Also, the tiny lady with the big mouth was threatening to sue me for grave bodily injury.

'Was she injured?' Toy asked.

'My doctor husband wrapped a cloth bandage twice around her shin just to cover a small scratch. Trust me, a child-size Band-Aid would have sufficed, but Gabe went overboard in order to give us a moment's peace.'

'Good for him. But like I said before, we're dealing with two quacks – pardon the pun – people in the magenta jumpsuits wearing the duck masks.'

'Yes, but Toy, don't you remember Melvinism and the Church of Melvin?'

Toy shook his head and laughed. 'I wasn't here for that, but I've for sure heard about it. Folks here really took him that seriously? That they worshipped him?'

'An egomaniacal man will do anything to be adored,' I said. 'My loser half-brother wrote the Gospel of Melvin, which is the most sacrilegious book that you can imagine. Allow me to quote just the very first verse: "Every word in this book has been divinely inspired, and thou dost know that they are true because they art contained therein."'

'Wow!'

'You see?' I said. 'You can't use a claim within a manuscript to prove its veracity.'

'But don't you do that?' Toy said.

'*What?*'

'You believe that the Bible is true because it says that it is true. Am I right?'

'That's different, because God wrote the Bible!'

'Magdalena—'

'And don't confuse me with facts,' I said. 'What I wanted to say before was that, for some strange reason, which I will *never* figure out, Melvin Stoltzfus is so stupid that he once sent ice cream by mail to his aunt in Florida. Yet somehow he was still able to attract a huge cult following with his made-up religion. Who just makes up a religion, I ask you? Who can claim to have found a book buried in a field, and then have over a hundred – make that two hundred – people believe him? It's bizarre!

'I refuse to call what he has "charisma", but whatever it is that he possesses, Melvin is able to manipulate others into doing his bidding. What I'm trying to say is, that even though it has been almost five years since this evil man was last seen out in the open, I'm sure it wouldn't have been any trouble for him to secure a partner in crime. And it is most probably a woman; they seem to be suckers for his scrawny physique and bobbly head.'

'Very interesting,' Toy said. 'Any guesses who this woman might be?'

'My guess is that this woman is someone whom Melvin knew when he was the head of his cult. She might even have held a high position in that organization. My first thought was a woman by the name of Zelda Root, but poor Zelda was built like Ida, except taller – which still wouldn't fit the description that Cheryl and the Hancocks gave. But then, as we both know, eyewitness accounts are notoriously inaccurate.'

'My sister had a double mastectomy as a pre-emptive procedure,' Toy said. 'What I mean by that is maybe you shouldn't rule out Miss Root. Her appearance could well have changed since you saw her last.'

'Good point. I definitely want Little Jacob as far away from me as possible. After supper I'll have Gabe drive our son into Pittsburgh, along with Ida and Cheryl, and they can all check into a motel there. Of course Agnes should go too.'

'Aren't you forgetting someone?'

'Of course! The Hancocks. My guests from Texas. What should I say to them, besides the fact that if they stay here, they could be brutally murdered?'

Toy squeezed my arm. 'Someone *else*, Mags.'

'No! *I* can't leave. Don't you see? I'm who Melvin wants! I'm the Melvin magnet. If I leave with my family, then he'll search until he finds us. So I'd just be putting everyone in danger. You have to trust me on that.' I started to walk faster to show that my mind was made up.

Toy jerked me to a stop. 'Don't be a fool. What do you propose to do? Remain here like the proverbial sitting duck, until a pair of magenta ducks swoop in and knock you off in the middle of the night? Because frankly, as fond of you as I am, I feel it's my duty to escort those folks back at your house to a safe place for the night.'

'You're choosing *them* over me?' Admittedly, I whined. In retrospect, I should have been slapped – gently, maybe with a dandelion – for having been jealous at a time like that.

'No. *You're* doing the choosing. And shame on you for putting me in this position, I might add.'

'Stop it, young man! Just stop it. I know Melvin Stoltzfus like the back of my liver-spotted hand; compared to me, you barely know him. But I tell you what, just to put your mind at ease, I will barricade myself in our master bath, which has no window, with a fully charged phone. Of course, I will have no weapons with me, except for the bestselling book of all time.'

'The first Harry Potter book?'

'No, silly, the Holy Bible.'

Toy sighed. 'Magdalena, you are as stubborn as a team of mules.'

'I take that as a compliment,' I said quite sincerely. 'Now let's put a move on it, because you'll want to get out of here before dark, and I need to prepare my hideout. But first I insist on feeding everyone supper, and don't be obstreperous and say you'll eat on the road instead.'

'OK, I acquiesce, but call me from your hideout the second you hear something going on outside. You promise?'

'Yes, sir, Chief Toy Graham. But you still haven't told me how to break it to the Texans.'

'Leave that to me,' Toy said. 'Come on, let's hurry.'

Although we walked back from that point at a good clip, I still had to do the evening milking, since I'd given Rebecca the day off.

Fortunately, Milchig, my dairy cow, wanted to be milked as badly as I needed to get the job done. Not wanting to take the time to pasteurize the milk, I poured it into a bucket and let Fleischig, the Angus calf, drink his full. Meanwhile Toy waited impatiently, peering out of the stall now and then, as if he expected to spot Melvin and his duck-faced accomplice at any moment.

When I was through, he practically dragged me from the barn to the kitchen steps. 'I'll help you throw together a quick supper,' he said. 'We'll make it soup and sandwiches.'

'Actually, supper is already made – I think. Susannah and Gabe's cousin Miriam drove into Bedford this morning and did the shopping for us. Miriam wants to treat us to something Australian.'

Toy opened the door for me. 'Kangaroo stew?'

'That's next week. Tonight it's to be a seafood salad.'

As the kitchen was devoid of people, Toy wasted no time in pushing open the swinging door to the dining room.

'*Voila*,' he said.

'*Voila* indeed,' I said. 'What have we here?'

Everyone was already seated at the dining-room table. In front of Gabe was an immense platter of Miriam's tantalizing Australian seafood salad. Beside him was a stack of dinner plates, one for every person at the table, except for Little Jacob, because our son was already chowing down on a small pizza.

'So what's going on?' I said. 'Why didn't you wait until I got back?'

Gabe was just about to pass the first heaped plate of salad around the table, but instead he set it down in front of himself. 'I tried texting and calling you, hon. You didn't respond to either. My calls kept going straight to voicemail. Ma was getting hungry, and frankly, so was I. We were all expecting to get something for lunch from the venders during the festival, but you know how that went.'

'Yah,' Ida said. 'Like my vurst nightmare.'

'It's Australian seafood salad,' Agnes said helpfully. 'Susannah and Miriam had it all prepared. Doesn't it look yummy?'

'We could eat it while it's still fresh, if everyone will stop yammering,' Delphia said. 'You – the chubby woman who was just talking – pass the bread down here, will you? And pizza kid – how about you pass me the salt?'

Agnes reached for the basket of freshly baked dinner rolls. Ten. But instead of passing the basket as she had been asked, Agnes set it down in front of her, and launched one of the pastries at Delphia's head, hitting the Texan woman's left temple. That certainly got Delphia's attention, but Delphia had asked for more than one, so Agnes launched a second, this one hitting Delphia's tongue, because her mouth was open in rage.

I was gobsmacked by my best friend's behaviour. Agnes is a college-educated, middle-class, God-fearing woman of a 'certain age'. Of course, I am all these things as well, and I have been known to behave in an unorthodox manner upon occasion, but this was *Agnes*. She wouldn't even pluck a grape from a cluster at the supermarket to see if they were sweet, when everyone *knows* that the grocer expects that to happen. Even *hopes* that it will happen in order to clinch the sale.

I can only guess what Delphia's response might have been had Gabe not intervened. It's possible that Little Jacob might have, following Auntie Agnes's example, lobbed the salt shaker at Delphia's head. True, it's difficult to hit a small target, but had my precious knocked out one of her veneers, or broken her nose, then she really *would* have sued us.

'Little Jacob,' his papa said sternly, 'take your pizza and go upstairs to room six. That's our temporary room for tonight. You'll have to eat it there by yourself.'

'Aw, no fair!' But already he was smirking, because Little Jacob knew he could get away with watching Gabe's TV if he kept the volume turned low enough.

'And no TV!' I said. 'You know that I can hear a toad toot a mile away.'

'How vulgar,' Delphia said.

'Please hush, sweetness,' Tiny said.

I waited until I could hear the door to room six close. I really do have exceptional hearing for someone my age. The reason for this is because I never had the opportunity to listen to loud rock and roll music. But this is not to say that I didn't want to do so. But Mama drummed it into me that Elvis with the pelvis was Satan incarnate. Therefore, I could either choose to wiggle my hips on my way down to Hell (whilst simultaneously going deaf), or remain rigid and frigid, and arrive in Heaven with my hearing so acute that I could hear an angel's feather as it brushed against a cloud.

At any rate, with my son out of earshot, it was time to 'lay it on them' as they say in the vernacular. I took a much-needed sip of water before tapping my glass.

'Friends, relatives, Romans, and visiting Texans, I regret to inform you that there will be no dinner tonight.' I leaned over

Gabe, removed the large platter of Australian seafood salad, and raced it into the kitchen.

'Very funny,' Gabe said.

I raced back, panting. 'Instead, I will be closing the inn.'

'Tell them why,' Toy said.

'Yes, why?' Agnes said. 'Is it worse than I thought?'

'Apparently so,' Toy said.

'Yes, much worse,' I said.

'What in the Billy Goat Gruff is going on?' Gabe said. (Actually, he said words that I refuse to repeat.)

I let loose a sigh that lifted yesterday's breadcrumbs off the table. 'OK, folks,' I said. 'Hang on to your chairs, because this is going to be a wild ride.'

Ida turned to Delphia. 'Dis von eez coo-coo, vhat I tell you?'

Delphia nodded in agreement. 'Like a shop full of Bavarian clocks.'

'*Quiet*, ladies!' It was the first time I had ever seen Toy lose his temper with a woman who wasn't committing a felony.

'An evil ex-police chief by the name of Melvin Stoltzfus is trying to murder me,' I said to Ida. 'He's been trying to kill me for the past five years.'

'Und did he succeed?' Ida said.

'*What?* Does it look like it? Obviously not!'

Ida shrugged. 'Nu? Den yore brooder eez not such a very goot killer.'

Both Hancocks laughed and Gabe chuckled a little. I am sorely disappointed to say that even Agnes may have smiled.

'This isn't funny, folks. Everything that went wrong today with the festival, including the rattlesnake on my car seat—'

'Whoa,' Gabe said. 'Rattlesnake? No one said anything about a rattlesnake.'

'How about Agnes's slashed tyres. Did she mention those?'

'Uh, I didn't tell them,' Agnes said.

'I agree with Magdalena,' Toy said. 'There is definitely a pattern of intimidation here that is consistent with the way a coward like Melvin Stoltzfus works. We – I mean, *I* – believe that Magdalena is his target, not any of you. But as long as you are in her company, none of you are safe. Therefore, it is necessary for all of you to evacuate these premises as soon as possible.'

'But we're paid up for three more nights,' Delphia said. 'We haven't toured any of the charming countryside.'

'You'll have to do that some other time,' Toy said. 'Tonight, I will be accompanying you to a very nice motel in Pittsburgh. Magdalena has elected to stay here in a safe location and act as bait.'

'Over my dead body,' Gabe roared.

'There will be a pile of dead bodies here soon if you folks don't skedaddle,' I said calmly. 'And no need to worry about me; I'll be just fine in our safe spot. Remember, darling, we designed it to be impenetrable.'

'Oh, *that* spot,' Gabe said. 'Is your cell phone fully charged?'

'You betcha, and the second I hear anything, even a toad tooting a warning, I'm going to call Toy, as well as Sherriff Stodgewiggle.'

'*Oy vey*,' said my Jewish husband and our Episcopalian police chief simultaneously. Sherriff Stodgewiggle was about as competent as the overstuffed armchair that he resembled, and I mean that kindly.

'How about you call Chief Toy's assistant, Officer Lucinda Cakewalker?' Gabe said. 'She'll be a lot closer than Pittsburgh.'

'Huh?' snorted Delphia. 'Isn't Lucinda a woman's name? I wouldn't even want *this* scrawny cop protecting me in a gun battle, much less a woman – unless it were a Texan like me.'

'*Was* a Texan,' Agnes said.

'That's what I said.' Delphia growled.

'You folks oughta see my little woman shoot,' Tiny said, beaming. 'Why, she can shoot a beer bottle off the head of a Yankee at three hundred yards.'

'There isn't going to be a shoot-out,' I said. 'OK?'

'Dang it,' Delphia said. 'Because I would for sure stay behind for that. I'd maybe even drop my plans to sue you for bodily injury suffered on what was supposed to be a hiking trail—'

'Ma'am,' Toy said, 'I heard about that, and I can assure you that what happened to you was the handiwork of this diabolical, escaped convict, Melvin Stoltzfus. For all we know, he's stalking the perimeters of this building right this minute.

'I advise you, Mrs Hamhocks, to throw together an overnight bag and evacuate these premises post-haste. That goes for all of you – except for the hero of the hour, our brave Magdalena Yoder. Magdalena, we will keep you in our thoughts and prayers.'

'It's *Hancock*, not *Hamhocks*, you idiot,' shouted Delphia.

'More prayers than thoughts, please,' I said. 'Thoughts never did anyone a lick of good.'

'Mags,' Agnes said, 'what do you want me to do with that platter of uneaten seafood salad?'

'Put it in the fridge, I guess,' I said.

'Who knows how long we'll really be gone,' Toy said. 'I think it's best to throw it out.'

'I agree,' Cheryl said.

'Waste not, want not,' I said.

'And risk getting someone sick?' Cheryl said.

'My sister's right,' Gabe said. 'It's best just to pitch it.' He blew me a kiss to make up for choosing sides.

'All right,' I said, 'I'll dump this fabulous-looking Australian seafood salad down the garbage disposal. You just see to it that you don't forget to take our son with you to Pittsburgh.'

'Dere von't be no problem,' Ida said, 'because I am taking da leetle von wiz me.'

'No,' I said calmly. 'Zee leetle von eez going wiz Gabe.'

'Mags, was that necessary?' my otherwise-dear husband said.

'Moving right along,' Agnes said, 'I'll help wash pots and whatever needs to be done in the kitchen, so that we can get this show on the road.'

'This is no time for tidiness,' Toy said. 'Time is of the essence. We can just put things in the sink and let them soak. Running the dishwasher now is a bad idea, because Magdalena needs to hear what's going on out in the kitchen.'

'Toy, how you do surprise me,' Agnes said softly. 'You've lived here for six years already, and you still don't understand Mennonite women. A well-raised Mennonite woman would never go to bed with a sink full of dirty pots and utensils. She'd almost rather be seen in public wearing nothing but her sturdy Christian underwear.'

Toy laughed. 'I rather doubt that.'

'My sturdy Christian underwear has never attracted cockroaches,' I said coolly.

'That does it,' said my loyal gal pal. 'We're doing the washing by hand, no matter how long it takes. Then since I'm already packed, I'm going to help Mags stock her safe place with whatever supplies she needs. In the meantime, you two Texans can mosey on down the Pennsylvania Turnpike.'

'Why, I never!' Delphia said.

Agnes waved the backs of her plump little hands at the Hancocks in a shooing motion. 'Now get along little doggies, as the cowboys say in that song. You too Cheryl and Ida. And Gabe, you and Little Jacob may as well head out with the rest. I'll be riding with the chief anyway, when we're through getting your wife squared away.'

Gabe looked at me. 'Are you sure that you really want to go through with this? I can't believe that I'm even asking, because it sounds so crazy.'

'I'm positive,' I said. 'It's the only way to draw the human praying mantis out into the open.'

TWENTY-FIVE

'A praying mantis, huh? I don't think that calling someone names is a very Christian thing to do,' Delphia said.

Agnes, who was already standing by then, marched around the table and leaned her impressive bulk into Delphia's space. 'And I don't think that what I want to do to you is very Christian either. So I'm warning you nicely: please don't say another mean word to my friend, Magdalena Yoder. If you do, you'll be sorry.'

Delphia's already wee face puckered even smaller until it resembled a rotten turnip. But to her credit, she didn't say anything. Although she could have behaved a mite better otherwise. Purposefully overturning her chair upon leaving the table was a mite rude, if you ask me.

However, after she left, her husband Tiny made a quiet apology before chasing after his rude wife. Then my husband and my two Rosen in-laws left to attend to their tasks at hand. That left just Agnes, Toy and me.

'Mags,' Agnes said, 'I love you like the sister I never had, but you're an utter fool to stay here by yourself. You know that, don't you?'

'Agnes, my dear, dear sister. While you were growing up in that more liberal branch of the Mennonite Church, weren't you forced to memorize Bible verses as a child?'

'Not really,' Agnes said, for she always tells the truth. 'I mean, we were encouraged to, but not *forced*. Were you actually forced, or are you exaggerating as usual?'

'Let's not quibble over vocabulary at a time like this,' I said. 'The point I'm trying to make is that if you'd memorized your scripture verses, then you'd know that in Matthew 5:22, Jesus said that anyone who calls another person a "fool" is in danger of Hell fire.'

'Then I take it back,' Agnes said. 'So there! Come on, Toy, we have dishes to wash.'

'Thanks, dear,' I said, and immediately set about transforming the master bathroom into a fortress. But not an armed fortress, mind you, just a place where I could hole-up safely, and comfortably, until Toy returned.

The first rule of any siege (beyond denying the enemy entry) is securing a water supply. So I began by filling up my sinfully large bathtub. The purpose of this water was only for drinking and flushing the commode, in the event that Melvin shut off my supply from outside. I bother to mention it because this tub, which I have named Big Bertha, has thirty-two sin-inducing whirlpool jets. At any rate, while the tub was filling I dragged in Little Jacob's mattress from his youth bed. Then I hit the pantry for food supplies. *Hard.*

Any rural woman worth her salt has a fully stocked larder, including salt and lard. I took both. The former was to season my food, whereas the second was part of my escape plan, if it came to that. (A greasy body can navigate tight spots better than a dry one can.) But in the main, I took tinned goods: tuna, peaches, pears, peas, tomatoes and even a lonely tin of sardines in yellow mustard sauce that had gone unnoticed for several years. Perhaps the most important items I brought back were the three large jars of extra-crunchy peanut butter, and to go with them, a carton of cheese-flavoured crackers.

At the last minute I remembered a manually operated can opener, a Swiss Army knife, my husband's medical bag, and most importantly, my King James version of the Holy Bible. I am quite sure that it is this version that Jesus Himself read when he was growing up in Nazareth, so it is of great comfort to me. You can bet your bippy that as I worked, I kept my keen hearing attuned to the low mutterings of my buddies at the sink. No amount of purposeful pot-clanking, and blasting of water, prevented me from hearing what was being said. So much for them keeping an ear open for Melvin, but at least so far, there was safety in numbers.

'I don't care,' Agnes was saying, 'she really is being foolish. Just plain reckless. She's not being fair to the people who love her.'

'Magdalena is exceptionally resourceful,' Toy said. 'She's one of the most capable women I know.'

'She's pig-headed,' Agnes said.

'In another time and place, I could see her working for the CIA or maybe the FBI,' Toy said.

'Maybe in this time and in this place, you should come back down to earth,' Agnes said coldly.

'Is that so?' Toy said. 'But hey, do you think that she really wants us to throw out this delicious smelling salad? There's no telling how long we'll be gone, and I'm pretty sure it will freeze OK. What do you think?'

I could hear Agnes banging about in the cupboards for a Tupperware container. 'Here,' she snapped. 'Pour it into this and shove it in the freezer anyway. Magdalena can pinch a penny so tight it will beg for mercy.'

'I'm still alive!' I called out. 'I can hear every one of your flattering words. Murdering Maniacal Melvin has yet to get me.'

'I was provoked,' Agnes said.

It was an excuse that I understood all too well. Although I believe that I am longsuffering, and do not easily lose my temper, neither do I hesitate to speak my mind. Some people, like Barbara Peters in particular, think that this character trait makes me sharp-tongued and mean-spirited, but I maintain that it does not, because I never say things with the intention of hurting someone.

At any rate, I most certainly did not hold Agnes's final

comments against her. On the other hand, I eschew sentimentality. When it was time for me to bid them *adieu*, I gave my friends Mennonite hugs (three slaps on the back) and told them I'd be praying for them. Then I gave them each a gentle shove out the bathroom door, starting with Agnes. I was afraid that if she dawdled for a fourth slap I would burst into tears, and she might get a Baptist hug, which would embarrass us both.

Toy stopped just outside the door. 'Magdalena,' he said, 'as you know, I'm not all that religious, but I do remember from Sunday school that Jesus ascended into Heaven from what today is the State of Israel. So should it really come to that, then—'

'Come to what, dear?' I said.

Toy's face clouded. 'You know what I mean. *It.*'

'Sex?'

'No! *Death*,' he whispered.

'Oh, go on,' I said.

'Well, we were talking before about where Heaven might be located. Now I'm the last person to venture an opinion since I'm not religious, but I just remembered hearing my Sunday school teacher say that Jesus ascended straight above what is now the modern State of Israel. So, like I said, if it should *come to that*, then head southeast, because that's where Israel is. But you have to cross the Atlantic Ocean and the Mediterranean Sea first before you get there. Just saying it's really far. But once you get there, I should think that you're pretty safe heading straight up. Anyway, just a thought from a backsliding Episcopalian.'

I couldn't resist and gave him two more back slaps for all the useful information. Although he could have been more helpful and given me latitude and longitude coordinateness. But as soon as their backs were turned, I shut the bathroom door and set about Operation Fortress.

Gabe and I remodelled the master bathroom immediately following our last run-in with the diabolical Melvin Stoltzfus. In essence we designed the bathroom to be an impenetrable safe room. It has solid concrete walls that are eighteen inches thick and a steel door. The ceiling is also concrete, reinforced with enough rebar so that it can host a hip-hop competition for elephants. There aren't any windows, but numerous camera feeds deliver views of the outside world, taken from various vantage points, both along the perimeter of the house, and also from inside. Although the room is soundproof, it is connected to each room in the house via an elaborate intercom system.

Three massive deadbolts on the inside keep the door securely locked. A special filtration system keeps the incoming air pure, and the vents are small enough so that neither Melvin, nor one of his enamoured minions, could possibly crawl through them – even after a year of continuous fasting. And yes, there is an escape hatch, should we ever find ourselves in the position to need one. Of course, I would never divulge that hatches' location, because doing so would make me even more stupid than I look. And yes, it is designed so that one can only crawl *out* of the safe room – not *in*. To that point, Gabe is even smarter than I give him credit for. It was in case I needed to use the escape hatch that I brought the lard.

After I was all squared away, I prayed. First I prayed for the safety of my loved ones, then for my own safety, and then I prayed that if the Good Lord willed it, Alison was still hanging in there and resisting the temptations of the flesh. Because once the walls of *that* fortress had been breached, there was absolutely no going back to the way things once were. No putting the stopper back in that bottle, so to speak.

As I sat there in my bunker, munching on a peanut butter-covered cracker, and musing about my daughter's sex life, I heard Susannah's voice coming through the kitchen intercom.

'They clearly liked your Australian salad! There's no sign of it anywhere. The pot's been washed, and the dishes have all been washed and dried and put away.'

'Susannah!' I yelled into the intercom. 'You're back early.'

Thanks to a hidden camera, I watched my sister literally jump out of one of her slides. She had to steady herself by grabbing the fridge door handle. I couldn't see Miriam from that angle of the video feed, but her exclamation of surprises was only slightly less vulgar than my sister's.

'Mags,' Susannah eventually got around to saying, 'where *are* you?'

'I'm in Heaven, dear,' I said. I was joking, so technically that wasn't a lie. Even if it was a lie, Susannah deserved it after all she's put me through over the years.

'*Really?*'

'Yeah, sorry sis that I couldn't hang around to say goodbye, but like they say, you never know when your number's up.'

Then Miriam's wheelchair rolled into view and the two women conferred for a moment. 'What's it like?' Susannah said. 'Do you see Mama and Papa?'

'I've seen Papa flapping about hither, thither and sometimes yon, but so far Mama's been at choir practice. We're all supposed to meet up later at Cloud Number Nine. By the way, I asked St Peter to check the master enrolment list for future members, and your name is still not on there.'

'*What?* Just because I'm a Presbyterian?'

'No, that has nothing to do with it. It's because—' Unfortunately my body betrayed me, and I was overtaken by what was perhaps the longest, and loudest, fit of sneezing that I had ever experienced. Perhaps one of the items that I'd brought in from the pantry had a wee coating of dust and I happen to be quite allergic to dust mite droppings. I'm guessing that the item in question was the tin of sardines in yellow mustard sauce.

'Aha!' Susannah shouted, looking all around her. 'People don't sneeze in Heaven. Even *I* know that. Nobody gets sick there.'

'Maybe this is Heaven-Lite.'

'Ha, ha,' Susannah said. 'Very funny, Mags, except that it's not. You're the last person I know who'd make a religious joke. Clearly you're not yourself. What's up with you, and where are you?'

'You're right, Susannah; I'm not fine. I'm hiding. And guess who I'm hiding from?'

'Gabe?' Susannah clenched her fists and began punching the air. 'So help me, Mags, if that New Yorker touched even one of your mousey brown hairs, I'll punch his lights out.'

'Calm down. It's not Gabe; it's the love of your life, Melvin Stoltzfus – or as you like to call him, Mely-kins.'

Susannah froze like a statue in our childhood game by that very same name. It took a second for her lips to thaw enough to enable speech.

'You're crazy!'

'That's beside the point. Come in here where it's safe, and I'll tell you what's been going on while you and Miriam have been playing. By the way, where is she? I can't see her?'

'You can *see* me?'

'Of course, dear. Didn't I always tell you when you were growing up that I had eyes in the back of my head?'

'That isn't funny. Where *are* you?'

'Go get Miriam, then I'll tell you.'

'She won't come.'

'What do you mean she won't come?'

'Well, she won't come right now. She's out in the backyard keeping watch for the stars. The last few evenings were either rainy or cloudy, but tonight it's clear, so she's determined to see what the sky looks like in the northern hemisphere. Mags, I thought we were in the western hemisphere.'

'That too, dear. OK, Susannah, so then you come alone, and we'll make this quick, so that you can get back out there. I'm in the master bathroom.'

'No way!'

'Yes, way. Now hurry.'

Susannah and the concept of speed have never met. I can honestly say that she is the laziest woman whom I have ever known, and that includes Tammy Schnell. Even as a tender-footed child, Susannah would stroll along a hot paved surface, with no more sense of urgency than a three-toed sloth going about its day. The fastest I ever saw her move was when she was a teen, and a car full of hormonal boys slowed down in front of our house and honked when they saw her standing in our drive. On that occasion, my sister took three consecutive steps towards the road without pausing to rest.

While I waited for Susannah, I prayed for Miriam's safety. I also ate the sardines in yellow mustard sauce. Then, because a watched pot never boils – in this case it was my sister – I took my mind off her pokiness by trimming my toenails with the Swiss army knife. I realize that in the telling of my story, some people might find me given to hyperbole; nonetheless, I wish to state the following: upon entering my little hideout, my toenails had been a perfectly acceptable length.

At last I heard her try to turn the doorknob. When that didn't work she pounded on it with her fists.

'Open up! Open up, for heaven sakes! I'm your baby sister, I'm not a terrorist.'

'Stand back,' I said, as I slid back the three massive bolts. Because the door is meant to keep us safe from invaders, it opens *out*, not in.

If I'd taken a video of Susannah's face when she saw the contents of my bathroom, I'm sure it would go viral. But when she stopped staring, she started laughing, and that was a reaction that I found far less amusing.

'You're a hoot, Mags. And a holler.'

'Now step aside so I can close the door.'

'Like I said before, you're nuts, Mags. You're certifiably crazy. You're wackadoodle dandy.'

'Am I?' I said. 'Consider the facts, toots. Your so-called Sweetie Pot Pie has sworn to kill me and has made three considerable attempts to do so. Everything horrible that has happened here in Hernia during the Billy Goat Gruff Festival, and leading up to it, have been directed specifically at making me look foolish or incompetent.'

Susannah plopped her patooty on a pile of pillows and almost fell backwards. 'Mags, you're paranoid. You're imagining things.'

'Did I imagine the rattlesnake curled up on the seat of my car? Or the sewage dumped into Main Street just as I was announcing the winner of the festival? Or Billy breaking free and running across the bridge without the wagon?'

'Oh stop,' Susannah said. 'You can't tie those things to my Mely-kins. The next thing you're going to blame him for is everyone getting sick from eating the Australian seafood salad that Miriam and I made.'

'*What?*'

'Nothing,' Susannah said.

'Don't say "nothing", Susannah. What did you mean about everyone getting sick?'

'Uh, no reason. It's just that that's the kind of thing you're likely to say, that's all.'

'Oh, really?'

'Yes, really,' she said, then started chewing her bottom lip. Ever since she was two years old, my sister has ratted out her own lies by her habit of self-mastication. It's a wonder that she can still whistle.

'Fess up, missy,' I hissed, 'or I'm calling your parole officer, and I'm telling them that you're a cannibal.'

Susannah laughed. 'I'm a *what*?'

'When you chew on your lip like that you invariably ingest some of your own cells, which are human, and that makes you a cannibal. So there!'

Susannah laughed so hard that she finally fell backwards and lay there kicking her legs in the air like a small child throwing a tantrum. I'd best try another angle.

'OK, then. I'll tell your parole officer that you spent the day with a woman who habitually drives on the wrong side of the highway.'

TWENTY-SIX

'All right, I'll tell you everything. It's this: Miriam Blumfield does not wash her hands after using the ladies' room. She peeled and deveined the shrimp with unwashed hands, and after baking the dinner rolls, she placed the finished rolls in their basket with unwashed hands. That's why I thought you might be sick. And it's not like she ran out of time for either of those tasks. She is just plain lazy. Mags, you always thought that I was lazy, but I'm telling you, the last few days with Miriam has been like watching that funny, hanging upside-down animal, that I've seen on *Animal Planet*, move through the trees. The cloth monkey, I think it is.'

'The *sloth*, dear.'

'Nah, Mags, it ain't a deer; it's some kinda monkey. It like, barely moves. That's how Miriam is.'

'Gotcha. Now run along, Susannah, and tell Miriam that she has exactly two minutes to get her behind in here, or else face the consequences.'

'Yeah, yeah, don't get your knickers in a knot. "Knickers" is what Miriam calls "panties", but I sure as heck don't know what

she'd call that getup that you wear. Maybe "battle armour".'
Susannah howled while I scowled.

'Can it, dear,' I said sternly. Although I must admit that I had
missed my sister's antics during her years in prison, if only in
the sense that one might miss having a case of influenza, because
it feels so good when the symptoms ease.

'Hey, sis,' Susannah said, 'before you push me out, I gotta
tell you about the two giant ducks that Miriam and I saw coming
out of the pond. The pond in our pasture.'

'You saw those ducks *too*?'

'Wait a minute,' Susannah said with a snort. 'Don't tell me
that *you* saw them! Does this mean that my big sister, Miss-
Holier-Than-Thou, Magdalena Portulacca Yoder Rosen, was
drinking on the sly?'

'Bite your tongue! I barely use mouthwash. I haven't seen
those characters, but others have. Were they actually coming *out*
of the pond?'

'Nah,' she said, 'but it looked like it at first, because they were
on the far side, behind a clump of cattails. Then they started
walking around the pond, and we thought they might be headed
towards the house, so we ran inside. But when we checked later,
we didn't see them again.'

'I see,' I said, although I didn't. 'Earlier you said that they
were giant ducks, but now you make it sound like they were
really people. Which is it?'

'Well, people, of course,' Susannah said. 'Duh, we were maybe
slightly tipsy, but we're not stupid, just because we both have
records. They were people in magenta jumpsuits, wearing cartoon
duck masks. Donald and Daisy Duck.'

'And you could identify the masks all the way across the cow
pasture?' I said.

'Give me a break,' Susannah said. 'I'm not old like you; you
probably have cataracts by now.'

'Did you call the police?' I said.

Her howls of derision were strangely comforting. At least I
had a sister, and she was out of prison, and could now deride
me in person, instead of through a thick plate of safety glass. I
waited, my heart full gratitude, until she at last ran out of steam.

'What would I tell the police?' she finally asked. 'That there were two idiots in costumes prancing about in our cow pasture? They weren't harming anyone. Sheesh, you really need to lighten up, Mags, you know that? Maybe you should go to prison. That would teach you the difference between the small irritations in life and the big ones. The small stuff, you gotta let go, or it will eat you alive.'

I rolled my eyes. I rolled them up, right, left, down and all around again. That was payback for all the times that Susannah had rolled her eyes at me when I was raising her. (I was twenty when our parents were killed, and she was eleven.)

Susannah was not amused. 'What is that all about?'

'Doesn't it look familiar?' I asked.

'It does not, and that's so juvenile! If you're not careful, your eyes are going to get stuck in the upward position.'

I rolled them up as far as I could.

'Stop it right now!' she yelled. 'You're just trying to get me mad, and it's not going to work.'

'OK, dear,' I said soothingly. 'Take it down a notch.'

'Don't talk to me like that,' she snapped. 'I'm not upset. I'm just highly irritated.'

'Understood,' I said.

'And just to prove that I'm not upset, I'm going to share with you what Miriam overheard that big Texan say to that little Texan out by the barn last night.'

'I'm all ears, dear,' I said.

'He said that they sure were lucky to find that house in Hernia to rent starting a week before the festival, and how it allowed them the time to do everything that they needed to do.'

'What? Are you sure you heard that right?'

'OK, that does it. I'm out of here. You're calling me a liar, and I'm not going to stand for it.'

'Wait! I'm sorry. That didn't come out right. It just doesn't make any sense, because if they have a rented house, then why are they staying here?'

Susannah shrugged. 'Maybe you should ask them.'

'Touché,' I said. 'If you don't mind me saying so, dear, it seems like you and Miriam have really hit it off.'

Susannah grinned. 'Yeah, she's cool.'

I decided to push my luck. 'Where did you take her this afternoon, after you guys were done making that salad?'

'Pittsburgh,' Susannah said nonchalantly.

'Oh?'

'Yeah,' Susannah said. 'Miriam wanted to see what American gay and lesbian bars were like, to compare them with the ones back in Australia. But it was too early to go bar-hopping, and so when we got as far as Monroeville, we stopped in at an Applebee's for supper, and then turned around and drove straight back here. She was anxious to hear what you guys thought about her Aussie seafood salad.'

'Is Miriam a lesbian?' To my credit, I asked the question very casually, like I might have asked: 'Would you care for another helping of green beans?'

'Isn't that wonderful?' Susannah said, as she carefully studied my face for a negative reaction. 'You know, about her being a lesbian. I think it's awesome, don't you?'

'I'm chuffed pink,' I said.

'Huh?'

'I'm plum tickled,' I replied.

'Whatever,' Susannah said, having failed to get a rise out of me. 'Hey Mags, Miriam wants to know if she should come out to her family. What do you think? Should she tell Ida and Gabe that she's a lesbian?'

I wagged a long, knobby finger as if it were a metronome. 'It's none of their business, and I can just hear Ida now, and she's saying something very judgmental.'

Susannah snapped equally long fingers. 'You're right. Besides, Miriam—'

'*Susannah! Susannah! Susannah!*' It was Miriam.

'That's bizarre,' Susannah said. 'The second I mentioned her name, she starts calling me. Do you think that she heard me?'

'I doubt it,' I said. 'But go ahead and respond; tell her where you are. She needs to get in here where it's safe.'

'Mags, I told you that Melvin is not—'

'Forget Melvin for a second. What about the Texan duo? Someone is after me – someone *muy loco*.'

'Mags, you know I don't speak Amish.'

'That was Spanish for "very crazy".'

'Anyway, after Miriam is safely seated on this child-size mattress on the floor, or reclining against her own pile of pillows, then we can theorize some more on what to do. So go ahead, tell her where we are.'

Had I not been so stressed, I might have laughed at poor Miriam's reaction when she heard Susannah's voice as it came seemingly out of nowhere, and then directed her to the master bathroom. Thank heavens Miriam was in her battery-powered wheelchair, and not using her unwieldy crutches. I was waiting at the door, and the second after she zipped in, I slammed that metal door behind her, and bolted it. But when I turned to tell her what was going on, she beat me to the draw.

'Come on, guys,' Miriam said breathlessly. 'Let's hustle. They're getting away!'

'Who?' I said.

'The Texans! Tiny and Delphia. Miss Yoder, Delphia took their rental car, but Tiny drove off in your car.'

'You mean he *stole* it?'

'That's correct,' Miriam said.

'Did you call the police?' I said hysterically, as was my wont.

'Yes ma'am. That good-looking policeman said he'd be right on it, and since he already knew your license plate number, you were supposed to just sit tight.'

'Then why did you tell us to hustle?' I said.

'I meant that Susannah and *I* should hustle,' Miriam said. 'Because before they took off, I heard Tiny on the phone talking to someone in a low voice, but not so quiet that I couldn't over-hear him, of course. Do you want to know what he said?'

'There will always be an England!' I screamed.

'No ma'am, that's not what he said.'

'I meant why would you even have to ask? Of course I want to know, you – you – fellow child of God.'

'Right,' Miriam said, 'although I am an atheist by the way. At any rate, on the phone Tiny was telling someone that he needed the materials to be delivered to the house tonight, and that the address for that house was 2032 Sweetbriar Lane. He said that only when the Mennonite witch and her inn lit up like a million firecrackers, only then would he feel like he'd gotten the venge-ance that he came for.'

I sank back down on the mattress. 'Was he speaking about me?'

'There'll always be a United States of America,' Miriam said.

'That's not a song lyric, dear,' I said, 'but I pray that you're right.'

'Mags,' Susannah said, 'what did you do that was so horrible to those poor people that makes them want to blow you to smithereens?'

'How should I know?' I cried. 'I've had hundreds of guests, and the worst thing that I've ever done was be brutally honest – you know, give someone a piece of my mind.'

'That means there are hundreds of people mad enough to kill you,' Susannah said. She wasn't joking.

'Thanks, sis,' I said. 'I get that you and Barbara Peters think I'm a terrible woman because I speak my mind. But do you believe that I should die on account of it? Or how about your little nephew?'

'Oh, come on, Mags,' Susannah said, giving me a sisterly push on the shoulder, 'don't be such a drama queen. Nobody said that you should die; I just said that you have a big mouth, and not everyone loves you for it. Tell you what, ignore what Toy said – he can handle your stolen car from his end, he's competent – and you come along with us to check out this place where Tiny and Delphia are expecting their delivery. That's probably where they're headed right now.'

'Yeah, come with us, mate,' Miriam said. 'Three is always better than one. What do the French call it? *Fromage au trois* – yes, that's it.'

'*Fromage* means cheese, dear,' I said. 'But OK, I'll go. Just let me write a note first.'

'What will you write?' Susannah said. 'That you can't be bothered to listen to a male authority figure? Or that you're intelligent enough to chase down your own clues?'

'Let's just skedaddle,' I said, and hopped to my feet with the nimbleness of a sedated moose. Trust me, it isn't easy jumping up from a mattress on the floor when one is as vertically enhanced as I am.

Outside night had fallen hard, and the darkness felt thick, as if it had a dimension to it. Normally, the parking area between the house and barn would have been brightly illuminated by a security light, but it must have burned out the night before. My feet were familiar with steps leading down from the kitchen, but how on earth the other two managed it was beyond me. I was especially worried about Miriam, who'd abandoned her wheelchair at the door, instead of taking the ramp meant for just such conveyances. Instead, after tucking her red lap robe around her like a long skirt, she hopped out the door like a one-legged robin.

'Get in the back,' she said to me. 'Susannah you're riding shotgun.'

'Do you need directions?' I asked.

Miriam didn't answer, which was just as well. Although I knew where Sweetbriar Road was, I had never heard of Sweetbriar Lane. The former was a two-lane, rural road that saw very little traffic except for farmers. If an area farmer had rented his house to folks from out of state, I would know. *Believe* me. Cousin Sam, who owns Yoder's Corner Market, is privy to all the gossip in the county, and outsiders are the number-one topic.

I thought that Miriam would program the address into her car's GPS system, but she didn't. As soon as I set my patooty on the back seat of her car, and had closed the door, off we went. I didn't even have time to buckle my seat belt. I was about to tell the poor foreign girl to turn right out of my driveway, when she made a reckless left turn. Then she stomped on the accelerator as if it was the head of the world's most poisonous snake and it was fixing to bite her. The speed limit along that stretch of Hertzler Road is forty-five mph, but Miriam was soon well above ninety. Maybe even over 100 mph. My thoughts had trouble keeping up with me at that speed.

I was flattened against the rear seat with so much force that my heart was squeezed out of my chest and into my throat. Fortunately, because my heart is so hard, and so small, I was in no danger of choking. But you can bet your bippy that I was terrified.

Quite possibly my sister, the ex-con, had given this woman drugs. Ever since her late teen years, Susannah had always dabbled in forbidden stimulants of one sort or another, as well as alcohol. I'm not saying that these things are the reason that she married her first husband, the Presbyterian, but drugs are definitely responsible for her poor judgment in falling for Melvin Stoltzfus. I suspect that her stint in the hoosegow did not help her go straight either. From what I've read, determined inmates can often find a way to get drugs into prison, as long as they are able to pay for them. The one thing that I do know about my sister is that as lazy as she is, if it's something that she is desperate to have, she will find a way to get it.

But if it wasn't drugs that had Miriam's foot practically pushing through the floorboards, then perhaps maybe it was the force of habit. Could it be that Australians always ignored the rules of the road? I base this theory on an advertisement that I saw on television for a popular Australian-styled steakhouse here in America. Its slogan was 'no rules, mate'.

Or could Miriam's bizarre behaviour have anything to do with the fact that she was an atheist? Didn't that open her up to demon possession? I'm just saying that a demon would love nothing better than to terrorize a nice, middle-aged, Conservative Mennonite woman like me. Then again, after the testimony of the other two women in the car, maybe I wasn't *such* a nice woman, what with my big mouth, and committing one of the worst sins a woman can commit, and that is to be sarcastic. After all, a sarcastic man is thought to be 'clever', while a sarcastic woman is labelled 'snarky'.

Of course, none of my aforementioned theories really mattered if the end result was a fatal accident. I was assured of my salvation and so I wasn't afraid of dying. Now that I knew the approximate coordinates for Heaven: southeast to Jerusalem for a very long way, and then up for a much, much longer way. However, I didn't want to head off for the Pearly Gates until I'd had a chance to see my darling daughter Alison again. And I had to smell the sweaty head of my little boy once more before I gave him his bath. Also, surely the Good Lord wouldn't begrudge me the mattress mambo one last time. Although, perhaps He would, having never danced it Himself – oh, how *could* such a sacrilegious thought enter my head at this moment? Another wicked thought like this, and I might have time to repent before becoming yet another highway statistic.

'Slow down!' I screamed. 'Slow down. I'm begging you.'

'Take it easy, sis,' Susannah shouted.

I will say this for Miriam. She had the reflexes of a cat in its prime, and the night vision of an owl. She was a foreigner, totally unfamiliar with our backroads and narrow country lanes, yet she managed to make a dozen right angle turns at harrowing speeds. We have more of these roads than I have spider veins on my thick, Yoder ankles, and after the fifth abrupt turn, I was completely lost. Periodically Miriam leaned into the horn just before a streak of light zoomed past. This I took to be another vehicle. Finally the stress became too much for me and I closed my eyes and resorted to prayer and reciting verses from the Book of Psalms in order to soothe myself.

Eventually I must have fallen asleep. Extreme stress can do that, you know – make a body sleepy. If perchance one does not agree with my observation, then I submit that said argumentative individual has never been subjected to the magnitude of stress that I have just described.

That said, it is my guess that at least two hours had passed when I was suddenly awakened by the car lurching to a stop. The moon had risen by then, and its light illuminated a small, dilapidated cabin. To put it kindly, it was a ramshackle shack. The structure appeared to be surrounded by dense forest, save for the small, weed-filled clearing in which we'd parked. A lit, low-wattage lightbulb hung suspended above the front door, which was inexplicably open. The interior of the cabin was dark, giving it an abandoned appearance.

'Looks like the bears have been back,' Miriam said, as she tapped a staccato rhythm on the steering wheel. 'Susannah, did you remember to put the cheese and salami back into the fridge before we left?'

'Maybe,' Susannah said. 'I mean, I think that I did.'

'I guess we'll find out soon enough,' Miriam said.

Then with a laboured grunt Susannah threw open her car door. When the overhead light came on, my first feeling was one of embarrassment. I had drooled on myself considerably and might even have had had a slight accident. But that feeling was fleeting, because I was startled into a new reality by Miriam turning to bark at me in a register two octaves lower than her normal voice, and in an American accent.

'Get out of the car! Now! Move it!'

Wasn't pinching oneself the way to tell if one was dreaming, or not? So I pinched. Hard. Then *really* hard.

'Ow!'

'You better get out, sis,' Susannah said quietly, 'if you don't want any trouble.'

I pinched three other locations. 'Ouch! Ouch! Ow-wa-wa-wa! I want my mommy!'

That's when Miriam reached into the back of the car, undid my seat belt, grabbed me by my coiled braids beneath my organza prayer cap and dragged me rudely, and painfully, from the car. And that's when I truly did want my mommy who, by the way, had not been all that cuddly, if I am to be honest. Clearly this was no longer a dream, but a case of two women under the influence of drugs.

'Dear,' I told myself, in the faintest of whispers, 'it behooves you to play along, because they are not themselves at the moment. Their minds have been hijacked by the chemicals that have entered their bloodstreams. Likewise, you must forgive them, as the Lord forgave those who crucified Him on account that they did not know what they were doing.'

'What is she mumbling?' Miriam hollered.

'I'm sure she's praying,' Susannah said. 'The poor deluded thing is always praying. As if that will do her any good.'

What that did was hike my hackles up into my armpits. I forgot about the pain, my drug-crazed kidnappers, and that I was being dragged by my braids, by a baritone-voiced Miriam.

I slapped my abductor's hands away while I struggled to my feet. When she attempted to grab me again, I shoved her hard. Yes, I know, slapping and shoving are both forms of violence, and I am a pacifist, but it sounded to me as if my sister was in danger of burning in Hell for all eternity.

'Susannah Priscilla Yoder Entwhistle Stoltzfus! Shame on you! If Mama and Papa could hear you say that praying doesn't do any good, they'd turn over in their graves with the regularity of a cement mixer. Has this foreign woman seduced you into becoming an atheist and abandoning the faith of our fathers that is living still, in spite of dungeons, fires and swords?'

'Oh, Mags,' Susannah moaned, 'you are such a dweeb. If you don't cooperate, you're going to be sorry. That's all I'm going to say.'

I gasped in horror. 'You *have* become an atheist, haven't you?

Don't you realize just how illogical that position is? If God was standing right here, then I could prove that He existed, but there are supposedly billions of galaxies out there, and God could be out visiting any one of them, on any given day that you searched. So you see, you could never prove that God *doesn't* exist; you can only prove that He does.'

'Ha,' Susannah said, 'you don't even believe that there is more than this galaxy, because if there were, your precious Heaven would be so far away, that angels would lose all their feathers commuting between here and there.'

'That's blasphemy,' I said, as tears of rage filled my eyes.

'That was clever,' Miriam said.

'Stuff it, dear,' I said to the not-so-dear Aussie. I didn't care anymore if she was Gabe's cousin. She now was about as welcome as a bad case of dandruff on a black Sunday dress.

Apparently Miriam didn't care about playing nice either, because she hauled off and backhanded me across the face. I lost my balance and crashed into Susannah, who then swore using words that I'm sure made Satan himself blush, if indeed even Satan knew their meanings, which I rather doubt.

Then, when I had regained my balance, I felt the barrel of a pistol pressed against my ribs. 'No more shenanigans, Yoder,' Miriam growled.

I looked wildly about into the night. All I could see were Miriam's car, the creepy little house, the two drug-crazed women, and trees and more trees. 'Think, dear,' I said aloud. 'Think.'

'She's mumbling again, sweet'ums,' Miriam said. 'Clearly she's delirious. I think we should put her out of her misery.'

TWENTY-SEVEN

'**B**ut Snickerdoodle, she's just stressed, that's all. Let me have a few minutes alone with her, and I'm sure that we can come up with a whole new understanding of the way things are.'

'Balaam's ass,' I cried triumphantly.

'Who said ass?' Susannah demanded.

'Me!' I said. 'I figured it out. If the Lord could make Balaam's ass bless the Children of Israel, instead of cursing them, then maybe the Devil can make Miriam sound like my nemesis, the evil, lily-livered, walleyed, pencil-necked, peanut-brained, totally incompetent Melvin Ichabod Stoltzfus.'

'Oh, oh,' Susannah said.

Miriam didn't say anything, but her gun sure did. It pushed me up three concrete steps, across a sagging wooden porch, and into the maw of the dark house. Susannah flipped a switch and a second low-wattage bulb illuminated what was the cabin's primary room. A stained pink and lime green sofa, and two matching easy chairs filled half of that space. What were the odds that both chairs would be stained as well, I wondered, and that both would have rips in their seat cushions with stuffing bulging out in corresponding locations? The floor was bare scuffed pinewood, where it was visible – that is to say, where it wasn't covered with dirty dishes, empty beer bottle, cartons of full beer bottles, crumpled newspapers, supermarket tabloids, discarded clothes, and a long, low cabinet upon which rested the largest TV screen I had ever seen in my life. Not that I have seen that many, mind you.

'Is this mess the work of bears?' I said.

'Put a sock in it,' Miriam said.

'Hopefully just the one sock, because it would be hard to find the sock's mate in this pigsty,' I said.

The barrel of Miriam's gun shifted from my side to the middle of my back. 'Sit,' she grunted, giving me a push with her weapon.

'Ow. That hurt, dear.'

'Stop calling me "dear",' she snarled.

Then, like a bolt out of the blue, it hit me. I knew the reason why Miriam was acting so strangely, why she was so mean and cranky. She was, after all, approximately my age. She and Gabe were first cousins who had been through college together, and Gabe is only a year older than I am. Miriam Blumfield, age fifty-five or thereabouts, was suffering from hot flashes. Trust me, I know from personal experience just how miserable they can make one feel.

I turned and grabbed her shoulders, having forgotten all about the gun. 'You are not alone, dear,' I said. 'We menopausal women share a common bond of silent suffering. And though we remain mute on the subject, our brows glisten with perspiration, and our underarms release torrents of sweat. Indeed, our entire bodies come alive with thousands of moisture-producing glands in places where they are *not* appreciated, and where they *are* wanted, our moisture-producing glands shrivel and die like seedlings planted in the sands of the Gobi Desert.

'Boy, I tell you – as if *you* don't know already – that when these things hit, they're enough to make even a saint get crabby and lash out. But if I might offer one suggestion, dear, lose the lap robe that you wear as a skirt. Firstly, it's quite unbecoming, and second, we already know that you have a prosthetic leg, so you're not fooling anyone. Why not show off your prosthetic leg? You're not Mennonite; you're allowed to be proud.'

Miriam responded to my wise words by pushing me into the nearest mutilated armchair. 'Susannah,' she said, 'do you have any idea what your whack-a-doodle sister is saying?'

Susannah giggled nervously. 'Um – I think she's saying that you're crabby because you're having hot flashes. Am I right, sis?'

'Duh,' I said, using a word that I had learned from Susannah herself when she was a teen.

Miriam approached my chair and stared at me with her one good eye. The eye patch with the electric blue iris painted on it was slightly askew, and I had a sickening feeling that I saw the glint of another blue iris behind it. Or was my mind playing tricks on me?

'And you think that's what's making me crabby, as you put it?' she said.

'Without a doubt, dear. Sometimes it makes even mild-mannered me feel out of sorts,' I said. 'Or worse.'

'Well, that's not the case here,' Miriam said, waving her gun. 'Do you want to know why?'

'If you want me to know,' I said.

'OK then, here goes,' Miriam said, and proceeded to hoot like the gibbons at the Pittsburgh Zoo.

'Hang on to your seat, Mags,' Susannah advised.

A nanosecond later Miriam dropped the lap robe. Beneath it she'd been wearing a miniskirt. Below this sinfully short garment were the *two* ugliest legs that I have ever seen on a woman. That's right: there were indeed *two* of them. Not only did she have two legs, but they were as skinny as the handles on croquet mallets, and her knees were as knobby as the heads on the ends of the mallets. What's more, the knobby-kneed legs were covered with black hair so dense that, had she been standing at the rear end of my Angus calf, I might have jumped to the conclusion that he had sprouted two extra, very long, knobby tails overnight.

'My word,' I said. 'Is that the fashion now in Australia, or do you have a French lover? In any case, it's a very practical look, I'll grant you that. Since your part of Australia is tropical and swarming with insects, no doubt those bristly underpinnings of yours function as a protective screen. Still, I should imagine that those woolly wonders have to be cleaned daily with a stiff brush and a strong disinfectant.

'Believe it or not, this is your lucky day,' I said helpfully. 'See how my cute little organza prayer cap is made out of white netting. Well, I propose that I sew a prototype of organza net leg-coverings for hirsute – that means hairy, dear – Aussies, such as yourself. Then the two of us go into business, mass producing my inventions. We'll make a killing, I promise you.'

'Enough!' bellowed Miriam. Then she unwrapped her ubiquitous scarf from around her neck. Bless the poor woman's heart, as they are wont to say in the South! That gal's head teetered on a neck that I was sure didn't have the circumference to support it.

'Get duct tape!' I shouted to Susannah. 'Quick! Duct tape fixes everything.'

'Shh,' she hissed.

'Shut up, Yoder,' Miriam said, as she whipped off her hideous black wig. Beneath it was a disarray of mousy brown hair, quite similar in colour to mine. It was truly awful, but more becoming than the synthetic mop of fibres she'd just whipped off. Being a kind Christian woman, of course, I felt obligated to give her constructive advice.

'Not that you've asked, dear,' I said, 'but your own hair, which at the moment makes you look like you're wearing a dead muskrat on your head, is an improvement over that hideous wig. My advice is to let that run-over rodent grow out, and then see if you have enough to pull back into a nice sedate bun. After all, you're a middle-aged woman, and it's time you act the part. And don't worry too much about your shiny bald pate; your bun and prayer cap should cover it nicely.'

'Is that so?' Miriam stalked around my chair on her black furry legs, her giant head bobbling to and fro on her spindly neck. When Miriam came to a stop in front of me, her head took a second or two to stop moving. It was a wonder she didn't suffer from motion sickness – or a broken neck. At any rate, something about Gabe's cousin was beginning to look very familiar, but I couldn't put one of my bony fingers on it.

'Yes, that's so,' I said. 'But as long as you're open to advice, might I suggest that you put your scarf back on? Really, dear, you are a textbook case for whiplash while walking, and unfortunately for you, I'm pretty sure that you'd have to sue yourself for damages.'

'Uh-oh,' Susannah said.

'You think you're funny,' Miriam said to me. 'Don't you?' As she spoke, she put her delicate feminine hands on her hips. This gesture is a 'no-no' in the Conservative Mennonite world, as it is considered a sign of arrogance. Of pride.

'I've never been funny in my life,' I said.

'She means it,' Susannah said. 'Mags doesn't have a sense of humour. She really doesn't know who you are.'

'Then she's the densest woman who ever lived,' Miriam said.

'Why I never,' I said. 'And here I thought you'd already reached the pinnacle of rudeness. Clearly you take after your Aunt Ida's side of the family.'

'Ha! For your information, I'm not even related to that old bag. I'm related to *you*!'

'To *me*?'

Susannah clapped her hands. 'Show her! It's time for the big reveal!'

'Whatever you say, sugar cookie,' Miriam said. She whipped off her blouse and then her bra, which was of the padded variety. Miriam's chest was as flat as a pancake, and smooth save for three limp black hairs just above her sternum that had been tied together with a pale pink bow. But the baffling woman did not stop with her torso reveal.

Next thing to go was the eye patch with the eerie neon blue iris painted on it. The second that ugly thing came off my heart stopped. There had indeed been a blue eye under that patch, but it was not aligned with her other eye. My very worst fears – aside from actually losing a loved one to death – is encountering Melvin Ichabod Stoltzfus in the flesh again.

I closed my eyes and prayed. By the way, God likes it better when our eyes are closed during prayer, even though all sorts of sinful images can pop up on the blank screens of our minds. Gabe once said that Jews aren't taught to close their eyes to pray, and that the only reason Christians are asked to close their eyes is so that they won't see their clergy stealing from the offering plates. I was not amused.

'Look at your sister,' maniacal Melvin chortled. 'She's fallen asleep.'

'No, she's praying,' Susannah said.

'Fat lot of good that will do her.'

I opened my eyes, but as I did so, I jumped out of my chair and shouted. 'Boo!' Right in Melvin's face.

The hairy-legged monster in the mini-skirt shrieked like a six-year-old boy and stumbled backwards. I was hoping that he would drop the gun, in which case I would pick it up and then make a run for it. Unfortunately, Melvin's small hand was much stronger than it looked.

'*Now* it's time for the duct tape,' he sneered. 'Get the duct tape for me, Honey-Bunny, will you? It's in the trunk of the car. Oh, and bring the noose, while you're at it. No use making two trips with those bears out there.'

'Aw Mely-kins,' Susannah whined, 'does your Pooky-Wooky have to go out alone? You know how afraid I am at night up here.'

'Speaking of here,' I said, 'where on earth *is* here? I assume that we haven't left the country.'

'We're on Cheat Mountain, West Virginia,' Susannah said. 'Mags, don't you just love that name?'

'How appropriate,' I said.

'What's that supposed to mean?' she asked, sounding more than a trifle deflated.

'Well, if you insist. Haven't you cheated justice by aiding and abetting a convicted murderer to escape?'

'Hey, I served my time in the lockup!'

'What are you doing now?' I asked pleasantly.

'You weren't supposed to tell her where we are,' Melvin said accusingly. 'We agreed on that.'

'Well, I didn't tell her about Thorny Flat,' Susannah said.

'Thorny Flat,' I said. 'My, what an intriguing name.'

'It's the highest point on Cheat Mountain,' Melvin said, puffing out his pigeon chest proudly. 'It's the second highest point in West Virginia at 4,848 feet. By comparison, the highest point in all of the United Kingdom is Ben Nevis at 4,409 feet.'

'My, you certainly are a font of knowledge this evening, Mely-kins – may I call you that?' Normally Melvin is as thick as a post, but curiously at the moment, he was as sharp as a tack, and that was worrisome.

Melvin's eyes bulged, as his face contorted with rage. 'No, you may not!'

'My Sweety-Poteety looked those facts up on the internet just to impress you,' Susannah said. 'And you *are* impressed, aren't you, Mags?' As much as my sister loved the man in the miniskirt, deep down, she knew that he was at least two sandwiches shy of a picnic basket.

I smiled at my kidnapper. 'Well, I am impressed. I never knew you shared my interest in topography.'

'Ha, wrong again for the billionth time, Yoder. I don't give a rat's behind about that so-called fancy handwriting. All those curly adornments on the letters make them too hard to read, if you ask me.'

'Which no one did, dear,' I said. Then I flashed him my pearly whites as an insurance policy. What was with me when it came to interacting with Melvin Ichabod Stoltzfus? No matter how hard I prayed, I just couldn't stop my lips from parting and allowing the most incendiary words from slipping out. It wasn't just a dance hall that was the Devil's playground, so was Magdalena Portulacca Yoder Rosen's mouth.

Alas, even a whackadoodle like Melvin can, if given enough time, recall a subject that had been derailed several topics ago. He stroked his baby soft, hairless chin, while first his left eye surveyed me, then his right. At last he bobbled his head in recognition of the retrieved memory.

'Duct tape! Susannah, go get the duct tape! *Now!*' She wobbled off on six-inch heels. How had I not noticed her crazy footwear before? I love my sister – sometimes quite dearly – but she can scarcely walk barefoot without wobbling. Well, maybe she could if she were sober.

As soon as her fairly ungenerous posterior had cleared the doorframe, my brother-in-law ran over and locked her out. My poor sister immediately began to pound on the door and scream.

'Don't worry about the noise,' Melvin said. 'There isn't another house for thirty miles.'

'I'm not worried about the neighbours, you lout. I'm worried about bears.'

'Nah, that racket is sure to keep them away. The only thing that it could possibly attract is one of the banjo-picking, moonshine-swilling mountain men that I've seen in movies. I mean, maybe there's hidden moonshine still up here, and one of those hillbillies is looking for a bride. I wouldn't blame him if he threw my little filly over his shoulder and carted her down to his cabin in the holler. I reckon she still has one or two more breeding years left in her, given that you spat Little Jacob out when you were older than dirt.'

'I beg your pardon!'

'Sorry. Long in the tooth, then,' he said. It was the first time he'd ever apologized to me, and I was touched.

I smiled gratefully. 'Let's just say that I played with God as a child.'

'Hey,' he snapped, 'don't be sacrilegious.'

'But I thought you were an atheist.'

'Yeah, I am. But it ain't gonna be any fun torturing you, if you're no longer that stuck-up, pompous, hard-nosed, judgmental, religious, old bigot you always were.'

'I will do my best to judge you,' I said.

'Good, that's all I want to hear,' Melvin said. 'But one more thing. You need to scream really loud and beg for mercy, to make up for all the torture that you've put me through. And I want you to ask for my forgiveness.'

'Technically, that's at least two things, dear,' I said. 'I can either scream really loud, or else I can beg for mercy. And asking you to forgive me is definitely a separate demand. So that's really three requests. Which one should I go for?'

Melvin pressed two petite, well-manicured fingers to his bulbous forehead as he considered his answer to my weighty question. Perhaps I should have asked it in a 'yes' or 'no' format to ease the pressure on his poor, overworked brain.

'Uh,' he finally said, 'I want to hear you beg for mercy. Yeah. And call me "sir".'

'Yes, sir,' I said, and gave him a crisp salute.

'Not now, you idiot. Wait until I let your sister back in. I want her to hear you beg for mercy.'

'Well, now that's just silly,' I said. 'You know that deep down in her heart, which is not quite as shrivelled as yours, she loves me. When she hears me beg, then she might take pity on me. After all, I'm the one who raised her, ever since our parents were squished to death between that tanker truck carrying pasteurized milk and the semi-trailer loaded with state-of-the-art athletic shoes.

'No, I think that for your sake, you would be much better off choosing door four: forcing *you* to forgive *me* and letting bygones be bygones.'

Melvin hooted with laughter. He carried on so loudly that I could barely hear Susannah as she continued to pound the front door and scream with fright and rage at being locked out. When Melvin finally ran out of steam I continued calmly.

'It's to your advantage, sweet'ums,' I said. 'Consider this: she might not be impressed by a self-righteous, Bible-beating hypocrite like me pleading with you to forgive her. One would expect that of someone of my ilk. Remember that Susannah received the same religious upbringing that I did. She memorized that scripture verse in which Jesus said that we are to forgive someone seventy times seven. That number, by the way, meant "boundless" back in His day.

'But I tell you what. If Susannah hears a hardened criminal such as yourself, a malicious malcontent, a despicable lowlife, a bottom-feeder worthy of the utmost contempt, ask a Conservative Mennonite woman, an upstanding deacon in her church, as well as a Sunday school teacher, to forgive *him*, I guarantee you that my sister will virtually melt with desire. I would even venture to guess that she will have such an intense hormonal surge that she might even drop one of her viable eggs from her dwindling supply into her breeding basket, and nine months from now you might be the proud papa of a baby mantis.'

'Huh?'

'All those words meant that if you asked me for *my* forgiveness, then she might make a baby with you tonight.'

'Gotcha. But just so you know, Yoder, even I no longer believe that the Easter bunny hides them Easter eggs. And babies don't come from eggs – they come from hospitals. Except for Thelma Denkler's baby. It came from a car, on account she wasn't able to get to the hospital in time to collect one of them free giveaway babies. Come to think of it, I never did figure out how the doctor managed to sneak that baby into Thelma's car, on account of she was still all the way out on Bontrager Road.'

I smiled kindly. 'I guess that's why they call it the miracle of birth. So, dear, now that you've agreed to ask for my forgiveness, go let my sister in. If the bears eat her, or a mountain man takes her to be his second squeeze, you won't be getting that highly sought-after moment of satisfaction, and Melvin Ichabod Stoltzfus Junior might never be born.'

Melvin's eyes momentarily aligned. 'A *son*? Is that a prophecy, Magdalena?'

'The odds are fifty percent "yay",' I said, 'and fifty percent "nay", and that adds up to one *hundred* percent all the lived-long day.'

He smiled happily. 'Yoder, I have half a mind to let you live.'

'No truer words were ever spoken, dear. So now that we've agreed that you're going to ask my forgiveness, and allow me to live, go let my sister in. If you wait much longer you might not be able to discern who the father of Susannah's son will be: you, the mountain man, or the bear – at least not judging by the hair on the poor child's legs. Besides, as we both know, Susannah has always been a mite on the wild side, and she might love a new romantic challenge.'

'Grr,' Melvin said.

I refused to laugh at his tasteless joke. 'Now go get her, Melykins, or you might be forever sorry.'

Remarkably, he did just that. Of course, I was right behind him. My plan was that when he opened the door, I was going to push him outside, and then slam the door behind him. How was

I to know that my baby sister, after all that her man had put her through, would be such a tattletale?

'Look behind you!' she shrieked.

Silly old me. Of course, I turned around and looked as well, proving that Melvin and I are genetically related.

Alas, Melvin was quicker to react. Once he got his oversized head turned, the rest of him followed on a forward trajectory. That is to say, without any additional effort, he ploughed into me like an icebreaker on Lake Erie during the winter of 1976. And although my feet are bigger than icebreakers, I was knocked off balance and fell over backwards.

While it is true that I have a hard head, I was nonetheless knocked unconscious. When I came to, the first thought that came to mind was that I had died, but as with many things I have attempted in life, I had not managed to do it very well. I arrived at this conclusion because I could not see, speak, nor move my arms and legs. How was I supposed to see my promised mansion in the sky, if I could not see? Or walk the golden streets if I had no legs? Most importantly, how could I praise the Good Lord eternally, if I could not sing? I did, however, hear a loud buzzing sound. Could that be insects gnawing away at my flesh?

But after a few seconds of trying an incomplete death on for size as my new normal, my head began to throb with pain, and the buzzing in my ears was replaced by human voices. I couldn't make out distinct words – not at first, not until I heard my name being called. Repeatedly. That, of course, could only mean one thing: the Archangel Gabriel had come to escort me home to Heaven.

'Mmmmmmph,' was all that I could answer him. Believe me, dead lips don't talk.

TWENTY-EIGHT

B ut as I lay there, praying that the Good Lord would not allow me to lie mouldering in an unmarked grave, something akin to a miracle happened. My hearing returned loud and clear.

'Take the tape off her mouth,' Susannah said. 'What if she throws up and drowns? I've heard of that happening.'

'Then I say good riddance,' Melvin said.

'But Mely-kins, you promised that you wouldn't really hurt her.'

'A man can change his mind, can't he, Sugar Buns?'

'But Apple Dumpling, if she dies, you'll be hurting me terribly. You realize that, don't you?'

Oh, Susannah, I thought, I love you so much right now. Why did I never see all that goodness buried deep inside you, hidden beneath a thick veneer of bluff, and indifference to familial affection? I have been so judgmental, and I owe you such a huge apology. Can you ever forgive me?

'How will it hurt you terribly, Carrot Cake?' Melvin asked of my sister.

'Because she's already practically a saint. If she goes missing and is never found, then she'll be *a legend in her own crime*' – she paused to laugh – 'get it? But even if they just find her body, then there will be a massive funeral, like Bedford County has never seen the likes of before. Not only are we related to just about everyone, Amish and Mennonite, but Mags has donated tens of thousands of dollars to the community since the inn became such a success. And as you know, she paid your salary out of her personal funds when you were chief of police.'

'Yeah,' Melvin growled, 'but she only gave me an *annual* raise; I wanted a monthly raise. That's when I started calling her Scrooge McYoder. I thought it would catch on, but those Hernia yokels were so clueless, they'd never heard of Scrooge McDuck.'

'What idiots,' Susannah said.

What a traitor, I thought. I am not going to take this lying down! Except that I actually *am* lying down – on the floor, I imagine – and my feet and hands are most probably restrained by that much talked–about duct tape. Aha! But they haven't done anything about my neck. I can still move my head from side to side to show that I've heard them talking. Then maybe they'll stand me upright; I've always thought fast on my feet.

So that's what I did. I moved my head vigorously from side to side like a lone windshield wiper in a downpour. So what if it ground my coiled braids, my crown of Christian glory, into the floor? Hair is washable. But if my baby sister went along with Melvin's plan and dispatched me to the Throne of Grace and then never repented, she would burn in a lake of fire for all eternity. This is stated quite clearly in the Book of Revelation 20:15. It was my duty to save my sister's soul, was it not?

'Oh, lookee here,' Melvin said, 'your big sister is trying to tell us something. Shall we let her put in a final word?'

'Hmm,' Susannah, 'maybe she'll just start preaching at us.'

'Ah, come on, Custard Cup,' Melvin cooed. 'This could be fun.'

I tried nodding this time.

'You better not preach at me,' Susannah said as she ripped the duct tape off my mouth. In that split second, I was unintentionally given a mini-facial that not only exfoliated that area around my mouth, but saved me a whole lot of tweezing time on my upper lip.

'You two are very clever people,' I said, when I stopped screaming and could speak again. 'I absolutely understand your dilemma about "dead Magdalena" versus "unexplained missing Magdalena". But there is a third option, you know.'

'Yeah?' Susannah said.

'Don't get your hopes up, Sugar Plum,' Melvin said. 'This one's as slippery as a greased snake.'

'Melvin knows this from experience,' I said. 'When we were in third grade he brought a greased snake to Show and Tell. The snake got away in the classroom and couldn't be caught – for the rest of the semester. Fortunately for all of us it wasn't a poisonous variety.'

'Oh, Mely-kins,' Susannah purred. 'Even back then you handled snakes. You were such a brave little boy. You are my hero.'

I snorted. 'Brave? After the glue incident I waited a week and then I put a bullfrog from Miller's pond in your Sugar Dumpling's lunch box. You should have heard him scream; it put the chickens off laying for weeks in six surrounding counties. Melvin, didn't you twist your ankle when you eventually climbed down from your desk?'

'Tch,' Susannah said. 'Magdalena, you're mean. And what's this about a glue incident?'

'Oh, that,' I said, trying to sound nonchalant. 'In art class your brave hero dribbled a bottle of glue along the length of both my braids, because they had the temerity to hang down over the top of his desk. The glue dried before I noticed it, and Mama had to chop both braids off when I got home because she couldn't untangle my hair.'

Susannah giggled. 'Oh, Snickerdoodle,' she said to Melvin, 'you were such a creative genius. If only you'd flunked more grades than just one, so that you and I would have ended up in the same class!'

'What a lovely thought,' I said. 'Your Sweetie Pie is twelve years older than you, dear. Can you just imagine a twenty-year-old man in your third-grade class?'

'I wouldn't mind if he looked like my Mely-kins,' Susannah said.

'Well, I should have been held back more times,' Melvin said, 'because the one C that I made in Home Economics was the highest grade I ever made, until I graduated from high school, but the school district's official policy was that no kid should be left behind.'

'And so I hired you as our chief of police,' I said. 'On that fateful day my brain was out to lunch – on Pitcairn Island in the South Pacific.'

Melvin's right eye regarded me sceptically. 'I don't think so, Magdalena. I remember that it was you who interviewed me for the job, and then gave it to me on the spot.'

'You're absolutely right, dear,' I concede. 'That was me – but just my body. My brain, as I said, was on Pitcairn Island.'

Melvin turned to his Sugar Buns. 'Is your sister putting me on?'

'Like a feedbag on a horse,' Susannah said.

'Moving right along,' I said, 'don't the two of you brilliant criminal minds want to know what your third option is?'

'Of course we do, Yoder,' Melvin said. 'We were just waiting for you to spit it out.'

'Well, dearies, my plan is to write my sweetie a Dear John letter in which I tell him that I have fallen deeply in love with one of my former guests and eloped with him.'

Melvin snorted. 'That's nuts, Yoder. I know for a fact that your so-called sweetie isn't named John.'

'Maybe she doesn't mean Gabe,' Susannah said, trying to be helpful.

'Take off my blindfold at once!' I thundered. 'And that's an order. If you two don't even know what a Dear John letter is, then you're never going to be able to pull off the Greatest Crime of the Century.'

Melvin snatched away my blindfold, and nearly took my right ear with it. 'Oh, yeah?' he said.

'Yeah,' I said. 'You'll be the laughingstock of criminals everywhere. At best you'll be given a two-star rating by the Criminal Code of Conduct Court, which means you won't be awarded the Golden Guillotine pin.'

'She's making that up,' Susannah said. 'You can tell that she's lying because her lips are moving.'

'I'm not so sure,' my nemesis said. 'I've heard that word before. Guillotine. I think it's German for "crime".'

'How right you are, dear,' I said. I was able to say it without moving my lips, even though I was lying through clenched teeth.

'OK then,' Susannah said, as she stomped one of her long, but narrow feet. 'What is a Dear John letter?'

'In essence, it's a letter in which a girl writes to her sweetheart and tells him that their relationship is over. The point is that she doesn't do it in person,' I said, 'but through the mail.'

'That's wonderful news,' Melvin said. I could hear him clap his womanish hands just to my left.

'Why is that such good news, Melvin dear?'

'Yoder, you're such a nincompoop. Because we can email your Dear John letter, then kill you, so that means it's as simple as eating our cake and pie too.'

'With a dollop of mixed metaphor on top as well, I suppose,' I said.

'You got that right, smarty-pants,' Melvin said.

'Well then,' I said, 'we should get started. Although, we do have a major hurdle to overcome first, and it's one that you, Melvin, might be afraid to even contemplate.'

'My man's not afraid of anything,' Susannah said. Oh, if only I could ever feel that strongly about the man that I loved.

'What is it that you think I'm so scared of?' Melvin all but bellowed. For a rather small, pigeon-chested man, he could produce a prodigious amount of volume when provoked.

'You're afraid to untie my hands and feet,' I said. 'That's what. I can't possibly write a letter with my hands tied together.'

'You can dictate the letter to Susannah,' Melvin said.

'I told you that you were afraid.'

'I ain't afraid! But why take chances when there are risks involved.'

'Because, silly – I mean, dear – the letter has to be in my handwriting. Gabe will recognize my handwriting; he most assuredly will not recognize my sister's. Trust me, I know this. She used to write to me from prison, asking for this and that, and my Dearly Beloved would invariably dissolve into fits of laughter when he saw her letters.'

'You showed him my letters?' Susannah cried. 'That's illegal! I could have you arrested for that.'

'No, you couldn't, dear. By then they were *my* letters. And the point I'm trying to make is that Gabe said that your handwriting looks like chicken scratches. He asked which of our hens had written to me. And was she asking for more feed, or maybe a week off from laying eggs.'

'That hurts my feelings,' Susannah whined. 'In your Dear John letter to Gabe, I want you to tell him to apologize to me for being so mean.'

'Will do, sis. *If*, of course, I had the means to write the letter.'

'Well, now you do,' Susannah said. She dove into her purse which, come to think of it, was large enough to accommodate my scrawny body, and a moment later she reappeared with manicure scissors. Meanwhile, Melvin picked his nose and glared at me with one hate-filled eye, while the other one followed a moth around the room.

'There, now that's much better,' I said. 'Now undo my feet, please, or would you prefer that I untie them myself? Mind you, they smell something awful, so I quite understand it if you prefer that I do the job.'

'Then do it!' Susannah said, and thrust the scissors at me, without pausing to consider if I even needed my feet in order to write the proposed letter. Of course I did not. By the way, pretending that my feet stank was merely subterfuge on my part; it should not be categorized as a lie.

Once free from all restraints I sat up and discovered that I had been lying on an unmade hospital bed in a small, windowless room. Once upon a time the walls may have been white – or shades of beige – and what were those fancy patches of grey and black? Were they mould? All this I could see courtesy of a fluorescent light fixture that hung at a rakish angle from the ceiling directly above me.

Susannah was sitting at the foot of the bed, a bottle of beer tucked between her thighs. Melvin was perched on a high white metal stool closer to my head. He had changed out of the skirt and into trousers, and if you didn't know him to be the insect that he was, you could easily mistake him for a man. Bright red lipstick, lavender eyeshadow, and sweeping false eyelashes were the only vestiges of Miriam to cling to his carapace.

'No cramps yet?' he demanded.

'Frankly, dear,' I said crossly, 'that's none of your business.'

'Not even a stomach ache?' Susannah said.

'What's going on?' I said. 'Did I wake up from a hundred-year sleep with the flu?'

Susannah giggled nervously.

'You're fit as a flute, Yoder,' Melvin said. 'Now write that letter before the symptoms hit.'

'Symptoms? What symptoms?'

'Stress symptoms,' Melvin said. 'It's been known to make people very sleepy. Too sleepy, in fact, to cooperate with their captors.'

'Is that so?' I said, although of course I already knew that. 'I'd hardly classify you as *too* stressful Melvin. You're more like a bad case of gas.'

Susannah giggled again.

'The letter, Yoder,' Melvin said. 'Write it! Now!'

After taking stock of my surroundings, and coming up with an exit strategy, I feigned calm impatience. 'Well? How am I to make bricks without any straw?'

'Dang it,' Melvin said (alas, he used another word). 'She must have had a concussion, and now the blood is playing pool in her brain. Your sister's gone plum loco.'

'Actually, Mely-kins,' Susannah said, 'it's a biblical reference. It's from the story of Jonah and the Ark.'

My bottom jaw fell into my lap and I had to cram it back into place before I could talk. 'My Land o' Goshen! It is indeed a biblical reference. Good for you, Susannah.'

My sister beamed proudly. 'Was I right about the story?'

'Oh, let's not quibble about details, shall we? That's how religious schisms start. My point was that I must have paper, and a pen or pencil, in order to write this Dear John letter. So would one of you please provide me with the necessary materials? Please. Pretty please, with sugar on top.'

'That's how she used to make me eat my vegetables after Mama died,' Susannah said.

'Hmm,' Melvin mused, 'I've always liked sugar on my cauliflower.'

Susannah made a face. 'No, not by putting sugar on them; she said "please". That was so manipulative. And I was only eleven!'

To his credit, Melvin vacated his seat on the stool near the head of the bed and walked around me to wrap my baby sister in his spindly arms. 'There, there, Fudge Bar,' he said, 'she's always been a big meanie. That's why we can't be showing her any mercy. You see that now, don't you?'

'Yeah, I guess so,' Susannah said. 'But she did one thing that was sort of nice.'

'Just one thing?' I said. 'Pray tell. What was that? Intervene with the bullies on the playground dozens of times, or defend you to your teachers and the principal when you carved graffiti into your desk with a hairpin, smoked in the bathroom, cussed at them like sailors, threw food in the lunchroom, and destroyed books in the library? Or was it when I pled with juvenile court judges not to put you into foster care, and then later on bailed you out of jail so many times that I have lost track?'

Susannah had the chutzpah to roll her eyes throughout my recitation. 'Nah, them things was to be expected on account that we're sisters. I'm talking about when I was like five or six, and you bought me a baby doll – you know, one of them realistic ones that you can feed water to in a bottle, and then it wets itself. I loved her so much. I even named her Mags, after you.

'But then you said, that if she was going to be named after

you, she had to be a Christian, so you took me over to Miller's
Pond and you baptized her. Then suddenly Aaron Miller, who
was like your age and drop-dead gorgeous, pops out of the bushes
and says "hi", so you let go of my doll.' Susannah addressed
Melvin. 'Guess what happened next?'

'They started making out like crazy?' he said, before guffawing.

'I've apologized for what happened next a million times,' I said.
'And after your baby Mags went floating away and eventually
sank, I bought you a new one with my hard-earned babysitting
money. Plus, Mama thrashed me within an inch of my life with a
couple of weeping willow switches.'

'See, I told you that the doctrine of pacifism is phoney baloney,'
Melvin said.

'It is not,' I said hotly. 'Mama didn't believe in striking anybody
else's children – just her own children. So there.'

'My papa whipped the living daylights out of me,' Melvin
said. He sounded proud of it.

'Boo hoo hoo,' I said, as I rubbed at my eyes with my newly
freed fists. 'That doesn't give either of you the right to kill anyone.
Most especially blood kin, and the mother of your nephew.'

'Little Jacob is only my half-nephew, on account of you're
just my half-sister,' Melvin said proudly. In all seriousness, the
fact that he had been able to figure out his relatedness to my
son, was a major accomplishment, given the man's math skills.

'But Mags,' Susannah said, 'yours and Melvin's birth mother
was no relation to me, so that means that Little Jacob isn't related
to me either.'

'Au contraire, dear. Our family genealogy is so tangled, that
you and me and Melvin are closer than first cousins – more than
a small amount of hyperbole aside. If you and your Mely-kins
have a baby together, it might even be born with horns and cloven
hoofs.'

'Really?' Susannah said.

I smiled. 'Would I lie at a time like this?'

'Yes,' my captors replied in unison.

'Well, I'm not lying when I say that you and Melvin are close
blood relations. But before we ponder the possible peculiarities
of your potential progeny any further, perhaps you should procure
paper and pen post-haste.'

Melvin stepped back from the bed, all the better to give me a menacing look as he stroked his hairless mandible with a claw-like forefinger. 'Maybe we would,' he said, 'if we could.'

'What is that supposed to mean?' I asked.

'That means, *dear*,' he said in a mocking voice, 'that we haven't got any paper or writing implements, as you call them, in the house.'

'How can that be?' I said. 'Don't you ever jot down messages? Take notes of some kind?'

'We're millennials, Mags,' Susannah said. 'We're not you old-fashioned boomers. Boom, boom! What does that stand for, anyway? Farts? Old farts! Get it?'

Susannah laughed until tears ran down her cheeks. My poor, misguided, lovelorn sister has always been worse at maths than Melvin, and apparently not very good at guessing one's age from one's physical appearance. Melvin is actually one year *older* than I am, which makes him a boomer, not a millennial.

'Boom, boom, you old fart,' Melvin said to me. But his eyes said, *You better not give my age away, Yoder, or your death will be more excruciatingly painful than you imagined.*

I sighed dramatically. 'When you're done having your fun, children, I suggest you fetch me the writing supplies before I change my mind and call the operation off. Then not only will you lose the only reasonable excuse for my disappearance, but you will also forfeit the million dollars I was planning to send you by money order when I made it safely out of the country – if indeed, you will consider that option.'

'We will! Won't we, Mely-kins? I always wanted to have a pink bathroom and a walk-in closet that can hold a hundred pairs of shoes.' Susannah draped herself around Melvin's narrow shoulders like a wet piece of tissue paper.

'Sure thing, Carrot Cakes,' Melvin said. 'Here, you take the gun. Now, don't let your sister out of this room, no matter how much she begs and pleads. Even if she has to go to the bathroom, she can just do it in her pants. Remember that she's a fast-talker, a manipulator – in other words, you can't believe a word she says. Magdalena Yoder is a big, fat, skinny liar.' He started out the door but turned back. 'I'll be heading down the mountain to the Bottoms-Up Bar and Grill. The bartender's gotta have something. If he don't, I'll keep on going until I get to town. I'll be back within an hour – maybe an hour and a half. You got all that, Sugar Lips?'

'Sure do, Mely-kins.' My sister blew him a kiss.

We heard his tiny girlish feet patter down the stairs, the front door slam, and then the engine of the car, as he drove down the mountain in search of writing implements.

Susannah stood very still listening to him go, as if she were a doe in the woods, and he was a predator retreating into the distance. When we could no longer hear the car, she whirled and threw herself into my arms!

'Thank God that evil man is gone,' she cried, as the gun clattered to the floor. 'Oh Mags, oh Mags, I thought he'd never leave.'

TWENTY-NINE

'Wait just one marshmallow minute!' I cried. 'What do you mean by that? Is this a trap?'

'O, Mags!' Susannah said, and threw herself at me, practically knocking me back down on the bed. 'I didn't know. I didn't know. I didn't know!'

I held her at arm's length as I slid to my feet. 'OK, tell me slowly, and clearly. What didn't you know, and what is going on?'

When Susannah resumed speaking, she was crying. To my knowledge, Susannah hasn't cried once since the day that we buried our parents.

'I didn't know that he was actually planning to *kill* you,' she said, sobbing. 'He-he s-said that he just wanted to make you suffer because your life has always been awesome, and his life has always been lousy. So he asked me to help him with some pranks during the festival. Magdalena, that's all I agreed to do. They were just harmless pranks, right?'

'*Harmless pranks?*' I screeched. 'You call killing two people "harmless pranks"?'

'What are you yelling about?' she asked between sobs. 'We didn't kill anyone!'

'The bodies in Sam's dumpster, Susannah.'

'Cousin Sam's dumpster?'

'Who else's? They were to be guests at the PennDutch until you and Melvin murdered them.'

'Honestly, Mags, I have no idea what you're talking about. I swear on a stack of—'

'Don't swear on the Bible,' I said. 'I believe that *you* didn't kill anyone. But I am convinced that Melvin did.'

'Oh Mags, I am so sorry for everything!'

This was not the time to lecture her, nor was there even any time to comfort her. She would always be my baby sister, no matter how stupid and misguided her actions were. I've lived too long to believe in 'unconditional' love, but I do believe in loving the memory of how someone once was.

I grabbed my sister by her shoulders, still at arm's length, and squeezed them gently. 'So what do we do now, Susannah?'

'We run,' she said. 'We have to get out of here before Melvin gets back.'

'Where to? Up to the top of Cheat Mountain, and hope that we can get cell phone service up there?'

She shook her head. 'It's too steep and rugged. We'd never make it up there at night. Especially without flashlights. Besides, what good would it do if we did? Neither of us has a phone.'

'Yes, we do,' I said, as I headed for the door.

'Mags!' she wailed, sounding just like me, 'we *don't* have phones. I left my phone in the car, and you—'

'Brought my phone,' I said.

'What? But Melvin had me search the pockets of your frumpy dress. There was zilch. *Nada.*'

I turned triumphantly. 'Susannah, dear, we are both a carpenter's dream: flat as a board on top. Ergo, we both wear an item of clothing that comes with its own twin phone storage pockets.'

'We do?'

'Susannah, where did you used to tote that nasty little teacup Yorkie dog of yours?'

'You mean my precious itty-bitty, widdle Shnookums?' Susannah said in a little girl voice.

'Yes,' I said with a growl, 'that very same mangy rat that snapped at me every chance his flea-bitten carcass came within an inch of me.'

'You know where I kept him,' Susannah said. 'In my bra, of course.'

'Well then,' I said, 'it shouldn't surprise you to learn that your older sis often stashes her cell phone in the top half of her sturdy Christian underwear. But never in the bottom half, of course, because that would be unhygienic, and besides, the periodic vibrations of incoming messages would undoubtedly lead to unintentional arousal. That is what's known as phone sex, and the pastor has preached that phone sex is the same as adultery.'

'Give me a break,' Susannah said. 'But OK, come on, we'll have to run down the mountain a ways in order to get a signal. I mean a *good* long ways, like clear down to the Bottoms-Up Bar and Grill.'

'Then let's get a move on, dear,' I said.

Of course, there was to be no running. One does not just wake up from a concussion and then hit the road pounding. Well, I guess that I could, if one was willing to put up with a miniature jackhammer in one's head, pounding away at one's skull. Besides which, Susannah has never run a meter in her life, unless it was away from work. Nevertheless, the steep incline of the mountain road kept us moving at a dangerous, and painful, pace. Had it not been for the full moon, I'm quite certain that the earth would have been happy to rise up and greet my face on several occasions.

Due to the brain-rattling conditions it was hard to carry on a conversation. However, it was imperative that I learn as much as I could about Melvin's latest diabolical scheme as soon as possible, lest Susannah switch allegiances again. It's been said that blood is thicker than water, but when it comes to my sister, the saying applies only if the blood in question has been congealed.

'Susannah, whose cabin is that?'

'Melvin's. I mean, he's renting it.'

'But why all the way out here?'

'He said that after he killed you, he was going to bury you in the woods out back, and no one would ever know where to look for you because the cabin was so remote. But Mags, you have to believe me: I didn't think that he'd actually follow through with it.'

The Devil made me want to reach out and swat her. Thank goodness I am as stupid as I look, for had I done so, she might have stumbled and rolled down the mountain all the way to Charleston, West Virginia, and I still had oodles more questions to ask.

'Susannah, how long had Melvin been planning this multi-prong attack on the Billy Goat Gruff Festival?'

'Is that a serious question, sis?'

'Silly me,' I said. 'In other words, ever since the first one. Because I came up with something good, he wanted to destroy it.'

'That's not fair, Mags. Did you ever think to honour him? Make *him* Hernia's Citizen of the Year? Think of all the years that he served this community as Chief of Police?'

'Sister dear, your hubby is a convicted killer. And you've got it wrong; he didn't serve this community – this community *survived* him.'

'Oh, Mags, you're so mean!'

'I'm being truthful. Now you be honest and tell me how he found the time and opportunity to pull off all those pranks if he had to be Miriam half the time.'

Susannah trilled triumphantly. 'My Mely-kins thinks of everything. Remember when my genius hubby – and that's what he is, Mags – hung out with that bunch of unemployed Shakespearean actors?'

'Oh, yeah. The last time he tried to kill me.'

'Right,' she said. 'Well, my lovey-dovey learned all about make-up and costumes and wigs, so he's been living in Hernia for the last two weeks setting things up. You know, like renting the sewage truck, filing the wagon traces, scoping out the snake-handlers' church. That kind of thing.'

'No way, Jose!'

'Yuppers. He's been living in a rented room on Cranston Street, on the poor side of town.'

'Economically challenged,' I said.

'What?'

'It's not nice to say poor anymore.'

'What about "rich"?' Susannah said.

'Economically blessed,' I said.

'Now you're just messing with me,' Susannah said.

'Perhaps,' I said. 'Susannah, where is that mini, mangy mutt of Miriam's – er, Melvin's, that goes by the name of Fi-Fi? He didn't leave it back at the inn, did he?'

My sister had the temerity to laugh. 'Oh, Mags, you and your need to alliterate. No, that mini, mangy mutt wasn't even Melvin's. He picked it up from a rescue shelter just for "operation Magdalena". We dropped it back off at the same shelter when we went into Bedford to pick up the ingredients for your Australian seafood salad. How did everyone like the supper that we prepared? You never did say?'

I groaned loudly.

'Mags?' Susannah said in alarm. 'Does your tummy hurt? Tell me!'

'No, Susannah. My stomach feels fine. Why do you keep asking?'

'Because Melvin poisoned the seafood salad.'

I managed to stop a few yards downhill. '*What* did you say?'

'I didn't do it, Mags. Melvin did it. I tried to stop him; honest I did. But he hit me, Mags. Hard. Right across the mouth. He's never done anything like that before. And then he just collapsed on the floor and bawled like a baby. Mags, I'm scared. It's like he's had a breakdown or something. Then when he got up – believe me, I've never seen his face look like that. Mags, there was nothing that I could do to stop him. I felt so helpless.'

I stared at my baby sister. Maybe it was the moonlight, but I was looking at a face that I didn't recognize.

'Let me get this straight,' I said. 'You couldn't think of a way to warn me? You couldn't text? Maybe leave a note with the salad when he wasn't looking?'

'I don't expect you to understand,' Susannah said, 'but it's like Melvin has this power over me. Sometimes I think that I would die for him.'

'Yeah?' I shouted angrily. 'Well, how about this? What if my Little Jacob had died tonight because his supper was poisoned?

Or my husband Gabe? Or Chief Toy? Or any of the others, all just because a convicted murderer was controlling your mind? Susannah, you are a bright and beautiful woman, yet you sold out your family for the approval of this . . . this . . . well, never mind.'

Susannah burst into tears, but I let her cry. I had no words of comfort for her at the moment; she needed to feel the total impact of her actions. For years Melvin had been obsessed with killing me, and surely Susannah, as his Sweetykins, knew that. Even a marble statue isn't that blind.

'Stop your blubbering, sis,' I finally said. 'For your informa-tion – not that you deserve to know this – we never did eat the meal that you two felons prepared for us. I suppose that if we had, we'd all be long dead by now. Is that it?'

'Well, not Little Jacob,' Susannah said between sobs. 'I knew that he was allergic to seafood. I remember you told me that once when you visited me in prison.'

'Uh-huh. But what about me, the woman who raised you since you were eleven years old? Were you really all right with me clutching my stomach, and writhing in agony like a python at a snake belly-dancing contest?'

Susannah let out a cry that was so mournful it was sure to make coyotes weep. 'But you don't *understand*!'

'Then help me understand,' I said. It wasn't so that I wouldn't press charges (I would, no matter what she said), but because I wanted to be able to forgive her.

My sister grabbed my arm and clutched it with fingers as thin and sharp as knitting needles. 'Melvin adores me, Mags.'

'That's nice,' I said. I sped up, as to pull away from her talons, but she surprised me by exhibiting speed for the first time in her life.

'You don't understand,' she said. 'He worships me. Frankly, I don't know why, but I can tell you, that it feels awesome. Mags, you're smart and drop-dead gorgeous, and you've always been able to get a man. Now you've got that handsome Jewish doctor—'

'Excuse me? *What* did you say?'

'I'm not anti-Semitic, Mags, you know I'm not.'

'It was that drop-dead gorgeous part. Were you mocking me?'

She let go of my arm. 'I know what it is now! It's that body-dysmorphic syndrome that you suffered from, isn't it? You haven't been cured, have you? Don't tell me that you still think that you have a horsey head, and a flat chest, yada, yada, yada. All you need to do is look in a mirror, Magdalena, and see the beautiful woman that Gabe adores. And Toy, for that matter.'

'Toy?'

Susannah groaned. 'Yes, you fool. That man is crazy about you too.'

'Ack,' I cried. 'Get behind me, Satan! I don't want to be beautiful! I'm *not* beautiful. I look like a horse, and that's that. Case closed.'

We walked in a state of high tension until we approached Bottoms-Up Bar and Grill where chaos appeared to have reigned. The large parking lot was jam-packed with pickup trucks and motorcycles, and there were vehicles seemingly abandoned willy-nilly along the embankments. Clearly this was one very popular nightspot for entertainment. One car belonged to the county sheriff or one of his, or her, deputies, yet I paused before entering.

Don't think for a second that I was reluctant to enter the establishment because it sold booze. My Jewish husband drinks wine, and the Bible states that Jesus turned water into wine, but even Samson couldn't have pried my dry, withered lips open wide enough to allow a drop of firewater to pass between them. I had seen how alcohol could ruin a person's life, and I had enough troubles, without yielding to any new temptations.

I turned to my baby sister. 'Before I go in, tell me, where is the real Miriam Blumfield?'

Susannah gave me a thin smile. 'On a European tour with the money that Melvin gave her.'

'What money? Where does he get money? He's a schlemiel, for crying out loud.'

'His mother, your birth mother, left him half a million dollars, Mags.'

'Oh.' To be brutally honest – and it is nobody's business but my own – I felt left out. Maybe even jealous. Elvina Stoltzfus was my birth mother too; she could have at least left me enough money to buy a can of beans. Maybe even a can of beans with franks.

'Don't tell me that you're jealous, Mags,' Susannah said.

'OK, I won't,' I said. 'But Susannah, I want you to please tell me how Melvin knew about Miriam, and where she lives?'

Susannah shook her head. 'You're not going to like my answer, sis. It's going to make you like my Mely-kins even less. You might even start to hate him, and that's the same as killing him in your heart, and that's a bad sin.'

I couldn't tell if she was joking, but I certainly was serious when I answered. 'Trust me, toots, I couldn't possibly dislike your Ooey-gooey Toffee Bar any more than I do already. So lay it on me!'

'Well, you don't lock your doors, do you?'

'Of course not. It's Hernia; no one locks their doors. Besides, what good would it do? My guests are always coming and going at their leisure. And trust me, no authentic eighteenth-century inn is going to have magnetic door keys.'

'That's what I thought,' Susannah said. 'And that's exactly why it was so easy for my hubby-dubby to sneak into the PennDutch like a billion times and plant listening devices and video cameras. You guys have been under surveillance for the past three years.'

Every hair on my head started to rise. I could even feel my bun struggle for lift-off against its restraining bobby pins.

'In our bedroom?' I roared.

She nodded.

'In the master bath? Anywhere near Big Bertha?'

Her eyes closed, she held her hands over her ears and nodded.

'I'm going to kill that man!' I shrieked. Then I gasped, for I realized she'd been exactly right. I did hate him, and it was the same as killing him – in my heart. According to Jesus, I was just as bad as Melvin Ichabod Stoltzfus, although I had yet to physically murder anyone.

I waited for Susannah to open her eyes, and then I gave her a 'Mennonite hug' – three pats on the back, as if I was burping a baby. I stepped back.

'Susannah, I'm going in now. I will, of course, be telling the sheriff the truth, and nothing but the truth. Would you like to make an honest woman of yourself and come in with me? I would imagine that if you turn yourself in and act as state's witness, you can make a deal for yourself. You might not even have to go back to jail. What do you think?'

My sister looked intently at me. I thought that I saw love in her expression. Maybe even contrition. Then she grabbed me around my bony shoulders and squeezed hard.

'Love ya, Mags,' she said, 'but I could never rat on my sweet Mely-kins.' Then she turned and ran off between two rows of pickup trucks and I never saw her again that night.

I am ashamed to say that I did not search for Susannah. I was emotionally broken, and physically exhausted. I just wanted the evening to be over, so I plodded straight to the door of the bar.

THIRTY

The following week, on her day off, Agnes invited me over to her house for coffee and stale pastries. It was a pleasant morning, just right for sitting outside on her back patio. To avoid contact with her uncles, I walked around to the rear of her house and phoned her when I'd arrived. When she answered the door, I handed her a thousand-piece puzzle with a dozen pieces missing.

'This will keep the old dears occupied,' I said, 'because it's missing a dozen border pieces.'

'Mags, you wouldn't!'

'You're right, not even I would stoop that low. It's just temporary.' I handed her a baggie with the missing pieces. 'Sneak these into the mix after our gabfest and we'll all have had a good time with no harm done.'

Much to my surprise, Agnes was pleased with my evil scheme. 'I shall sneak the missing pieces into the mix surreptitiously. Goodness me, I don't know why I haven't thought of that before, given that they are such puzzle freaks.'

'Well, unfortunately I only thought about it after one of my disgruntled guests swiped a handful of pieces out of a puzzle we'd set up in the parlour.'

'Was it that tiny Texan married to a Texan named Tiny?'

'No, this was a long time ago,' I said. 'By the way, I am so glad to get that tiny Texan out of my mousey brown hair. Him, I could stand, but *her* – never mind, I refuse to gossip. I'm turning over a new leaf.'

'So then we won't discuss her,' Agnes said. 'But please, best girlfriend, tell me how you stormed into the Bottoms-Up Bar & Grill with your guns blazing.'

'Ack! I didn't have any guns, and nothing was blazing. It just looked like a safe place to make a phone call. Besides, you've already heard the story.'

'I know, Mags, but I get such schadenfreude out of hearing it. Indulge me one last time, and I'll drive you straight into Bedford and to that nail place I was telling you about that takes "walk-ins". I asked your pastor, and he assured me that pedicures are not sinful.'

As my fubsy friend poured me a second cup of coffee, I considered her offer. Gabe has reneged on his private wedding vow of giving me a weekly foot rub. I had never had a pedicure – not because I thought the process itself was sinful, but that my response might be quite inappropriate. Confidentially, even the *prospect* of a stranger touching my tootsies gave me shivers of delight. Tiny shivers that were still manageable. Who knew what might happen when someone actually touched my feet.

'OK, it's a deal,' I said at length. 'But if I run out of the salon screaming something about Satan having to get behind me, it will be all your fault.'

'I'll be right behind you, laughing my head off,' Agnes said. 'Now humour me.'

'Well, it was a dark and stormy night on a deserted mountain road,' I began. 'Correction. It was a bright moonlit night, and the parking lot was jam-packed, as you already know. When I stepped inside, it took a minute for my eyes to adjust to the dimness of the bar. At first, I didn't see that burly guy standing right inside the door.

'"Hello sweetheart," he said to me. "There's a cover charge of twenty dollars and a two drink minimum."

'"I'm not your *sweetheart*, dear," I said. I attempted to bypass his bulky frame, but he kept stepping in front of me, demanding that I pay him twenty bucks. What chutzpah.'

'Go on,' Agnes said breathlessly.

'Then I remembered the tactic we girls used on Melvin in elementary school when he'd corner one of us in a school corridor and try to plant a booger on us. "Melvin, your shoes are on fire," we'd scream. He'd look down at his feet, and we'd make a run for it. It worked every time.'

'Yes!' Agnes said gleefully. 'But then what?'

'"I'm going to be sick!" I shouted at that big man in the bar. He jumped aside to avoid my vomit, and I ran into the middle of the room, where I found myself surrounded by a crowd of gyrating men. Agnes, you know that I don't have a judgmental bone in my body, but if I did, I could have sworn – if I was a swearing woman – that I'd landed in Sodom and Gomorrah.'

'Hmm,' Agnes said. 'If dancing is a sin in your book, is homosexual dancing any worse than heterosexual dancing?'

'I really wouldn't know which is worse, dear,' I said drily, 'since I've never seen straight men dance. But these gay men were pretty good in my estimation. Anyway, what's important to the story is that suddenly I became aware that there was a man on stage singing in a high tenor voice – a very *familiar* high tenor voice. The song that he was singing was "Somewhere Over the Rainbow". That's one of Gabe's favourite songs, so I stopped moving and paid attention, and that's when my eyes nearly popped out of my head.'

'Because?' Agnes coached.

'Because it was Melvin. *Our* Melvin Ichabod Stoltzfus in full Miriam make-up: lavender eyeshadow, sweeping false eyelashes, overly rouged cheeks, and bright red lips. Although he was shirt-less, he had on men's trousers, and men's shoes.

'But I must say that his voice sounded just like the Judy Garland record that Gabe has. Everyone there in the bar must have thought so too, because they'd stopped gyrating, and now the partners were swaying in those sexually suggestive postures that makes dancing so sinful.'

'And then?'

'The song ended and the dancers clapped and cheered so enthusiastically for Melvin that I couldn't hear myself think. The patrons went on to beg Melvin to perform another song, which he did, and it was just as beautiful as the first, and met with just as much enthusiasm. Then Melvin spotted me, and he had a total meltdown on stage. He blithered, blathered, and squealed like a house full of parrots and pigs. At first his many fans supposed he was doing a comedy routine, but when he pointed at me repeatedly and said the most ungracious things, they turned.

'I watched, transfixed by the spectacle for perhaps longer than was necessary. Finally I came to my senses and took refuge in the ladies' room. The only reason I was able to do that unnoticed by the brute at the door, was because he was using the men's room! At any rate, I was in the ladies' room when I called Toy who, as you know, called the local sheriff. By the time Sheriff Jowlstump arrived, the wonderful bar patrons – drinkers and dancers, though they were – had subdued the malevolent Melvin, and he was tightly bound with leather belts. Of course in the interim, I'd called Gabe, but I had to call three times before I got through.'

'That's because he was talking to Alison,' Agnes said. 'So what was your immediate reaction to learning that she didn't get on the plane to Puerto Rico after all? Relief? Or were you disappointed that she put off doing her volunteer work?'

'Don't be silly,' I said. 'In fact, when I learned that Alex was one of her girlfriends, and not a boyfriend, I was so relieved that I did the one-step dance.'

Agnes laughed. 'Pray tell, what is the one-step dance?'

'Well, dear, there are several variations of the one-step dance. Mine was called the Jumping up and Down for Joy dance, and Little Jacob's is called the I Have to Pee So Badly dance.'

'Gotcha,' Agnes said. 'Once on a trip to Florida I did the I Stepped in a Nest of Fire Ants dance. Say Mags, now that this ordeal is over, and Alison is on her way to being a doctor, are you finally happy?'

'I'm content with my life – well, sort of.'

'Just sort of?' Agnes demanded. She was suddenly angry. 'Mags, you have everything!'

'I know,' I said, defensively. 'Wealth, health, husband, children – whatever order you want to put them in, but I miss Granny Yoder.'

Anger faded from Agnes's face. 'Still no sign of her, huh?'

'Zilch, zip, nada. But last evening, after supper, the oddest thing happened. I asked Little Jacob to go into the parlour and see if I might have left my reading glasses in there. When he came out he said that there was an Indian man sitting on the floor beside Granny's rocker. He said that the Indian spoke to him in the language that Freni sometimes mutters to herself in.'

'Swiss German?'

'Right. So I followed him back into the parlour but I didn't see anyone, even though Little Jacob insisted that the Indian man was still there. I told Little Jacob to ask the man his name.' I paused to gulp down some of my pale coffee, which was fast getting too cold.

'Don't stop *there*, Mags! What was the Indian's name?'

'Joseph Hochstetler.'

Agnes frowned. 'That is not an Indian name.'

'No, but it is the name of my eighth great-grandfather. Joseph Hochstetler was kidnapped by the Lanape Indians when he was a boy and adopted fully into their tribe. He was given to an Indian family to raise as their own son, and when he was rescued ten years later, he didn't want to leave his new family.'

Agnes shivered. 'Mags, this is very weird.'

'It gets even weirder,' I said. 'Little Jacob said that this Indian sitting cross-legged in our parlour has blue eyes.'

RECIPES

Moreton Bay Bug Salad with Sesame Dressing

NOTE: Morton Bay or Balmain bugs (these are not really bugs, but are a little like a flat lobster – much smaller though), are from a bay hear Brisbane. A quick internet search will bring up the definition so you're not grossed out by the word 'bug'.

You could substitute lobster for the 'bugs'. If you're anything like me, I would substitute anything I like in a recipe. You could possibly use squid (calamari), prawns, or scallops. I think being inventive with a recipe to change it to suit those in the family will always work. It is, after all, a salad.

Serves: 6

INGREDIENTS
  12 cooked Moreton Bay Bugs
  1 cup brown rice, boiled in salted water until tender
  1 bunch green asparagus, trimmed, blanched and sliced
    (see notes)
  6 cups mixed baby salad greens, to serve
  ¼ cup flaked almonds, toasted (see notes)
  Sesame dressing:
  ¼ cup rice vinegar
  ¼ cup peanut oil
  1 tablespoon sesame oil
  1 tablespoon light soy sauce
  2 teaspoons grated ginger
  1 small red chilli, seeded and finely chopped
  1 teaspoon sesame seeds, toasted (see notes)

METHOD
Make sesame dressing: combine ingredients in a screw top jar and shake well. Set aside until needed.

Slice bugs lengthways and remove the meat from the shells,

remove the digestive tract (grey thread) running down the middle of the tail meat. Cover and refrigerate.

Place rice, asparagus and salad greens in a large bowl. Add dressing and toss well to combine. Divide between plates, top with bug tails and sprinkle with almonds.

NOTES

If asparagus is thick and woody, discard the woody bottom section and peel the spears with a potato peeler. Blanch asparagus in well-salted boiling water for 30 seconds to 1 minute, then refresh in ice water, or cold running water, to stop the cooking. Toast sesame seeds and almonds in a dry frying pan for a couple of minutes, tossing gently to prevent them burning, or under a griller (but watch them closely).

Seafood Salad

> Prep Time: approx. 15 mins
> Cook Time: 2 mins
> Difficulty: Easy
> Serves: 4

INGREDIENTS

> 2 small/medium whole squid, cleaned, hood scored and
>   cut into squares, tentacles cut in half
> Olive oil
> 2 tbsp fish sauce
> 2 tbsp caster sugar
> 2 tbsp water
> Zest and juice of 1 lime
> 1 long green chilli, finely chopped
> 1 small handful Thai basil leaves (or substitute coriander)
> 1 small handful mint
> ¼ green papaya, julienned (see notes)
> ½ punnet of cherry tomatoes, quartered
> 6 large, cooked prawns, peeled and cut into thirds
> 2 cooked Moreton Bay or Balmain bugs, remove from
>   shell and cut in half
> ¼ cup crispy fried shallots

METHOD

Preheat a grill pan or barbecue. Season the squid with a little salt and massage it in with a drizzle of olive oil. Add it to the hot pan or barbecue and flash fry for one minute on each side. Once cooked, remove from pan and allow to cool to room temperature.

In a large bowl combine fish sauce, sugar, water and lime juice and zest. Whisk together until the sugar dissolves, then add the chilli. Toss the herbs, papaya and tomato in the dressing. Add the seafood. Toss again. Serve topped with fried shallots.

NOTES

This recipe uses Australian tablespoons and cups: 1 teaspoon equals 5ml; 1 tablespoon equals 20ml; 1 cup equals 250ml. All herbs are fresh, unless specified, and cups are lightly packed. All vegetables are medium size and peeled, unless specified. All eggs are 55-60g (about 2 ounces), unless specified.

If you can't find green papaya, you could use green mango, cabbage or cucumber – something to give the salad texture.